Catch Me

CARLIE JEAN

Copyright © 2025 by Carlie Jean

All rights reserved. This book or any portion thereof may not be reproduced or used in any manner whatsoever without the express written permission of the publisher except for the use of brief quotations in a book review.

This is a work of fiction. Names, characters, places and incidents either are products of the author's imagination or are used fictitiously. Any resemblance to actual events or locales or persons, living or dead, is entirely coincidental.

Printed in the United States of America
First Printing, 2025
ISBN: 9798310690684
Kindle Direct Publishing

Line editor: Emily at Fairy Plot Mother
Developmental editor: Salma R.
Proofreader: Como La For
Cover Designer: Cat Imb at TRC Designs
Formatting: Qamber Designs

For the man who made me believe that romance novel love is real. Our story is my favorite, and I can't wait to keep writing it with you.

Content warning

Explicit sexual content

Mention of past parent death, anxiety, emotional abuse and alcoholism

Contents

Prologue 1
Chapter 1... 7
Chapter 2.. 14
Chapter 3.. 20
Chapter 4.. 27
Chapter 5.. 32
Chapter 6.. 42
Chapter 7.. 48
Chapter 8.. 56
Chapter 9.. 59
Chapter 10.. 63
Chapter 11.. 76
Chapter 12.. 81
Chapter 13.. 87
Chapter 14.. 96
Chapter 15.. 107
Chapter 16.. 115
Chapter 17.. 126
Chapter 18.. 138
Chapter 19.. 142
Chapter 20.. 150
Chapter 21.. 162
Chapter 22.. 167
Chapter 23.. 174
Chapter 24.. 186
Chapter 25.. 194
Chapter 26.. 206
Chapter 27.. 211
Chapter 28.. 218
Chapter 29.. 229

Chapter 30 243
Chapter 31 250
Chapter 32 256
Chapter 33 265
Chapter 34 270
Chapter 35 274
Chapter 36 280
Chapter 37 286
Epilogue 290
Bonus scene 294
Group chat 297
About the Author 305

Playlist

Catch Me
Carlie Jean

Shooting Star - Bad Company
Cowboys Cry Too - Kelsea Ballerini ft. Noah Kahan
All of The Stars - Ed Sheeran
You Are in Love - Taylor Swift
For Your Love - The Yardbirds
King of Broken Hearts - Ringo Starr
Taste - Sabrina Carpenter
Free now - Gracie Abrams
I'm With You - Vance Joy
Don't Stand So Close To Me - The Police
Until I Found You - Stephen Sanchez, Em Beihold
Use Me - Dallas Smith
Let Me Love You - Mario
Just Like Heaven - The Cure
Wonder - Shawn Mendes
You Are The Best Thing - Ray LaMontagne
A Drop in the Ocean - Ron Pope
I Fall Apart - Post Malone

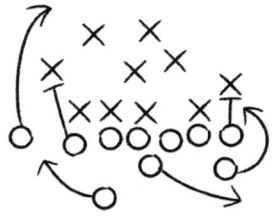

Prologue

Theo

First day of classes - Freshman year

There's something to be said about the paradox of a new beginning feeling like the end.

How moving forward in my life feels like I'm drifting further away from my true self and closer to this made-up version of me.

"Remember, son, today marks the start of working towards your dream. There's no time for mistakes or laziness now." My dad's reprimanding tone is just as intimidating over the phone as it is in person.

Most freshmen are excited and nervous to start their new chapter at college, but me? It feels like signing my life away to the man currently giving me an earful early in the morning.

"I'm well aware, Dad," I tell him, my eyes tracking everything going on around me as I walk to my first class of the day. There are professors walking around with briefcases and coffee, a group of students taking pictures in front of a building, and an underlying sense of urgency in the air, like everyone is in a hurry to be somewhere.

It makes my skin prickle with anxiety.

"Coach Davis is aware of your extra training sessions with Rob, and expects you to perform and show up to each team practice regardless. I scheduled the sessions early in the mornings to avoid it overlapping with any team commitments," he explains, making my stomach coil at the idea of early mornings every day for the next four years.

But I do what I do best, and please everyone around me.

"Thanks for doing that, Dad. I want to be the best, and that's going to help me stay in peak shape which will improve my game play. Do you think I'll get the attention of scouts this year?" I ask, sounding more interested than I actually am.

"If you work hard like you've been doing since you were a boy, then yes. You're a freshman, but you've got the skills to outperform the starting quarterback. When you get your chance to show it, don't hold back."

"You know I will," I assure him.

I hear my dad clear his throat, his telltale sign that he's about to bring up something that will make us both uncomfortable.

"Theo, I know there will be a lot of girls trying to get with you, but you need to be careful. Those girls are only looking for one thing. Don't get seriously involved, you hear me? If you do need to, you know … please wear protection," he utters the last part, sighing as he does.

"I know how to be safe, Dad." I chuckle uncomfortably, wanting to get the hell off this topic. "The way my schedule is looking between personal training, team commitments, and my classes, I won't even have time to look at girls. So, don't worry."

"Good, keep it that way and get to class. You have a reputation to uphold as soon as you step foot on campus, so make it a good one," he ends the phone call with one last demand, hanging up before I can even say goodbye.

Catch Me

I pocket my phone as I arrive early for my elective creative writing class, my hands clammy at the idea of sitting in my first ever university lecture. I wrap my fingers around the fidget cube in my pocket and fiddle with it, my breathing slowly steadying with the distraction.

I open the door and find a grand lecture hall, which looks like it could fit a thousand freshmen, completely empty. My dad always *enforced* the idea of being as good a student as I am a football player, which means showing up early to my classes and getting the best seat where I won't be distracted.

So here I am, early as fuck, and taking the seat smack dab in the middle of the front row.

I look around the empty room, wondering how the hell high school is over already. Those four years flew by, and I'm worried these four will go by just as quickly.

This all feels way too grown up for me.

I'm used to being the goofball, the outgoing one, the life of the party. My fun persona is the only time I get to feel genuine joy, because otherwise, I'm following someone else's orders.

But right now, everything suddenly feels more serious. It's like I'm at the beginning of that LIFE board game, and every little action will determine how my life moves forward.

It'll decide if I'm worthy of getting scouted by a professional football team and going pro.

It'll tell my father if I'm worthy enough too.

Our professor already posted the syllabus on our course website, so I reach into my bag to begin the readings to avoid falling behind, even though we literally just started. With how busy I'm going to be, I'll take any chance I can to stay on top of things.

I'm about to pull out my textbook when the lecture hall door swings open, revealing the prettiest girl I've ever laid eyes on. My previous whirling thoughts come to an absolute halt as I take her in.

She's short, with killer curves, and long, dark brown waves cascading down to her waist. I admire her as she takes in the room, her eyes wide in shock. But there's a smile on her lips too.

A devastatingly-gorgeous smile.

God, she's so beautiful.

Her eyes finally find mine, and her smile instantly disappears, a wave of embarrassment clouding her face upon realizing she isn't alone.

And holy shit, she's got the prettiest shade of brown eyes, a honey-like hue.

A long moment passes before I decide to break the silence with some humor, hoping it'll bring that smile back. "I guess we're the teacher's pets, huh?"

"I, uh—I guess so." She chuckles softly, placing her backpack on the seat at the end of my row.

I pretend to sniff myself. "Do I smell bad or something?"

Her head snaps up, confusion written all over her face. "What?"

"Is that why you're not sitting next to me?" I smile, letting her know I'm just teasing.

Pretty Girl's lips open, close, then open again. "Well ... I thought it might be weird to sit right next to you. I don't even know you."

"We can change that, if you'd like."

"You can get to know me from here," she says, sliding into her seat, unbothered as she begins taking her things out of her bag.

"Alright, what's your name?" I ask, starting off easy.

"Marcela Bass, and you are?"

"Theo," I purposely leave out my last name. She has no idea who my dad is, and I want to keep it that way. "And your major?"

"English, you?" She looks over to me briefly, then opens her pink notebook.

"Biology."

Marcela's head swings back to me. "Why are you here then? In a creative writing class?"

I shrug, deciding to take out my notebook as well. "I needed an elective and this seemed like fun."

She says nothing to that, and from her soft tone and slight hesitation, I get the vibe that she's shy. Nothing wrong with that, I've always been able to talk to anyone. I twist my body to face her. "How are you feeling about your first day as a freshman?"

With her head buried in her notebook, she softly says, "Good."

"You're not nervous at all? C'mon, I can't be alone in this," I plead, being dramatic.

"You don't seem nervous," Marcela points out, still not looking at me.

"It's my charming personality, isn't it?" I wink, not that she sees it.

She finally turns to me, pity on her face. "I—"

The doors open, and a slew of students make their way into the room, cutting her off. People quickly fill the space between us, and class starts shortly after, but it doesn't stop my eyes from darting her way every thirty seconds for the entire lecture.

That happens every class of the first semester, she always sits at the end of the row, and I'm in the middle. Always keeping her distance.

When creative writing comes to an end in December, it's the last I see of her until sophomore year. She works as a waitress at Beers 'n' Cheers, our local on-campus sports bar.

You could say I'd become a regular—or at least tried to—between my insane school schedule.

I take every opportunity to talk to her, throwing in some harmless flirting whenever I can. She never flirts and is always nice, until she finally tells me she has a boyfriend, and I instantly back off.

Do I ever lose hope though? Fucking right, I don't.

Call it delusion, but I call it fate. There's a reason we showed up early to that creative writing class, We were meant to meet that day. She intrigues me, on top of being the prettiest girl I've ever seen, and she made me smile on a day I was dreading the most.

Despite all of the obstacles between us, I know there is more for us.

Now that she's single and we're both heading into senior year, I know all of this pining for her won't have been for nothing.

Over the years, I've gotten to know Marcela, and I've grown to like her.

A lot.

That's my girl, and when given the chance, I'm going to do everything I can to show her that.

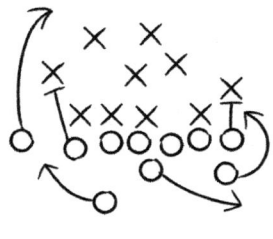

Chapter 1
Theo

I breathe in the early September air, but my lungs tighten at the thought of playing another season of football.

My dad would have a coronary if he ever found out how much I hate playing the sport he raised me on. From the moment I could walk, he made sure I had a football in my hand. An ex-NFL player himself, he knew exactly how to create a prodigal son.

I'm amazing at what I do. Not to sound too full of myself, but I know with the raw talent I possess, along with how hard I work, I'm on the trajectory to become one of the greats. Just like my dad was, before his career-ending knee injury two years before I was born.

After my mom passed away from a rare form of cancer when I was four and my sister was nine, he stepped up and did everything he could to raise us. It was a rough time for our family, and I like to believe my dad tried his best.

So, being the people pleaser I am, I want to carry out his dream for me, no matter how much I dread being on the field.

Not wanting to spiral further, I plant my ass on the grass near the local sports bar on campus to catch my breath after the run mandated by my trainer for the upcoming season. I lift the hem of my shirt and wipe away the beads of sweat on my forehead while I pull out my phone with my free hand.

The screen reads 7:00 p.m.

"Shit," I yelp, fumbling with my phone to pull up the stream to my best friend's baseball game.

This past summer, Ryker was drafted by the Detroit Panthers as their starting third baseman, skipping a rookie's typical years in the minor league. He's *that* good.

I'm doing my best to watch every game, but with the preseason camps and my own personal training, it's been tough.

The livestream plays on my phone, having tuned in at the perfect time. Camille, Ryker's wife, is the head of social media for the Panthers and is currently interviewing the team before the game begins.

Their story is one for the books.

In a matter of two days last year, I found out Camille was a runaway princess, and proceeded to marry her off to my best friend to save her from an arranged marriage.

Then there's Jasmine, who is opening up her café this fall. I'm so damn proud of her, and I know her fiancé, Elio, the ex-NHL legend, is too.

To top it off, the first friend I made at Rock Land University, Aurora, is working her ass off playing for the USA's national volleyball team. Her boyfriend, Cameron, is thriving as a coding wizard for Disney.

All of my friends are doing amazing things, and I couldn't be happier for them. I only wish I was as excited about my future.

My chest pinches at the reminder that football is all I've ever had.

I pull out the fidget cube I always keep in my pocket for moments like this. It distracts me from my anxious thoughts, allowing me to center my breathing and calm down.

I look around campus, seeing freshmen walk around with excitement in their steps as they head toward Beers 'n' Cheers. Instantly, my mind goes to freckles, honey-brown eyes, and curves that have plagued my dreams since I laid eyes on her three years ago.

Marcela.

As if I conjured her, she exits the bar, slinging her tote bag on her shoulder as she crosses the parking lot.

Before I know it, I'm on my feet and jogging toward her.

"Marcela," I huff, coming to a halt at her side.

Those honey eyes I can't stop thinking about widen for a moment, her freckles more prominent with the sun-kissed tan of summer on her skin.

"Hi." She brushes a dark-brown strand behind her ear.

"Hey." I wave.

Did I just fucking wave?

I shake it off and try to act like I'm not talking to the girl who's been on my mind forever.

"How was work?"

"It was busy, which made it go by quickly, thank goodness," she half-yawns, her exhaustion clear.

I'll be honest, I can't figure out why she works there since her social energy tends to run out quickly.

"How tired are you?" I ask.

Marcela shrugs. "A decent amount, why?"

"Walk with me? If you're up for it, of course," I add, always giving her the choice, because I know she likes her quiet time.

"Just for a few minutes," she answers, pulling at the hem of her cardigan.

"Oh, what a lovely few minutes this will be then." I smile, my heart fluttering like it does every time she talks to me.

Fuck, I need to get a grip.

"Should I be concerned?" she asks with a raised brow and a smile.

"Not at all, you're always safe with me," I assure her, watching as the sun begins to dip behind the pine trees on the path.

Marcela doesn't respond, which I've gotten used to. I usually fill in a good portion of our conversations, but it doesn't bother me in the slightest. I'm a man who loves to talk.

"How do you feel about it being our final year of school?" I question, guiding us up the grassy hill toward a quieter path.

"I'm excited for it to be done. I can't wait to get away from this place," she admits, shocking the hell out of me.

I watch as she fumbles to change the subject. "But, uh, how about you?"

I shrug, not wanting to lie to her. "I'm dreading it."

Marcela's head whips my way, confusion written all over her face. "How come?"

"I hate playing football," I mutter under my breath, just as we reach the top of the hill. I run a hand through my hair, messing up the strands.

Silence falls between us as the weight of my confession settles. I just admitted to her something I've never spoken out loud to anyone.

Marcela remains quiet, heading to the wooden bench that overlooks campus. It's my favorite place to go when I need to quiet my mind as I look at the stars, distancing myself from who I need to be on campus, versus who I'd like to be.

She sits on the bench and her gaze meets mine. "What part do you hate? If you want to talk about it, that is, sorry if I'm overstepp—"

"You're not." I move forward, planting myself next to her.

Marcela nods, giving me the time needed to gather my thoughts.

With a deep breath, I find myself telling her everything I've been holding on to. "Randy Miller was the most exciting player in the game twenty years ago. He had so much promise until he tore his ACL, unable to ever play a game again. Miller eventually had a son, and he vowed that the boy would live out his dream, doing whatever it took to make sure it happened. Even if it's not what Theo wanted."

I'm not sure why talking in the third person is making this easier, but it does.

"Knowing how much it meant to Miller, Theo did what was asked of him. Always. Even though no one ever asked him what *he* wanted from life. So, he became who his dad wanted him to be, until shit got real, and it's now senior year. Time for Theo to be drafted, but he's sick of it. He hates the sport that took his dad away from being a dad. He hates the beating his body takes. He hates the limelight."

I tilt my head back, eyes closed as I inhale deeply because that familiar feeling of anxiety is creeping its way into my system, and I need to center myself.

Marcela's soft voice seeps into the swirling thoughts in my head, "That's really tough. I'm sorry you're dealing with something so heavy. I know what that's like."

I crane my head toward her, seeing her shoulders stiffen at what she let slip again. It seems like neither of us can keep our lips sealed tonight.

She shakes her head, conveying without words that she doesn't want to talk about it. And as someone who wants to know everything about her, I hate it, but need to respect her privacy until she's ready.

"Thank you." I clear my throat, wanting to escape this somber mood we've stumbled into. "Alright, let's get back to fun Theo." I clap my hands.

Marcela rolls her eyes and smiles playfully.

"What have you been reading lately?" I ask. It makes her perk up, her honey eyes lit with excitement as she twists her body to face me.

"I recently finished the first book in the First Bite series. It's about a vampire who falls in love with a human. I know it's a beloved trope, but it gets me every time. This series is my newest obsession," she explains, going into detail about the characters.

Listening to her talk is easily my favorite thing, especially when I know talking isn't always easy for her.

"Sorry, I went off on a tangent." She tucks a loose strand behind her ear, before fiddling with the hem of her dress.

"Don't be. I feel like I just read a book without even reading it. I loved it."

"You know that does exist. Audiobooks?" She smirks.

"Yeah, but audiobooks don't come with you getting all excited. That alone makes it better," I say without thinking. And as always, as soon as something flirty comes out of my mouth, she shuts down.

"Yeah," she replies, chuckling awkwardly. She suddenly stands. "I need to get going."

"I'll walk you to your apartment," I say as I stand as well, towering over her.

She looks up to me, about to protest as she always does.

I speak first. "I need to make sure you get home safely, would that be okay?"

Marcela sighs, giving up easily for once. "Alright, let's walk."

And we do just that. We walk in a comfortable silence on the short path to her apartment that's just off campus.

We stop outside the doors to her complex, and Marcela turns to me.

"Thanks for walking with me, and for taking me up there. It was a nice breather after work." She smiles faintly.

"Not a problem, and it can be our shared quiet space." I chuckle. "And thank you for listening. I appreciate it."

For once, someone listened to me. She didn't pry or try to give me solutions. She just listened to me. She knew I needed to vent and gave me the space to do so.

Marcela nods, and flashes a shy smile before turning on her heel and into her building. I watch until she rounds the corner and then head back to the football house.

I take my time, enjoying the solitude in the cool air. I've always loved walking at night, away from the intrusive eyes of people around campus.

Everyone knows who I am, and they're all waiting to see what I do for the team this year.

Talk about fucking pressure.

And all I want is a life away from that demand.

Chapter 2
Marcela

There is nothing more freeing than taking your bra off after a long shift at work, and that's exactly what I do once my front door is locked and my tote bag is hung up.

I exhale a deep sigh, but the anxiety in my chest fails to dissipate.

I'm expecting a call from my mom tonight, and I've been stressed about it all day, because I already know how it's going to go.

We'll do our small talk, and she'll update me on any family gossip. And then I'll hear my stepdad in the background, drunk as a skunk, making some kind of comment that's going to upset me.

My mom met my stepdad in Costa Rica while he was vacationing there. She worked as his private chef at his winter home, and they ended up falling in love. Within a year, we packed up our home in Puerto Limon and moved to Colorado where he lived with his four-year-old daughter Jade.

I was only two at the time, so I don't remember much from my time back home.

We usually visit once a year, and every time, I fall in love with the way the world is there. Every morning, I would wake up in my grandma's house, the smell of her cooking always getting me out of bed quicker than normal. She typically made gallo pinto and fried eggs, my absolute favourite. We'd eat breakfast together, catching up and exchanging stories, in which she'd teach me new words in Spanish that I then would practice with my mom once we got back home.

The smell of black coffee would linger throughout the house, a scent that I associated with her as she always had fresh coffee ready to go. There was the constant sound of a fan on to keep the humidity out, mixed in with the background noise of the TV that had the local news station on.

I'd then spend the rest of the morning at the beach, reading in my own bubble surrounded by the sounds of nature. Some mornings though, I'd wake up earlier than my grandma so that I could watch the sunrise on the beach. Watching the fading night sky turn into a light blue with hints of orange and pink while the world was still quiet was stunning. It was pure bliss, and I long for that sense of peace I always find when I'm there in my life now.

I wish we'd go more. I'd love to be closer to my mom's family there and our culture. Being there always feels like hitting the slow motion button, allowing you to relax and enjoy life.

Sometimes, it makes me wish we'd never left, because every time we do go, it makes me wonder what my life would be like had I grown up there.

That's not to say I hate my life in Colorado, because I have a good life and grew up with everything I could ever need. My childhood was great... until I learned what it was like to live with an alcoholic.

My stepfather never once laid a hand on me, Jade, or my mom. But his words were scarring.

I think it's where my love of books began to grow, because when I was immersed in reading, his words couldn't hurt me. I could, for a little while, forget the way he made my mom cry, the way the wall sounded when his fist went through it, or how loud his yelling was.

I've always wondered why she never left him. As a kid, I thought it was a no-brainer. Someone's being mean to you? Walk away and get help. That's what my second grade teacher, Mrs. Denis, told me.

But now I realize how complex their relationship is, and how scary it must be for my mom to leave him and start over all on her own. Especially when he hasn't let her work since we moved in with him, claiming he wanted her to focus on raising us. If she left him, she'd have nothing—at least until a divorce was settled and she took half of what she was owed.

Which would be a lot, since Chris is the CEO of Bass Hotels, a five-star hotel chain known across the globe.

My phone buzzing in my hand causes a ripple of anxiety to shoot through me, but I push through it and answer the call, ready to get this over with.

"*Mami.*"

"Marcie, *¿Qué es la vara?*" My mother's sweet voice pours through the phone.

"*Estoy cansada,*" I tell her honestly. "Work was busy, so I'm looking forward to curling up with a book before bed."

"You work so hard. Make sure you rest and take care of yourself," she chides, forever the helicopter parent.

"I do, don't worry, Mami. How are things at home?" I ask with a swallow.

"*Maravillosa.* Your dad and I just finished dinner, I made olla de carne," her voice lifts excitedly, always passionate over food. "Actually, here he is now, he wants to talk with you," she tells me, making my stomach drop.

"Marcela." My dad's crisp, boardroom-like voice carries through the phone, signaling he's not drunk. *Yet.*

"Hey, Dad, what's up?"

"I'm not one of your friends. I'm your father. Treat me with respect, Marcela," his icy numbing my entire body.

I should've known better than to address him so casually. This is all my fault.

"I'm sorry, Dad. I hope things are going well. Is there anything I can do for you?" I say, my voice calm and collected when I feel anything but that.

While I did not think he deserved the title of being called my dad, it was a sign of respect I knew I had to show him. I'd learned the hard way what happens if I don't.

"I'm checking in to see how school's going. You still have a 4.0 GPA?" he asks.

"Yes," I breathe. Even though school hasn't even started, it's better not to argue for fear of triggering him.

"Good, I pay for your tuition and apartment, and I expect you to return the favor by doing well. You're a part of the Bass family, and we don't fail," he reminds me. His plan is to have me work for the family company, even though I have no desire to have a career in that field.

"Of course," I say quietly.

"Speak up when you're talking to me," he scoffs, and I hear my mom whisper something in the background. "I don't care if she's shy. She needs to speak up," he tells her, as sweat beads on my forehead.

"Sorry, Dad. I'm just really tired," I raise my voice, desperate to placate him so he doesn't yell at my mom all night.

He sighs into the phone. "It's always an excuse with you."

"How's Jade?" I switch the focus to her, since she's his pride and joy who can do no wrong, despite how troublesome she can be.

"She's doing great. She's in LA auditioning for some roles," he explains. Jade is an aspiring actress and moved there a year ago to pursue her dream.

"That's amazing," I tell him genuinely, because I am so proud of her. The best thing he has ever given me is my sister. We haven't talked as much since she moved, but we were really close growing up.

"Let's hope you can make us just as proud." His comment is meant to come off as motivating, yet it feels like a threat.

"I will," I say with a yawn. "I need to get to bed."

His tone switches to the one of the caring father he pretends to be. "Of course. Get to bed, sweetheart."

"Night, Dad."

I hang up the phone and immediately go to my room, where I strip out of my work clothes, shower, and settle in bed with my favorite blanket, e-reader, and a cup of chamomile tea.

As I get lost in a world of vampires, the anxiety from the earlier phone call begins to fade. In its place is a sense of comfort in knowing I'm safe here, and that one day, I can rescue both my mom and myself from him.

Once I graduate, my plan is to work for my dad for a few years while I get my master's in English literature, with the hopes of finding work at a publishing house. Then, once I'm able to, I want to tell my mom that we don't need him. We can be free of him. I can take care of us and all of the bills from divorcing him.

And once all is said is done, maybe then I could pursue my true dream of being an author. But first and foremost, I need to take care of my mom.

It's in these quiet moments of dreaming of the future where my mind wanders off to a fairytale world, where my real father would have still been here.

He died of a heart attack before I was even born.

I've always found it odd how you can grieve someone you've never met, yet I do. Because I wish I could've known him and the life the three of us might have had together.

All I have are the beautiful stories my mom has shared with me over the years, and the only photo she saved that now sits on my dresser. In the frame is a picture of my mom pregnant with me, and my dad with his hands on her belly. It was taken a week before he passed.

It's the only picture of us I'll ever have, and I'll cherish it forever.

Once my eyes grow heavy, I set my e-reader on my side table, shut the light off, and snuggle under the covers.

But sleep doesn't come as easy as it does most nights, because I can't get the conversation with Theo out of my head.

He hates football? That was a plot twist I didn't see coming. He seems so happy and silly, I never would have thought he hated anything in his life.

And then there's the flirtatious comments. We're friends. I know it's harmless and a part of his charming personality, but I clam up every time.

I have my ex to thank for that. I'll never believe a thing a man says to me again, because Hunter said he loved me and wanted a family with me—only to make out with my one and *only* friend.

I don't understand why Theo would want to flirt with *me*. We're complete opposites. We come from two different worlds, mine much quieter than his. Although I'm happy with my looks, I also know I'm not the type of girl who would be seen on Theo Miller's arm.

To be honest, I don't think I've ever seen Theo with a girl. And when I think about him with someone else, I hate it. For no good reason either, because Theo and I are friends. That's it.

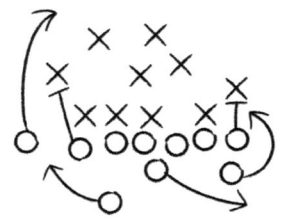

Chapter 3
Theo

I wake up in a cold sweat as my alarm goes off at 4:30 a.m., my usual schedule now that classes are starting today. My personal trainer, Rob, whom my dad hired, has me doing extra conditioning in the morning before classes, on top of the practices and team workouts that I already have later in the day.

To say I'm exhausted, even thinking about it, is an understatement.

I quickly get up and dress in athletic shorts, a T-shirt, and my running shoes, before bounding out of the football house, a house that all junior and senior players live in, to meet Rob at the track where I spend the next hour.

By the time I leave the track at six, I'm drenched in sweat from the brutal conditioning we just did.

As I walk through the front door of the football house, I'm hit with the smell of bacon, making my nose curl in distaste. Growing up on a farm and seeing the animals as my friends, I have refused to eat meat since I was a kid.

"Theo, you want some eggs and toast?" Dale, the kicker for our team, asks.

"Yes, please," I tell him, taking a seat at our large dining room table.

"I'm not your dad. Come get your own food," Dale snickers, dumping the scrambled eggs onto a large serving dish.

"Can't a man catch a break?" I groan, my muscles screaming in protest as I get up from my chair to load my plate up with eggs, three slices of toast, and some olives.

Yes, olives. I don't think there's anything better than a green olive stuffed with red peppers. It's my go-to snack.

Dale, who is apparently the only person awake in the house, groans when he sees my plate.

"Dude, you and your olives."

"Why does good old Theo always get so much judgment? I'm a guy who likes olives, sue me," I defend myself and my exquisite taste.

"They're gross," he mutters.

"I could say the same about your bacon." I raise my brow at him.

"Touché," he agrees easily, knowing my aversion to meat.

"How is Robin doing?" I ask, because Dale told me last week that she's pregnant. They've been dating since freshman year, after meeting at a party the first week of school.

"She's stressed. And I'll be honest, so am I." He runs a hand through his hair. "We didn't plan on starting a family until after I got drafted and we're settled in our careers."

"Fuck, I'm sorry. That's a lot to deal with. I know your family will be supportive. Your parents are great. What about hers?"

"We haven't told them yet, they're very … traditional, you could say," Dale sighs.

"Hey, look on the bright side. You have a woman you love—your soulmate—and once this year ends, you'll be leaving school with not only a spot in the NFL, but a mini version of you both. How awesome is that?" I try to reassure him, because if I'm honest, I envy him a little.

Not the baby part, per se, because I'm not ready for that. But I envy the fact that he met his person so early on, that they fell in love, and now get to experience more of it.

I want that.

"Fuck, I know." He rubs his finger into his temple. "I can't wait to start a family with that girl. She's my everything. And we're both happy and want it, it's just shitty timing."

"Everything will work out how it's supposed to," I tell him, and myself. Because my belief in fate has me convinced that I'll get my girl somehow, someday.

"I hope so," he says before chugging the rest of his strawberry milk. Leaning forward, he looks around to make sure no one's there and whispers, "Did you hear the rumor about tonight's practice?"

I lean forward too, and whisper back, "No, what?"

"We're getting a transfer on the team."

My eyebrows pinch together. "What? This late in the season? Who is it?"

Our first game is this Friday, and after having pre-season training for this past month, it's really late for someone to be added to our roster.

"Rumor has it, Hunter Johnson is going to be our new wide receiver. Even though he was a previous quarterback, he was having some trouble with that position, so they're trying something new."

There is no way I just heard that right. Hunter is joining our team. The guy who cheated on Marcela, and is the scum of the Earth in my books? This means I will have to see this guy almost everyday, and fucking trust and throw to him during games?

Please let this be only a rumor.

Catch Me

I must not hide my disdain well, because Dale's looking at me with confusion. "What's up? It's all good. Your position is safe. It'll just be weird throwing to someone we haven't played with for years, like the rest of the guys."

"You're right," I say, plastering on a fake smile, the one I know he's expecting. "Where did you hear this?" I ask him, finishing off the last bite of my toast.

Dale pins me with a dumbfounded look. "Did you forget Robin's dad is our assistant coach?"

"That I did." I stand, rounding the table to grab his cleared plate, and clap him on the back. "Good luck telling him you knocked up his precious daughter."

"You dick," he half-groans, half-chuckles.

Later that day, I walk through the hallways of our stadium toward the field where practice is being held, my mind a mess.

If Hunter is actually here at our school, that means Marcela will be forced to see him, because our team loves to celebrate wins at the bar she works at. My gut twists at the idea, knowing how much it will hurt her to see that piece of shit.

I plan on texting her about it to warn her, but I decide to wait to see if the rumor is true first.

The late afternoon sun shines down on me as I exit the tunnel, the crisp turf under my feet familiar. The stands are a mix of our school colors, forest green and white, with our famous coyote logo on the jumbotron.

I scan the group of people here. It's still early, so there are only a few players, the coaching staff, and our trainers. I come to a stop when I see none other than Hunter Johnson standing on Rock Land University turf.

Fuck me.

I've never liked the guy—even less so now. He used to play at the University of Aspen, our rival school, which instantly made him enemy number one.

Add in the fact that he hurt my Marcela?

He's not even an enemy anymore. He's nothing. Doesn't exist.

Sadly, he'll have to exist in my world once more if he's about to be my goddamn teammate. For now, I avoid him, instead walking over to my friends to chat before practice begins.

"Did you see who's standing over there?" Will, the center, whispers.

"Fucking Hunter Johnson. What is Coach getting at with this shit?" grumbles Cory, our tight end.

Dale chips in. "Probably out of his hands. Hunter's dad is a fucking state senator, and if he wants his kid going to a new school in his senior year, then it'll be whatever Daddy says."

Before we can say anything else, Coach Davis claps his hands, signaling that he wants our attention. We all turn toward him, finding Hunter at his side.

"You boys know I don't beat around the bush, so let's get to it. I know there's been some confusion as to why Hunter is here with us. He no longer wanted to be a quarterback, and with his previous team already having a solid wide receiver, he wanted to transfer out. Since our best receiver graduated, we are more than happy to welcome him to the team," Coach says, his tone even and practiced.

Definitely something Hunter's dad wrote for him. Which has me wondering why Hunter's *really* here.

The team is silent, nodding as Coach goes on, "I expect you to welcome him to our family with respect. If I find out otherwise, you'll be personally meeting with me and the dean. Got it?"

"Yes, sir," we all say in unison.

Coach Davis doesn't mess around and expects perfection from us. He's taken teams to the championship more times than I can count. He joined RLU two years ago, and it's been his goal to get our team to win its first ever championship.

Coach instructs us to line up to run one of our plays, so I take my position behind the center, ready to go.

I watch as Coach instructs Hunter and the other two receivers, and I instantly know the play we're doing. We're running a flood play, placing three receivers at one end of the field, which will force the defense to decide who to cover once the ball is snapped to me.

Will snaps me the ball as soon as I yell "Hike!"

My eyes quickly scan for an open player as the defense works to get closer to me. I see that Hunter is open, but because I can't stand the guy, I decide to make a run for it.

I'm tackled down after only gaining a yard.

"Again," Coach orders, his near-black eyes on me.

We set up the same way, and once the ball is snapped to me, somehow Hunter is open again.

I run the ball, not wanting to throw it to him because fuck. That. Guy.

And just like last time, I'm tackled.

"What in the hell are you doing?" Will says so only I can hear. "Hunter is open, throw him the damn ball."

We do it again, and this time, despite Hunter being wide open, I throw the ball to another receiver who's somewhat covered. The ball is tipped away and intercepted, causing Coach to blow his whistle.

"Miller," he barks, and I jog toward him instantly.

"What's up, Coach?"

His gaze hardens when he looks at me, but I don't flinch. After growing up with a father like mine, you get used to this.

"Is there a problem? Hunter is wide open and you're making stupid decisions," his weathered voice is harsh. "I won't have you as my starting QB if I can't trust you to make the right choice."

I swallow down what I'd really like to say, simply nodding before I return to my spot behind Will. This time, when Hunter is open I throw him the ball and he catches it, gaining us ten yards before he's tackled to the ground.

And I hate every second of it. I hate that he's good and we have to work together, when all I want to do is repeatedly throw my fist at his face.

When practice finally ends, I make sure to shower and change quickly to avoid running into Hunter more than necessary.

Knowing what he's done to Marcela, I don't know if I can fake being nice to him, but I can't let personal issues affect my game and the team dynamic this year.

My dad will be watching, which means there's no room for disappointment.

Fake it 'til I make it.

It seems to be the motto I've lived my entire life. Why stop now?

Chapter 4
Marcela

I don't think I've ever woken up happier than I did today, because it's my *final* first day of school.

Senior year, at last. One day closer to being free of my stepfather, because he won't be able to hold over my head anymore that he's paying for my future.

I'll be a *true* adult, able to go where I want, do what I want, and set boundaries with the people I couldn't before.

A smile unfurls as I make my way across our beautiful campus. Today's a good day. I have my favorite iced coffee, with one shot of espresso and brown sugar syrup. I'm wearing a light pink mini dress that flows at my waist, with white trim and bow shoulder straps, complete with wedge sandals. It's girly and very me, making me feel even better.

I continue to ride that high all the way into my first class of the day, Literary Criticism.

Sitting at the end of the first row, like I've always done, I begin unpacking my tote bag. I take out my laptop, along with my notebook and pens.

When I finally look up, I freeze at the sight of who just walked in.

No.

It can't be.

My eyes must be playing tricks on me, that's all.

There's absolutely no way that my ex-best friend, Ruby, is here right now. But I'd recognize her red hair anywhere. It's so dark that it's nearly purple, and her eyes are a vibrant green that pop against it.

She smiles brightly, and I turn around to see if there's someone behind me, because there's no way she has the audacity to engage with me. When Ruby walks toward the first row, my nerves skyrocket. What does she want? We haven't talked since I received a video from a random number of her making out with my boyfriend.

My only friend and my boyfriend, who I had been with since high school.

She tried calling a few times, but I never answered. She eventually ceased any attempt to make amends. The only person I talked to afterward was Hunter, and even then, I broke up with him over the phone, because I couldn't bear to hear either of them deny what happened or admit it to my face.

He tried to fight for us, but when I sent him the video I received, he immediately turned things around on me. Blaming his infidelity on the fact that I didn't visit him enough. That I didn't have sex with him enough. That *I* just wasn't enough.

I broke up with him right then on the phone and haven't heard from him since. Thank God.

"Marcie!" she squeals, giving me the most awkward side hug as I'm still seated.

I don't hug her back.

The worst part is that despite how much I hate her, I can't find it in me to be as rude as I'd like to be. If I could, I'd tell her not to call me that. That she lost that privilege when her tongue dove into my boyfriend's mouth.

But I've always been too shy to voice how I really feel.

"Hi," I say quietly.

Ruby slides into the seat next to me, and I feel myself cringe. How did I go from feeling so good today to wanting to claw someone's eyes out?

"How are things? I haven't heard from you in forever. I miss you!" she lays it on thick, batting her fake lashes at me. "I transferred back this year because of that."

Ruby had switched to the University of Aspen last semester, claiming she needed a change of scenery. Which is where my ex-boyfriend goes to school. I wonder if things fell apart for them, and that's the reason she's back here now.

Not that I'd take her back as a friend. But I'm curious, nonetheless.

"And look," Ruby whispers, taking her hand in mine, "I'm really sorry for what happened with Hunter. But when you know you're meant to be with someone, you can't let anything stand in the way of that. We're so happy together, and we'd love it if you could accept us. We both have missed you so much. It can be like old times, the three of us always hanging out. Except I get to kiss Hunter now," she blushes and giggles, as if it's a joke.

Something inside of me breaks. Maybe it was the drastic change from riding high to now feeling so low that I lose it on her.

"How could you do that to me?" I hate the way my voice cracks at the end of my question, my bubbling emotions threatening to burst. "You were my *only* friend since we were kids. You've always had everything. Any guy you wanted. Why *him*?"

I watch as Ruby's demeanor changes from placating to defensive.

"Because he was the only man I couldn't have, Marcie. I wanted him for years. Do you know how intoxicating that is?"

"No, I don't, because friends don't do that to friends. I would quite literally throw up if I so much as thought about wanting another girl's boyfriend, let alone my best friend's," I say, incredulous at the things she's saying to me right now. "And stop calling me that. We're not friends and will never be again."

A snarky grin appears on her face, her eyes lighting up like she enjoys this. "I guess if we're having one last conversation, let's end it with two truths and a lie, hm?"

I'm frozen, unable to move or do anything but listen as Ruby digs the knife deeper into my chest.

"Okay, first, we never did anything behind your back until you got the video. That was the first time. Second, I came back here because I missed you. Third, Hunter said I'm a better fuck than you ever were."

I'm shoving my things into my bag as fast as I can, my vision blurring with tears. Letting her know she's hurting me is killing me even more, but I can't help it.

"Don't worry about leaving, I'm not even in this class. Just thought I'd pop by to relay the information," Ruby says, standing and running her hands over her skirt. How she knew I was in this class is startling, but then she leans down and whispers in my ear, "In case you were wondering, the lie was number two. I came back to get the satisfaction of being with him in front of you."

In front of me? *What?*

Is he … does that mean … Hunter is here at RLU too?

"See you around, *Marcie*," she winks, strutting out the door.

I slump in my seat despite the tension radiating throughout my body.

Beneath the initial hurt and anger, there's a layer of confusion as I try to figure out what I ever did to Ruby that would cause her to treat me like this.

As the lecture starts, I find myself unable to focus as my brain whirls with everything she admitted. For some reason, I believe nothing happened prior to the video, not that it changes anything. But then there's the comment about the sex ... as if I wasn't already shy when it came to intimacy.

The fact that I've never felt comfortable, worshipped, or entirely turned on by Hunter speaks volumes to me now, but at the time, I thought something was wrong with me.

Now, I'm thinking it was my body telling me that he wasn't the one.

Most concerning of all, she mentioned wanting to be here so she could rub their relationship in my face, meaning Hunter is also here.

My stomach caves in at that while my fingers twitch with the need to write, to get lost in a fantasy world where *I* call the shots. Where I don't get hurt.

I'm over it happening to me in real life.

My stepdad. Hunter. Ruby.

Three people who shouldn't have purposely hurt me, but did.

The excitement I felt this morning has vanished. Instead, it's replaced with a tightness in my chest that I fear won't go away until the year ends.

I can't wait to get away from this place, where I'll never have to run into Ruby or Hunter again. A place where the hold my stepdad has on me will no longer exist.

Until then, I'll have to make it through each day the best I can.

Chapter 5
Marcela

My feet drag as I head to my last class of the day, a night class I willingly picked to free up my days during the week. That way, I could have more time to work on my book during the day, when my creativity flows best.

I've been writing stories anonymously on an online platform for the past few years. It's been a way for me to practice storytelling and escape the world for a bit. My words give my voice the power it lacks in reality.

Something I wish I had when I faced Ruby today.

My good mood is replaced with anxiety and dread at having to see Hunter around campus.

My fingers wrap around the door handle to the building, when a much larger one wraps around the top half of the handle, pulling it open.

Startled, I remove my hand and turn quickly, finding Theo grinning at me.

"Did you forget we have the same class tonight?" he winks, holding the door open for me to walk through.

"Kind of," I admit, walking past him.

"You wound me," he holds his heart as he comes to stand in front of me, making me stop.

I shake my head at him, unable to pretend because of the mood I'm currently in.

"What's wrong?" Theo asks, switching from playful to concerned in seconds.

I shift from one foot to the other, not wanting to replay this morning to him despite Ruby's words running rampant in my mind.

"It's nothing," I muster a smile, then look away.

"I hate when you do that."

My eyes snap back to his light blue ones as confusion takes over. "Do what?"

"Act like things don't matter when they upset you," he says softly, never raising his voice, even though I can tell he's irritated. I always do this whenever he asks what's bothering me. "Anything that takes that beautiful smile off your face is a problem."

If only he knew how much his composure means to me. When you come from a household where a man's scream would echo off the walls whenever something displeases him, his calming presence feels like a breath of fresh air.

I inhale a breath while my eyes scan the entryway to make sure no one's around to hear us.

"I saw Ruby this morning. She's back at RLU for the year, and she didn't have the greatest things to say," I swallow down the emotion clawing at my throat. "It's thrown me off since. To top it all off, she mentioned something about Hunter also being here, and I don't know if I can deal with having to see him after … everything that happened."

Theo's jaw clamps down, his eyes hardening. "What the hell did she say to you?"

"It's not worth repeating, and I'd really rather not say."

He mumbles something under his breath while running a hand through his light brown hair.

"What is it?" I ask him, sensing that he's stressed about something.

His eyes find mine, and my heart sinks, because I already know what he's going to say. "Hunter's at RLU," he confirms, making my stomach twist.

"H-how?" I murmur.

"I found out this morning that there were rumors of him coming here, but I didn't want to send you into a panic if they weren't true. But he was at practice," he says. He looks apologetic, as if any of this is his fault. "Coach said something about Hunter wanting to become a wide receiver and that position wasn't available at his school, so he came here. Dale thinks something is up though, so I don't know what the real reason is."

My mind whirls at the information, because his friend is right. Something has to be up, because all Hunter ever talked about, since I met him in our freshman year of high school, was being a quarterback. There's no way he's throwing that dream away in his last year of college. It makes me wonder what really happened, but before I get lost in the what-ifs, Theo snaps me out of it.

"You okay?"

I look up at him, not sure how to answer his question. "I don't know," I reply honestly. "I know I will be. I always am. But I'd be lying if I said I'm not scared to see him. I haven't since … since he cheated on me. And seeing him with Ruby…"

"What makes you scared of him?" Theo questions, looking at me with sorrow in his eyes.

"He never hurt me physically, if that's what you're thinking," I confirm. "It's more so the fear of how I'll feel. I don't love him anymore. I'm not sure what we even had was love. All I know is

I don't want to see them gloating around campus, happy and in love when what they did hurt me so badly."

Theo nods, going quiet for a moment. He clears his throat and says, "If anything ever happens and you're uncomfortable, call me. Okay?"

I don't tell him it's fine. Instead, I surprise myself.

"Okay," I smile faintly.

"And you're a badass, you can handle this. Don't let them think they won, when they lost out on the best person I know."

I fall silent at that. Whenever he says something that sweet, my instinct is to not believe him. I do my best to ignore it for the sake of our friendship.

I chuckle and shake my head. "Thanks."

Theo flashes a wide grin, and I know he's about to try to uplift the mood even more.

"No problem. That's what friends are for, right?" he winks, ever the charmer. We walk toward our class together, and I slide into my usual spot at the end of the first row. I expect Theo to go to his usual spot in the middle, but he surprises me by dropping down into the seat next to me instead.

"Don't tell me in the last three years you've become an end of the row guy," I tease, sliding my tote bag onto the floor.

"Nah, just a *you* kind of guy," he says casually, as if it's as simple as saying the sky is blue.

His words are meant to be sweet, but after everything that has happened today, they don't hold much weight. I brush off his comment, because my brain needs a break—something I plan on giving it later when I curl up in my pajamas with a cup of tea to try to get some writing done. While I usually prefer writing during the day, I need it more than ever tonight.

Professor Grum walks in then, wearing a casual brown loungewear set. I like her already.

"Welcome, beautiful earthlings!" she beams, clapping her hands together to get our attention. She adjusts her large, green-rimmed glasses. "How wonderful is it that we're all on this planet at this time? That we get to experience the mountains, the trees, the oceans and the stars above?" She gestures wildly with her hands. "If you don't feel that way, I suggest you find another class, because this semester we are going to love the hell out of this planet and learn just how freaking cool it is."

Theo chuckles beside me, and I can't help but do the same. She's quirky, but keeps it real. My kind of girl.

Professor Grum stops in her tracks, holding a finger up in the air. "And if you don't like being outside, that's going to be a problem. We will spend lots of nights staring at the stars during our astronomy section. Fair warning now."

No one gets up and leaves, maybe out of fear or because they want to stick around. We'll never know, because even if *I* wanted to drop the course, you can bet I wouldn't be walking out right now. I'd do it from the comfort of my bed and laptop at home.

About an hour into our three-hour class, I notice Theo's neck craning as his jaw dips and his lips part out of the corner of my eye. I know how seriously he takes school to keep his spot on the football team, and I've never seen him fall asleep before.

Concerned, I gently nudge his elbow with mine.

His head shoots up instantly, his eyes flying wildly around the room until he realizes where he is. "How long was I out?" His voice is raspy, and I do my best to ignore how good it sounds.

"Not long," I whisper back. "Long day?"

"Something like that," he murmurs back, then takes a sip of his drink.

He remains awake for the rest of the class, and it's ten o'clock by the time we exit the building. Campus is nearly empty at this hour, save for the students leaving our class, giving it a quiet and calm atmosphere that it lacks during the busier days.

I turn to walk home without a word, hoping he'll be on his way to get a good night's rest.

"Ah, ah," Theo tsks, falling into step with me. "Where do you think you're going?"

"Home, and so should you. You seem exhausted. Go take care of yourself, please?"

"A gentleman always takes care of the woman first." He waves me off with a cheeky grin. I ignore his innuendo, because in my experience, that wasn't the case. Ever.

"I'm serious." I halt, forcing him to stop and look at me.

When he does, I almost forget what I was about to say. I know we're friends, but God, why did he have to be so good-looking? From the messy, light-brown hair that makes you want to run your hands through it, to his strong jawline, light blue eyes, and the best smile I'd ever seen.

I shake off the thoughts, focusing on what I meant to say. "Theo, I don't live far from here. Go home and sleep. You need it. How early do you have to be up tomorrow?"

"Four fucking thirty," he groans.

"Exactly," I say, patting him on the shoulder. "Good night. I'll see you around." I turn on my heel and continue walking, but of course, Theo falls into step beside me.

"You're funny, Marcela. Anyone ever tell you that?"

"No, actually. No one's ever said that."

"Sounds to me like you've never had a good friend, have you?"

I know his question wasn't meant to hurt, but it does regardless, because it makes me think of Ruby and how I never truly knew her.

Growing up, I thought she was the best friend a girl could ask for. But now, when I look back at our friendship, I recognize how she controlled everything. How she made it all feel like a competition between us. How she made fun of me for my passions.

Maybe she was never the friend I thought she was. Maybe I was so lonely that I clung to the first girl who stuck around, because despite loving being alone, I also craved friendship. I never had that with anyone, and I apparently still don't.

I don't realize how long I've been lost in thought until Theo brushes his hand gently against mine. "What's going on in that head of yours?"

For the second time tonight, I find myself opening up to him.

"I'm realizing that I've never had a genuine friend, you know? Ruby never treated me like one. I was more like someone she could compete with and control, because I didn't want to lose her. Even when Hunter and I were dating, I didn't see him as someone I could tell everything to. We didn't have that kind of relationship," I explain as we walk, the cool air wrapping around my legs and making me shiver slightly.

Theo's jacket is wrapped around my shoulders before I can say otherwise. I tug it closer, reveling in the warmth it provides.

"To think anyone has treated you with anything less than the respect and love you deserve makes me want to toss them through a wall." His voice is laced with anger as his jaw ticks. "And don't you dare say it's okay, because it's not."

"I know," I answer quietly.

"And I hope you know you do have friends. Aurora, Jasmine, Camille ... me," he adds in, with a soft smile.

I realize he's not wrong. Over the last couple of months, I've grown closer to the girls. We have a group chat where we talk daily, and have already hung out a couple of times.

And as much as I want to push him away, Theo has wedged his way into my life. So much that I think I'd miss his antics if he didn't want to be in it anymore. He's always had my back, cared for me, and wants the best for me.

That's what a friend is, right?

"You're right. I do have some pretty great friends now," I smile at him, letting him know he's included in that statement.

Theo pounds a fist over his chest. "I've never been more honored to be anyone's friend."

"Stop it," I shake my head, doing my best to stifle a giggle.

"So tell me, did the human hook up with the vampire yet?" he asks, referring to the book series I'm currently reading.

The entire walk back to my apartment I fill him in on what he's missed since the last time we talked about it. He listens attentively, asking questions every now and then and reacting in ways that make me laugh.

When we make it to my building, I turn to face him, feeling better than I have all day.

"Thank you."

"You never have to thank me for making sure you get home safely."

"Yeah, that, but also for making me feel better about everything. It's nice knowing I'm not alone in dealing with this," I admit while taking his jacket off.

"Keep it." His hands rest on top of mine, stopping me. "And you're never alone, we've got you. Once you're a part of the squad, there's no going back."

"The squad?" I arch an eyebrow.

"It's what I call our friend group. Nice and simple. Even though Ryker still likes to say he's not a part of it, that asshole is *so* in."

I laugh at that, because that is something the grumpy Ryker would do.

"Good night and get home safe. Text me when you do." I go to turn away when Theo grabs onto my hand, spinning me into him.

"Being my friend means you don't get to leave without a Theo-style hug." He smirks, and before I can ask what that means, he wraps his arms around my back and lifts me in the air, spinning me around.

I clutch onto him, a wide smile breaking across my face. My body feels more protected than it ever has before. Wrapped in his arms, it feels like nothing could ever hurt me. The feeling is so odd, it makes me question what in the world I was doing with Hunter if I've never felt that until now.

Once he sets me down and I catch my breath, I say, "That's some hug."

"Best one you've ever had, I know. It's going to be hard to ever top." He smiles, his lone dimple appearing.

"Bye." I chuckle, heading into my apartment complex.

"Bye, Marcela!" he shouts back. Without looking, I know he keeps his eyes on me until I round the corner and am out of sight.

Once inside of my apartment, I decide to text him to keep him company on his walk, because that's what a good friend would do.

At least, that's what I tell myself.

Me

> You should carry pepper spray on you on Tuesdays when we have our night class.

Theo

> You worried about me or something?

Me

> Maybe. But that's what friends do though, don't they?

Theo

> They do.
>
> I like that you care, but I don't need pepper spray. Our campus is relatively safe and my place is only five minutes away.

Me

> Okay good.

Theo

> I'm walking through the door now, get some sleep.

Me

> You too, night.

    I planned on writing tonight, but since Theo made me feel better and allowed my mind to clear a bit, a wave of tiredness has settled over me. As I attempt to fall asleep once my nighttime routine is done, the only thing that keeps playing in my mind is the haunted look on Theo's face at the idea of waking up so early to train for a sport he hates.

    It makes me sad that he's doing it anyway, despite how unhappy it makes him. But if there's one thing we have in common, it's that we know how to fake it for the people we love.

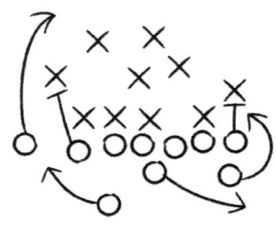

Chapter 6
Theo

By the time Friday rolls around, I'm more than exhausted. Every bone in my body aches from the practice sessions and the extra training my dad has me doing.

I can barely keep up with trying to do all of that—get enough sleep, eat enough food, and stay on top of my schoolwork. This year more than ever, I find myself lacking the motivation to do it all, probably because this is a glimpse at what my life will look like once I'm drafted.

To top it off, I haven't seen nor heard from Marcela since Tuesday. Which should be normal, since we're not dating. We don't need to talk everyday, but fuck, I wish we did.

"Last home opener game tomorrow boys. How we feeling?" Will claps his hands together as we walk toward the front doors to Beers 'n' Cheers.

Every night before a home game, the guys on the team and I come here as a tradition to hype ourselves up. Sans alcohol, of course, because Coach would kill us.

"That's fucking wild." Dale sighs. "Where the hell did the last three years go?"

"Tell me about it," I mutter to myself, because that's not something I'd usually share with them. The Theo they know rarely ever complains.

We easily find some teammates at our usual table. I follow Dale and Will over while I scan the bar, looking for her.

I spot Marcela taking an order from a couple at a booth. She looks stunning, as usual, with her hair up in a ponytail and wearing her uniform—black leggings and a T-shirt.

A hand lands on my shoulder. "C'mon, lover boy, it's guys' night," Dale says as I turn to face him.

I shrug him off with a chuckle and take a seat next to him at the large table.

The guys share their feelings about tomorrow's home opener, while I take another glance over at Marcela.

"You're oddly quiet," Cory pipes up, getting my attention.

"Yeah, QB, where's your leadership? You should be leading us in a chant to get us pumped up," Will goads me.

"Nah, think about how much more powerful it'll be tomorrow in the locker room. If we do it now, it loses its edge," I supply, making up some story, because I simply just don't care enough to get hyped right now.

"That's fair," he says, pointing a finger at me.

"You think we got a chance at the championship this year?" Cory asks, looking right at me.

I smile widely, hoping it's convincing. "Hell yeah. We're looking stronger than ever, and I'll be damned if Theo Miller leaves RLU without bringing home a championship title."

Our table erupts in cheers while fists slam the table.

At that exact moment, the front door of the bar opens and none other than Hunter walks through, heading straight for our table.

The table quiets as he approaches, and I look for Marcela to see if she's noticed that he's here yet. I sigh in relief when I don't see her on the floor, she's probably grabbing food from the kitchen.

"What are you doing here?" I ask through gritted teeth.

"Am I not allowed to join my teammates? We are all brothers now, right?" Hunter grins as he takes the seat in front of me.

It's quiet for a beat until one of the guys speaks up, "Yeah, for sure, man."

"Miller, how's it going?" He leans forward on the table, locking his gaze with mine.

"Great, you?" I say curtly, because there's no point in pretending that I like the guy. We've never gotten along in the last three years we've played against each other. While I'm faking that I like him, I don't have to pretend to be his best friend either.

Hunter's smile widens, looking way too comfortable. "Never better. I've been getting everything I ever wanted these days."

I ignore him and my eyes naturally dart to look for Marcela again, but I still don't see her anywhere. My knee bounces uncontrollably at the thought of how she'll feel when she sees Hunter is here. I know it's inevitable that she'll run into him, despite how much I wish it wouldn't happen.

Hunter clears his throat to catch my attention. "Let's lay it out right now, Miller. I know we've had some bad blood because of our school's rivalry, but now that I'm here, what's your issue with me?"

The team is occupied with their own conversations, oblivious to the one Hunter and I are having. Except for Dale, whose eyes shift to mine, letting me know he's listening.

"I don't have one," I say flatly.

His brown eyes narrow as he folds his arms across his chest. "Bullshit. You never want to throw me the ball when I'm clearly open and good at what I do. What kind of quarterback would mess up our chance at scoring if it's not over some personal issue?" He asks, raising his voice enough to get the team's attention.

The table quiets as everyone listens in.

"You got a problem, Hunter?" Dale jumps in, already on the defensive.

"Not currently, but I will if Miller here can't throw to me when I'm open," Hunter retorts, and I hate that he's not wrong. I should be doing what's best for the play, but I'm letting my personal hatred for the guy win.

"It's called getting used to a new player on the team. That's it. I'll do better." I settle on the safest answer, because no one on the team knows why I hate the guy. And they never will, because that's Marcela's story to tell.

"I hope so," Hunter muses, throwing his hand up to get the attention of the waitress, who thankfully isn't Marcela.

While the team places their orders, I take the opportunity to leave the table in search of her. Luckily, I don't have to look too far, because she's exiting the kitchen with a tray full of food.

She looks at me, and without saying a word, she knows exactly why I'm looking seeking her out. I watch as she peers around me, where I know she'll get a view of Hunter seated with the rest of the football team.

Her eyes widen, then harden, and I can see her knuckles turn white from how hard she's gripping the tray.

I move closer to her, just enough so she can hear me. "Which table is this for?"

"Seven," she mumbles, eyes still glaring at Hunter.

I grab the tray and deliver the food to the table, smiling at the customers who look confused to be served dinner by their school's quarterback. I ignore the questioning looks and return to Marcela, who now looks like she's seen a ghost.

"Fuck this," I whisper to myself as I take her hand—which fits perfectly in mine—and lead us down the hallway and out the back exit.

She removes it once we're outside, coming back to her senses as she takes a couple of deep breaths. I find myself doing the same, the mindful act bringing me a sense of calm I desperately need. Seeing that look on her face made me want to slam my fist against his nose.

"I-I have to get back in there and work," is the first thing she says, moving to get back inside.

My brows furrow as I stop her. "Marcela, you just saw your shitty ex for the first time in months, and you're worried about work?"

Her mouth parts, then closes, and opens again. "I guess so," she finally says.

"It's okay to take a second. Your feelings are more important than work."

"Seems like you should take your own advice," she snaps, and I'd be lying if I said I'm not slightly turned on by her sudden attitude. While I don't love that she's upset, I do love that she's sticking up for herself.

I put my hand to my chest, feigning offense. "You know how to hit a man where it hurts. Jesus."

She squeezes her eyes closed. "I'm sorry," she whispers. "I didn't mean to—-"

"It's okay. I like when you put me in my place," I smile, then take a step toward her. "But talk to me about what happened in there. You okay?"

Catch Me

Her honey eyes glance down for a beat, but when she looks back up at me, all I see is hurt on her face. My stomach twists at the fact that Hunter's the reason behind it.

"I don't know, honestly. I was shocked to finally see him, and then I was angry. Really freaking angry for what he did. And now I'm upset, because I'm going to have to see him and Ruby happy and in love all over campus or here at work," she admits, her voice thick with emotion. "How is it fair that they get to parade around their joy, when they're the ones in the wrong?"

"We don't know if they're happy together, and even if they are, you're the one who won. Two shitty people are together now, and you're free from both of them," I try to convince her, because I can see that, as much as this sucks, she's better off without them.

"I'm trying to tell myself that, but sometimes all I can focus on is how badly they hurt me and it feels like I'm the one who lost. And I really don't want them to see that they're hurting me," her voice quiets as a tear strolls down her cheek.

My heart pinches at seeing her like this. I fucking hate that they did this to her, of all people.

Marcela's the most selfless person I know. Why would anyone ever want to hurt her?

I wrack my brain for the right thing to say, when an idea pops into mind. Not my greatest idea, but somehow still not my dumbest. And I can thank Jasmine for this one, because of the book she told me about the other day.

"What if you showed them that you've moved on and you're happy?" I say, my voice nearly trembling with nerves at the crazy idea I'm about to propose.

Her face morphs into confusion as her head tilts to the side. "How would I do that?"

"Be my fake girlfriend."

Chapter 7
Marcela

Be my fake girlfriend.

I play the words on repeat in my mind, trying to be sure that I heard them correctly. Because there is no way Theo is asking me to fake date him, like we're in some kind of romance novel.

Absolutely no way.

"Theo …" My voice trails off, because I don't even know how to respond to that.

"Hear me out," he holds his hands in front of him. "If we pretend to date, it'll drive them crazy seeing how happy you are, but more so how much it doesn't even bother you that they're together, because you'll be with me."

I run my fingers through my hair as a stress headache blooms across my forehead. I don't hate his suggestion when he puts it that way. It would be so satisfying to walk by Hunter and Ruby with Theo on my arm, showing them that what they did didn't break me.

It's all I want.

"What would you get out of doing this?" I question him, because why would *he* want to do this?

"Other than getting to fake date the girl of my dreams, it would help get girls off my back," he shrugs, always saying the sweetest things like it's nothing.

I roll my eyes at that. "I'm not the girl of your dreams, and I highly doubt you haven't been with anyone since you came to RLU."

Theo steps closer to me again, his fingers resting under my chin as he tilts my head up. "That's where you're wrong. I may joke around, but I don't lie."

Shocked by his confession, I back away from his touch. "But, Theo … that could be a problem. The fact that you have me on this pedestal and flirt with me … it would make this fake dating thing complicated, and I don't want to hurt you. Because if we do this, all of it would be fake."

With a seriousness I never see from Theo, he nods, eyes intently on mine as he speaks. "If the only chance I get to be with you is a fake one, then I'll take it. I'll take anything you give me."

"I don't want to hurt you," I whisper.

Theo's lips morph into a lopsided grin. "Yes, I flirt with you, because you're beautiful. It's hard not to. And yes, I think you're an amazing person, but that doesn't mean I have feelings for you. I can do this. Let me do this for you."

We stare into each other's eyes, not knowing what we are looking for. I need to know that he's being honest. Because how could he have feelings for me to begin with? It never would have made sense, and he just confirmed it.

He's just a natural flirt, that's all.

"Okay."

His bright blue eyes bounce between mine, lips parted slightly. "You're saying yes? You're gonna be my fake girlfriend?"

For whatever reason, excitement races up my spine as I say, "Yes."

Theo wraps his arms around me as he lifts me into one of his famous Theo hugs.

Once I'm back on the ground, I take a few steps away from him. "We need some ground rules, to make sure lines don't get blurred. I don't want to lose our friendship."

I finally feel like I have a good person in my life, and I'd hate to lose him over this.

Theo takes my hands in his, his thumb running gently on top of them. "We will always be friends, okay?"

I nod, and he continues. "Tell me what you're comfortable and not comfortable with."

My eyes dart to our joined hands. "I don't think we need to touch unless either of them are around."

He releases my hands instantly. "That's fine, but remember that we're not just faking it for them. We're faking it to the entire school, otherwise word will get back to them."

Shit, I didn't think of it that way.

"Okay, what are we telling … the squad?" My voice is unsure, because I don't know if I'm in the friend group enough to refer to myself as a part of it.

Theo smiles, "We can tell *our* friends the truth, because they'll never believe for a second that we're actually dating."

I want to ask what he means by that, but he speaks again.

"So, no touching when we're alone is our first rule. What about when we're in front of people, specifically Hunter and Ruby? What are you comfortable with, PDA-wise?" he asks, ever the gentleman.

Heat rushes to my cheeks. "Uh … we can hold hands, hug."

"That's all?" Theo raises a brow. "Could I do this?" he asks, wrapping his arm around the small of my back, tugging me closer to him.

"T-that's kind of like a hug, so yes," my voice is breathy, and I don't know why. We're friends practicing how to fake-date. No big deal.

"What about this?" His voice dips lower as he spins me so that my back is against his chest. His muscular arms wrap around my stomach, holding me close, as his face nestles into my neck. "This okay?" His lips brush against my skin, sending a shiver down my spine.

"Yes," I mumble softly, unable to think straight. I'm blaming it on the emotions of tonight, and not on any other reason. Like, that I may be attracted to him.

Theo draws back, coming to stand in front of me. "How do you feel about kissing?"

My mouth goes dry at the idea of kissing him, because of course he's hot, but that would make our friendship hard to get back to once this is over.

"No kissing. I want to be able to be friends after this."

He grins, that lone dimple appearing. "Afraid you'll kiss me and fall in love?"

I shake my head and scoff a laugh. "Not at all." I redirect the conversation to another topic. "How long do we do this for?"

"I say the entire school year, unless you want to stop at any point. This is all on your terms."

"If you want it to be over at any time, that's fine. You have a say in this too, you know," I remind him, because it's not just me who's benefiting from this. He'll be off the market and girls will leave him alone. So if he wants to go back to that, he can.

"Okay, I think that covers just about everything. But one last thing." He swallows, looking serious once again. "While we do this, you're mine and I'm yours. I can promise you I'll be loyal, but I expect the same from you."

While I don't think I'll ever truly believe that statement from a man anytime soon, I nod anyway. "I promise you that's nothing you need to worry about. I know how awful it feels, so I'll never do it to someone else. Fake relationship or not."

Theo holds out his hand to me "So, we have a deal? You're gonna be my fake girlfriend, Marcela?"

I put my hand in his, shaking it. "We do, but I have one final question."

"Yeah?"

"Are you going to give me a silly nickname like you do for everyone else? Like AV baby, Jay bay bay, Millie moo…" I trail off, listing what he calls the girls in our friend group. He's known for his silly nicknames, and a part of me has been curious as to what mine will be.

"I give them silly nicknames … but you're different. You're my girl." He smiles shyly.

I can't help but smile back, because even though it's a part of our charade, it's my favorite name in books. There's something so soft, yet possessive about *my girl* that hits me right in the chest every time I read it.

"But I like the sound of Celly too, if you do," he adds.

"I do, both are good." I smile, liking their simplicity.

"You ready to go back in there?" Theo asks, concern edging in his voice.

I stand tall, feeling more confident than before. "Yes. I have to go back to waiting tables, so I'll see you around."

I debate hugging him after what we just agreed on, but I get too flustered and end up leaving him outside without another word as I hustle back to work.

Catch Me

It's my job that forces me to be way more social than I'd like, but it also lets me meet so many different people, which helps when it comes to my writing. When you're an author, anything or anyone can become inspiration. Suddenly, the stranger in the booth is the villain of a story.

As I round the corner, I see my boss and Aurora's brother, Nate, at the end of the bar, who signals me over.

"I'm so sorry for running out like that," I apologize to him once I'm close enough.

"Don't worry about it. You're my best server. I know you wouldn't have done it if you didn't have a genuine reason. I covered your tables while you were taking a break," he tells me while wiping down the bar.

I sigh a breath of relief. "Thank you so much."

Taking a glance around the space, I look to see who needs drink refills then head behind the bar to fulfill them. While I wait on my tables, I purposely ignore the area the team is sitting in as I get through the rest of my shift.

All of the worry about running into Hunter fades as I busy myself, so much so that I forget anything except for the tables I'm serving. Until I run square into him with a tray full of drinks.

"I'm …" I can't find it in me to say sorry, because I don't feel bad. He deserves a lot more than being soaked in beverages.

Hunter's eyes don't leave mine as we look at each other for the first time in five months. Unease prickles my spine at the fact that we're partially hidden from anyone else. I don't want to be alone with him.

"Marcela," he drags out my name, making my skin crawl. "Still clumsy as ever I see. How've you been?"

I want to tell him off. To scream at him. To make him feel exactly how he made me feel. But my mom raised me better than that.

"Never better." I smile widely, and thumb behind me to the bar. "I have to go remake these drinks, so …" I turn to do just that when he grabs my hand, turning me back to him.

Before I can tell him to let me go, Theo steps between us. "If I see you touching my girl again, we're going to have real problems. And not just on the field."

Hunter chuckles, looking between Theo and me. "This is why you don't like me, huh Miller? Over some lame puss—"

Theo has Hunter pinned against the wall in seconds. "Don't you dare finish that sentence."

"I'm just saying, bros before ho—"

"We're not bros. If you want any chance of playing this season, I suggest you walk away. *Now.*"

I watch with bated breath as they stare at one another with clenched jaws as anger radiates off the both of them.

Theo lets him go, and Hunter scoffs as he walks right out of the bar without another word.

Once he's gone, Theo turns to me. "You okay?" he asks softly while his hand gently lifts the one Hunter grabbed, inspecting it.

"Yeah, I'm good," I say as I let out a relieved breath. "You didn't have to do that, you know."

A puzzled look crosses Theo's face. "You're my girl now. I'm not allowing anyone, especially not Hunter, to manhandle you like that."

"Thank you," I tell him, giving his hand a squeeze before letting it drop. "I really need to get these drinks to their tables."

"Did you drive here tonight?"

I halt and look over my shoulder. "Yes, why?"

"I have to get going and get a good sleep in before the game tomorrow, but I wanted to make sure you weren't walking home alone. I can make sure Nate walks you to your car."

I want to tell Theo he doesn't need to do that, but knowing him, it's pointless. "Okay, good luck tomorrow."

"I better see you there with my number painted on your cheek," he winks, shooting me a boyish grin.

I'm his fake girlfriend now, so I guess I have to act like it.

"My ass will not be out for people to see," I joke, making his eyes widen as he laughs.

"Oh, you've got jokes now too? Listen, I'm the funny one in this relationship," he says, making me laugh.

"I'll see you tomorrow." I smile, giving him a wave and then return to the bar.

As I finish up the remainder of my shift, all I can think about is how good Theo is at faking his enthusiasm for football, but I really hope he's also good at separating real feelings from our fake relationship too. Because if one of us falls without the other to catch us, this could turn out very poorly.

And I make a silent prayer to the universe that it won't be me.

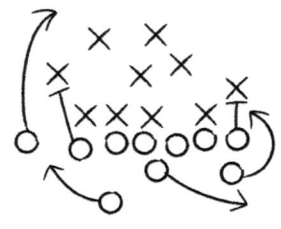

Chapter 8
Theo

Marcela is my girlfriend.

The girl I've been losing my mind over for the last three years is mine. Well, in a fake capacity, but I'll take what I can get.

I feel bad that I told her I don't lie and then lied to her face. The truth is that I like her.

A *lot*.

Of course I do, how could I not? She's perfect.

But I didn't want her to worry that I couldn't handle this, or that our arrangement would hurt me in the end. Without a doubt, it'll crush me, especially after getting used to having her as mine. If this is what will help her move on from the pain those assholes caused her, then I'd do it over again.

No matter how much it hurts me in the end.

And it's not like there's anyone else she'd rather do this with, it's just me she trusts. Which is a privilege I don't take lightly. So, as excited as I am, I need to keep my emotions at bay and focus on making sure this works for her.

I'm about to call it a night and toss my phone on my bedside table when it vibrates with my dad's name flashing across the screen.

Great.

"Hey, Dad," I answer, sitting up in bed with my back against the headboard.

"You've got a big game tomorrow. I'm surprised you're still up," he points out.

It's only ten o'clock, but I don't bother bringing that up.

"I'm excited. Can't sleep just yet," I lie, because my excitement is not related to tomorrow's game. Not even close.

"I remember those days," he hums. "I'll be there tomorrow, and I can't wait to cheer you on in the stands."

My stomach knots wildly, knowing if I make a single mistake he'll lecture me about it for days.

"What about Ally, David, and Mason?" I ask, referring to my sister, her husband, and my nephew.

"We'll all be there, cheering you on as you do great things tomorrow," he confirms, sending anxiety coursing through my veins.

I grab my fidget cube I keep close by to give my hands something to do and distract myself.

"Can't wait," I say, mustering what I hope sounds like joy into my voice.

"How're classes going? You staying focused?"

Here we go.

"It's only the first week, but they're good. And of course, I always am." I roll my eyes, not that he can see.

"That's what I like to hear. At this point in your career, women are only after one thing and it's your future dollar signs. Keep to yourself, get me?" His commanding voice hits me right in the stomach, where my anxiety permanently lives, igniting it further.

I can't hide Marcela and I being together from him, even if it's fake, like I'm able to do with my hatred for football. I told her I'm in on this, and if my dad sees, then I'll deal with the repercussions of it when the time comes.

He's dictated my career, but I'll be damned if I let him dictate anything that relates to her.

"Yeah, Dad. Listen, I'm going to get some sleep. See you tomorrow." I hang up on him before he can respond, needing to center myself before I drift off. Otherwise, I'll toss and turn all night, which isn't ideal before a game.

Plugging my phone to its charger, I roll over in bed and start doing breathing exercises. After a couple of minutes, my stomachache goes away and my spinning thoughts begin to settle.

Thankfully, I dream of honey-brown eyes and freckles that night.

Chapter 9
Marcela

I can do this, I tell myself repeatedly as I stare at my reflection in the mirror.

Today's the first official day of being in a fake relationship with Theo, and we're about to announce it to everyone. Knowing Theo, he's going to make it obvious.

My long brown waves are in a high ponytail, and the number seven—Theo's number—is drawn on my cheek with black eyeliner. It's a crisp fall day, so I opted for my white, long-sleeved RLU shirt, black vest, and black leggings paired with white sneakers.

The apple crisp oatmeal I made this morning gurgles in my stomach as the nerves begin to work their way into my system. I check my phone to see that I still have an hour before the game starts and decide to write for a little while.

I'm about halfway into my romantic fantasy novel online, set underwater with two royal mermaid families at war. Naturally, the princess is in love with the enemy's son.

Although I don't remember much of my life back home in Costa Rica, my mother always says I loved the water, which explains why I'm so drawn to writing an entire novel set in it.

I'm currently writing the scene where the male main character is protecting the female main character from his family, brutally beating a man up.

Fluttering erupts in my stomach when I think back to last night, how Theo defended me with ease, and the way he threw Hunter, who's a bulky guy, against the wall like it was nothing.

We're just friends, but that was hot.

I've always loved protective men in fiction, and that definitely made me more attracted to Theo than I should be.

My fingers fly over the keyboard as I get in the zone, where nothing else matters. Writing is my safe space, a solitude that I create all on my own.

That is, until my phone rings with an incoming video call from Aurora, Jasmine, and Camille.

I answer, and within seconds, I see all of their smiling faces.

"Marcela!" they all shout.

"Hey, what's up?" I smile back.

"What is that?" Jasmine notices instantly and that's when I realize that the number I put on my cheek is very visible.

"This? It's just a coffee I'm making," Camille turns her camera to show us her latte with a flower design on top.

"No, she's talking about the number on Marcela's cheek, and the fact that she looks like she's going to RLU's football home opener today," Aurora supplies, raising a brow.

All three of them stare at me through the screen, waiting for me to answer.

I swallow once, and with a sigh, I give them a shortened version of what's going on.

"Ruby and Hunter are back at RLU, and because that's been hard for me and I don't want them thinking they won, Theo offered to be my fake boyfriend. So, I'm going to his game as a real girlfriend would."

They're quiet for a moment, then they all erupt in excitement.

"This sounds like that book I was telling you about," Jasmine says.

"Fake dating is a real thing that happens?" Camille questions.

"Apparently so," I shrug.

Aurora chimes in, "I only say this with love, but please be careful. You know Theo has been after you forever … and I'd hate for him to get confused about what this is."

"That's a good point," Camille agrees.

"I know, and we talked about that. He said he doesn't have feelings for me, and wants to do this to help. We're friends, and friends help each other," I tell them, hoping they're not upset with me. "I would never do anything to hurt him."

"We know that, and we're not upset," Aurora says, reading my mind. "I'm just looking out for the both of you. That's all."

"I appreciate that." I let out a breath. "I don't even know how to be a fake girlfriend. What do I do?"

Jasmine perks up at my request for advice. "Well, it's the same as being a normal girlfriend, except it doesn't mean anything. It's all for show for someone else, kind of like you guys are actors portraying love interests in a movie. When the scene is done, you go back to your normal lives. But," she drawls, a wicked gleam shining in her eyes. "That's not how it goes in books. No, instead you feel things with those fake touches or gestures until eventually you can't distinguish between what's real or fake."

My stomach drops because that absolutely cannot happen. "Jasmine, you read too much fiction," Aurora says with a laugh.

"I kind of hope that happens," Camille says dreamily. "Imagine if she and Theo fall in love from this? I would be so happy. Of course, if that doesn't happen, I'll still love you two."

"Don't get your hopes up," I tell her honestly. Not wanting to dwell on it, I get back to my original question. "What should I do today? Is there anything a girlfriend would do at a game?"

"When Cameron comes to my games, he cheers me on. Even if he's not screaming the loudest, the fact that he's there is enough for me." Aurora blushes, turning to smile at who I'm assuming is Cameron off to the side.

"Elio doesn't play anymore, but if he was playing hockey, I would wear his jersey and cheer him on. That's all you can do really," Jasmine adds.

"If you wanted to really sell it, I would post a selfie at the game with his number visible in a story on social media. It would be a cute soft launch. Or if you want to go with a hard launch, post a video of the game where you zoom in on Theo, and tag him with a heart," Camille suggests.

All of this sounds very out of left field for me, because I dated Hunter when I was fifteen and this stuff didn't exist back then.

"What is a soft launch?" I ask, dumbfounded. "I haven't dated in a while, so I'm not really familiar with it."

Aurora chuckles. "A soft launch is when you subtly post the person that you're dating. So not their face or name, just mysterious posts that leave people guessing. Whereas a hard launch is full force, balls to the wall, tagging the person and showing their face."

We all laugh, when my alarm goes off.

The game.

"I have to go. The game is gonna start," I tell them. Although right now, I'd much rather stay here and talk to them.

Jasmine claps her hands. "You've got this and we love you!"

"And we expect a full report later on what happened," Camille adds before we all say our goodbyes and hang up.

Here goes nothing.

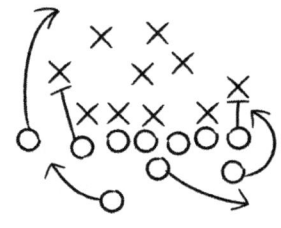

Chapter 10
Theo

The roar of the stadium pounds throughout my entire body, while a sense of dread follows in its path.

Don't get me wrong. I'm good at doing my job on the field, so there is a sense of excitement there, but it's dulled by the pressure and every other reason why I hate playing this game.

Add in the fact that I know my dad is in the stands critiquing me, and that leads me to want to be anywhere else but here.

I rest my forehead against the bathroom stall, my go-to place to center myself before I go out there and pretend to be someone else.

Along with taking deep breaths, I think of the things that *do* bring me joy.

My friends.

My sister and nephew.

The animals at the farm.

Sunsets.

Her.

A sense of calm washes over me at the thought of the last one, and with one last breath, I head for the locker room where I know everyone is waiting for me to deliver a speech of a lifetime.

As soon as I open the door, pandemonium begins. Everyone starts cheering, slapping helmets and huddling around me in a sea of dark-green-and-white jerseys.

I hold my hand up, signaling them to quiet down.

My gaze sweeps over the group of guys surrounding me, guys I have spent the last three years playing with. We've bonded on and off the field and have had each other's back through the chaos that is being a student athlete. If there's one thing I'm grateful for, it's that football has brought so many amazing people into my life.

Minus Hunter, of course.

"For the seniors, our last home opener is minutes away," I start, swallowing before continuing. "It's the last time we'll have this experience together. It's the beginning of the end for us. But one thing that remains will be the bond that we've created. No one can take that away from us."

Applause breaks out around me, but I know what they're waiting for, so I dive right in.

"The men in this room are the hardest working players in the game today. The Florida State Sharks better give it their all, because we're coming out of the gate at one-hundred-ten percent."

The claps get louder, so I stand on the bench, raising my voice.

"This season is ours. We've worked way too damn hard these last few years, building up our team, to not take home the championship. I'll give all I have to each and every game. Every bead of sweat, of blood, is for you boys. That trophy belongs here at RLU."

The team whistles and shouts, getting pumped up like I knew they would.

"Coyotes," I drawl, and they start howling back at me.

"Who's gonna bring it home?"

The howls get even louder.

"I said, who's gonna bring it home?"

"Coyotes!" everyone shouts and whistles, while some still howl in the background.

Then, we're charging through the tunnel for the first time this season. I lead the team, running out onto the field past the cheerleaders and smoke machines, while the crowd goes absolutely insane at the sight of us.

My eyes instantly flick to the spot where I got a ticket for Marcela, and I swear my heart expands in my chest when I see her. She's on her feet, clapping with the biggest smile on her face and *my* number painted on her cheek.

Even though our relationship is fake, it means the world to me that she came, because I know how uncomfortable these types of events are for her.

Then I look for my dad in his usual spot, just a few rows behind where Marcela is sitting. His signature cap is pulled low over his face to avoid attention, but I'd know that hat anywhere. It's a basic black and white New York hat that used to belong to my mom.

To avoid getting in my head, I shift my focus to my sister and her husband,, who are on their feet beside my father, cheering and pointing me out to my nephew Mason.

I give him a wave and jog over to our team's bench where I'm instantly surrounded by the coaching staff as we decide our first play.

As we set up on the field and wait for the game to start, I feel the need to not only impress everyone here and my dad, but Marcela too.

And there are no negative feelings attached to it. Instead, it's exciting.

I've never had a girl come to a game before, considering I only had one short-lived relationship in high school. Besides, I haven't been interested in anyone since Marcela came along. It makes me want to show her how good I am, and it's with that in mind that I play one of the best games I've ever had. I throw six touchdowns, and we keep their offense at bay for the majority of the game, only letting them score three times. We win our first game of the season 42-21.

And the best part was that I didn't have to throw to Hunter once, because he was never open. I call that a win alone in my books.

I jump off of the bench when the clock reaches zero, but instead of running to my team, I run to her. Because I'd imagine there is nothing that is going to piss off Ruby and Hunter more than seeing this.

I watch her standing behind the rails, biting her bottom lip in what I'm assuming are nerves, with her eyes locked onto mine.

"Celly," I yell, and everyone in the section looks at me, watching as I stop right in front of her.

"Great game, Theo," she says, looking genuinely proud.

It makes me grin, and I like hearing her say that more than I should, especially when she's wearing my number.

"You ready for a Theo hug?"

Marcela's eyebrows narrow. "I'm up here and you're down there."

I wave her off. "Lean over the railing and I'll lift you."

"What if you drop me?"

"Do you really think I'd risk hurting you?"

Her face softens at that, and she leans her arms over the railing, allowing me to lift her up and into my arms.

Nothing has ever felt as good as it does with Marcela in my arms. It reminds me of slow mornings at the farm when everything's quiet, and I'd watch the sunrise, reminding myself of all the things I'm grateful for.

It's the fullness in the stillness.

I spin her around, fully aware that there are thousands of people watching. Not only in the crowd, but at home too, as I'm sure there's a few cameras on us right now.

"Remember, do not kiss me," she whispers into my ear.

"Is on the forehead okay?" I whisper back as I set her down on her feet.

Her hands squeeze my forearms where they're still holding onto me, and she gives me a slight nod. I lower my head and press my lips to her forehead. I can feel her cheeks lift as she smiles, and it hits me then that I never knew a kiss on the forehead could feel so *right*.

Her skin is warm under my lips and there's a buzz running through my veins at the contact. It's dizzying and fucking terrifying, because what if we ever have to actually kiss?

I might die.

I pull away, noting the slight flush on her face as I do. Before I can look too much into it, a reporter shoves a microphone in my face.

"Theo Miller, amazing job on the field today. You sure are living up to expectations to be just like your father," the reporter says, her short blonde bob making me instantly recognize her.

Kelly Karson—the most intrusive sports reporter in college right now.

My arm wraps around Marcela's waist, pulling her into me. I don't want her getting lost in the crowd and I feel much better with her close.

"Thanks," I give her a curt nod, ready to get Marcela out of here, when Kelly speaks up again.

"I'm dying to know, who is this lovely lady right here?" Kelly's bright green eyes dance with mischief as she looks between the two of us. In my entire college career, I've never had a girlfriend, and she knows this story is going to sell. *Theo Miller Loses Focus During Last Year Because He's Too Busy With Girlfriend*, or some shit like that.

"My girlfriend. Next question," I smile, doing my best to come off respectful yet charming.

Kelly clearly doesn't like my answer, but moves on. "Do you think the Coyotes have a chance to finally win the championship this year?"

"We're going to give it all we've got, and hopefully that's enough to get the job done. Thank you for the questions. We need to get going," I plaster a fake, wide smile on my face as I wave to the camera and then escort Marcela away from the madness.

The action on the field is dying down as players from both teams are leaving to their respective tunnels for post-game debriefs, one I need to attend myself. I find us a quiet corner in the hallway, out of sight from anyone lingering. As soon as we're alone, Marcela steps out of my arm, putting space between us.

"I'm sorry if that was too much for you," I tell her, apologetic. I know how she likes her space and that was probably her worst nightmare.

"No, it's okay. I knew this was expected territory, but I do appreciate you respecting my privacy with the reporter. Even though everyone online will have it figured out in a few minutes."

"Shit, I didn't even think about that."

"Honestly, it only rubs it in their faces more, so I truly don't mind."

"Ah, so you *are* in it for the fame," I tease her, crossing my arms over my chest.

She rolls her eyes, but laughs. "Oh, yes, because there is nothing I want more than people stalking me and ruining every ounce of privacy I have in life."

We both laugh at that, but it's cut short when we hear footsteps coming down the tunnel. Marcela steps closer to me, not quite touching me, but I notice it all the same.

My dad's tall figure comes into view, making my stomach twist instinctively.

"Hey, Dad." I shake his hand once he stops in front of us. "Pretty good way to start the season, huh?"

"You made me proud today, son," he admits as he lets eyes that match mine sear into me. But today he's genuinely proud, I can see it there.

The nerves in my stomach begin to settle until he turns his gaze to Marcela.

"And who is this?" he asks.

"My girlfriend, Marcela. Marcela, this is my dad, Randy Miller," I introduce them.

Marcela sticks out her hand, "It's nice to meet you, sir."

My dad scoffs. "Don't call me sir, but it's nice to meet you too," he says as he shakes her hand, a playful smile on his face that I don't see too often.

I'm surprised by the gesture, but I know my grandma taught him to never disrespect a lady. His real feelings about this will come my way later. I'll receive a phone call once we're both home, where he'll warn me that I better not throw my future away for a girl.

"What are you studying?" my dad asks her.

"English literature," she replies, her shoulder brushing against mine.

"Do you want to be a schoolteacher or something?" His tone is genuine, not accusatory like I'm used to.

Marcela shakes her head. "My plan is to get a master's degree and work at a publishing house."

"That's good. I like that you have goals of your own."

I keep my eyes from rolling, because it's clear to me he's trying to see what her intent is in being with me.

She gives him a slight nod and smile.

"Alright, I better get going. Your sister's waiting to drive me back to the farm. I just had to come say congratulations on a great game and … to meet your beautiful girlfriend." My dad gives a genuine smile as he waves. "See y'all at the next game."

I'm a little bummed that my sister and nephew didn't come to find me, but Mason's probably in need of a nap, which means my sister is probably exhausted.

"See you, Dad. Tell them I say hey."

"Bye," Marcela says softly.

Once he's out of view, Marcela steps away from me.

"Sorry about him." I run a hand through my sweat-soaked hair, yanking on the strands.

"Don't be. I get it. He's looking out for you. It's what every parent does for their kid."

It suddenly dawns on me that I don't know anything about her family, but as much as I want to ask, I realize right now isn't the best time. I need to get into the locker room for a post-game debrief and a shower.

"I have to meet the team," I thumb toward the end of the hallway. "Are you okay to get home?"

Marcela groans. "Yes, *Dad*, I'll be fine to walk to my car."

I step closer to her and whisper in her ear, "If you want to call me daddy, I'm more than okay with that."

Her cheeks turn red as her eyes widen. "That's not what I meant."

"Sure, Celly," I wink as I begin to walk backward. "Text me when you're home safe."

I watch as she does her best to suppress a smile before turning and walking the opposite way. My heart nearly comes to a stop, because her ass in those leggings should be illegal.

Fuck. Stop. You can't have these thoughts.

We're friends, pretending to date to help her through a tough situation. I can't think of her that way.

Despite how much I wish I could.

As I walk out of the football stadium, I open my phone and see a message from Marcela telling me she's home safe. I text her back and then open my group chat with the guys to find a few unread messages.

Ry Guy

> When were you going to tell us about your girlfriend? And that it's fucking Marcela of all people?

Eli Oldi

> You have the biggest mouth in the world, how did you not tell us the second it happened?

Ronnie Boy

> I'm happy for you man, I know how long you've wanted this.

I frown at that, because I'm about to tell them how this is all for show and ruin their excitement.

CARLIE JEAN

Me

Just got done from post-game debriefs, so I was a little busy. Don't get too excited though, we're fake dating.

Eli Oldi

Is this some kind of prank or something? It sounds like a book Jasmine just finished.

Me

It's not. Her shitty ex and old best friend are back here at RLU, so we agreed to fake date so they don't think they got the upper hand, you know? Keep it quiet though, otherwise that would defeat the whole purpose and those two would have a field day with that information.

Ry Guy

What the fuck.

Ronnie Bo

Ryker you can't judge. You pretended to be friends with benefits with Camille when deep down you knew you wanted way more than that.

Ry Guy

I like quiet Cameron more than blunt Cameron.

Eli Oldi

> Can we focus here? Theo, you sure you can handle this? According to Jasmine you've had a crush on Marcela since... the day you guys met right? Can you really keep it casual?

Me

> I'll try. I have to, for her. I'd do anything to help her.

Ronnie Boy

> You'll hurt yourself just to help her?

Me

> I'll be good, you guys know I don't take anything too seriously.

I try to remind them of the Theo they know so that they're not as worried. But I'm not quite sure if I'm doing it for myself or for them.

Ry Guy

> Just be careful Theo.

Ronnie Boy

> Agreed, we care about you and don't want this to go south when you guys eventually do fake break up.

My stomach sours at the thought already, but I keep that to myself.

CARLIE JEAN

> Me
>
> Appreciate you guys. I need to get some sleep though, being the best quarterback and carrying the team is exhausting.

Eli Oldi

> Cocky fucker. You're not wrong though, great game today.

Ry Guy

> Seriously, the team is looking great. You better bring home the championship this year.

Ronnie Boy

> Aurora was cheering you on through the screen. You did so well, man. it's crazy how talented you are.

> Me
>
> Thanks, guys.

Once I put my phone away, I toss and turn, unable to sleep because their words play on repeat in my mind. Not about me getting hurt once this is over, because I know without a doubt that will happen, but the present reward is worth it.

No, what's playing in my mind are their comments about me as a football player. The guys have no idea how much I loathe being one. They always hype me up and tell me how great I am, which I know, but it doesn't help ease my guilt over despising something others would kill to be doing.

I could play for a few years and make enough money to never work again. But I don't care about that. Don't get me wrong,

I want to be able to provide for my family forever. I just don't care to make millions at the cost of my mental well-being.

What's the point of making all that money if it'll make me miserable?

I'm sick of my body feeling beat up all the fucking time. I hate the pressure of the game and the pressure I'm subjected to from my dad. Besides, football itself isn't very safe, like what happened to my dad. I'd be furious at myself if I got injured playing and it ruined my quality of life, all because I didn't have the guts to pursue what I really want.

It's on nights like these that I think of my mom, and what she'd say if she were here.

I don't have many memories of her because I was only four when we lost her, but my sister does. She told me all about her once I was old enough to understand.

Ally said that my mother was the most understanding and loving person there ever was. She was soft-spoken, yet fierce when protecting loved ones. She was raised on the same farm we were, and she spent her life doing what she loved—helping animals.

When she met my dad, he was this city guy who'd never been to the country in his life, but once he saw it through her eyes, he fell in love.

So much so that even after she died, he continued her family's legacy just to preserve her memory and passion. With my sister's help, they've elevated it with horse riding classes, holiday special events, and a year-round market with produce grown on the farm.

I'd like to imagine that she'd tell me to follow my heart and do what makes me happy. As a kid, that seems like the easiest thing to do. If it makes you happy, do it. If it doesn't, don't.

But no one tells you just how complicated that truly is as an adult.

Chapter 11
Marcela

I let out the world's largest sigh, blowing a hair out of my face.

I've been sitting at my desk for what feels like forever, unable to get a single word typed in my manuscript. Writer's block is the absolute worst, especially when writing has always come so easily to me. But now, for whatever reason, I find myself unable to get in the zone this morning.

Not even my morning tea or my gallo pinto could perk me up enough.

I'm wondering if it has anything to do with the fact that photos and videos of Theo and I at the game have gone viral.

Seeing it from an outside perspective, I can see what they mean when they gush about how romantic the gesture was. But knowing that it's all fake sends a twinge of guilt through me at the fact that we're lying to everyone outside of our friend group.

My phone lights up with a social media notification that I ignore, like the other thousand new requests to follow me. My eyes catch the wallpaper photo of my mother, and it reminds me that I'm going to have to tell her about Theo too.

Catch Me

And my stepdad.

Although he wasn't happy when he heard about what Hunter did to me, he surprisingly took my side for once. My dad used to love Hunter. Probably because Hunter is exactly what he was like as a kid. Privileged, from an important family, well-connected, and cocky.

Honestly, when I think about it now, I don't know what I ever saw in Hunter.

I'm not sure how my stepdad is going to react to me dating Theo, especially if he's had something to drink—which is more likely than not—but I'll have to call them soon.

As if the universe read my mind, I get a text from my mom.

> **Mamá**
> Come over Saturday for dinner. I'm making tamales. Bring your new boyfriend too. Dad and I can't wait to meet him.

I close my eyes as my stomach hollows. Dinner means too much time for my stepdad to get drunk beforehand. But if my mom is going all out and making tamales, which we usually do only on holidays, I know there's no changing her mind.

> **Me**
> Sure thing, love you.

> **Mamá**
> Love you too Marcie girl.

Unease seeps into every pore of my body, giving me the itch to write and get lost in another world so I can forget about mine. But I need to get to my class before I'm late.

On my walk across campus, all I can think about is how Theo didn't sign up for all of this. When we made a deal to fake-date, we didn't ask to endure each other's family drama.

After his game on Saturday, I could sense that Theo didn't want to talk about his dad and why things felt strained between them. Just like I don't want to have to explain that my stepdad is an alcoholic who has no filter when he's drunk. And how any time someone raises their voice at me, my body tenses and I'm back to being the little girl hiding in her room, trying to drown out the noise of her parents arguing.

I also don't want Theo to think that my mom is weak, or ask why she hasn't left yet. Because trust me, I've wondered that too. But the solution isn't always that simple, and it's why I've never once asked my mother, despite wanting to more than anything.

I mull over calling it quits with Theo, but it won't make anything better.

I do my best to focus on the present, taking in the piles of colorful leaves on the sidewalk and the laughter of the people I walk past. Today's our second day back on campus since the game, and for the second day in a row, I'm getting stares, waves, and friendly smiles from people who never would've looked my way before I started dating Theo.

It makes me slightly uncomfortable, because I'm happily a wallflower who likes to skate by without being noticed. But I smile back at them anyway, doing my best to be polite despite wanting to sink into a black hole from all the attention.

I'm about to enter the lecture hall when I spot Ruby walking my way. Now I *really* need that black hole.

She stops right in front of me, her lips pursed tightly, painted red to match her hair, indicating she's far from happy to see me.

"Are you kidding me?" she scoffs, crossing her arms over her chest.

I don't say anything. I merely look at her in confusion, because the fewer words we exchange, the better.

"You played the victim card by saying how hurt you were and *blah, blah, blah,* when you've already moved on too?"

Is she serious right now?

"Just because I've moved on does not take away from the fact that what you did was wrong. Although I'm in a much happier relationship, it doesn't mean I've forgiven nor forgotten what you and Hunter did," I say with a confidence I didn't think was possible.

Ruby rolls her eyes. "God, you are so sensitive. You have a new man. Stop being obsessed with my relationship."

I blink, dumbfounded. What did she just say? Was she always like this, and I never realized?

With a forced smile I tell her, "I hope you both find the happiness I have with Theo."

"And I hope for your sake you learn a thing or two about how to please a man, so that this one doesn't cheat on you too."

It takes every ounce of my control to appear unaffected when her words deliver a sucker punch to my stomach.

I thought Hunter and I had a good sex life. Not amazing, but good. He was a selfish partner, always ensuring he came. Though I never did, because he always refused to go down on me. Even though he never did it to me, I did it to him a couple times until he told me to stop.

I found it odd at the time, but now I'm wondering if it's because I wasn't good at it.

The idea shoots a hole in my confidence, leaving me feeling insecure and uncomfortable.

I don't say another word, because if I did, the words "fuck you" might slip out, even though I've never said them to anyone before. Instead, I sidestep Ruby and push through the doors to my first class.

But Ruby's words run on a loop in my mind all throughout the day. Would Hunter not have strayed if I was better at sex?

Maybe I wasn't a good girlfriend at all. Things seemed good in high school when we saw each other every day, but when he got a scholarship at Aspen and we went to different universities, things started to feel different.

I thought we were happy, but when I compare what we had to the love stories I read about in books, it makes me wonder if what we had was love at all.

The sex wasn't amazing. He didn't do much for me. No buying me flowers on Valentine's Day, no random thoughtful gifts, no surprise visits or phone calls. And he always preferred hanging out with his friends.

I'm beginning to think that the only reason we stayed together so long was because it was comfortable. That's not to say I didn't love him once, because I think I did at one point, but it changed somewhere along the way.

This was probably for the best, but I just wish it didn't require breaking my heart and ruining all my trust in people in the process.

Chapter 12

Marcela

"Alright!" Professor Grum claps at the front of the room. "Tonight is perfect for some stargazing. Not a cloud in that wonderful sky."

Theo and I begin to pack our things into our bags, since the lesson is being moved outdoors.

"Bring your belongings and follow me," our professor instructs. We all stand, following her out of the building and around the darkened pathways of campus until we reach the hill Theo brought me to a few weeks ago.

"Spread out, lay with a friend, and soak up the stars. Tonight, I want you to merely stargaze. Admire the beauty of the sky and see if you can find any constellations. There will be a discussion post on this next week, so be ready to share your findings. Whether that's something in the sky, or something the stars unleashed inside of you."

Everyone settles in different spots on the grass, and I'm about to sit when Theo takes my hand, sending a chill up my arm.

"Let's go over here," he gestures to a spot a bit farther from the group. I follow him with my hand in his, reminding myself that this is totally normal behavior because everyone here thinks we're dating.

I set my tote bag down in the grass, thankful that I was dressed appropriately for the cold weather in my oversized pink sweater and thick black leggings. Theo looks just as comfortable in his matching dark-gray sweatsuit that's molded perfectly to his muscular—wait, no. No thinking anything about his muscles.

I shake myself out of it, attempting to rid myself of those kinds of thoughts as I sink down to the ground.

I'm about to lay down on the grass when Theo says, "Wait."

I sit back up, looking at him with curiosity as he pulls out a sweater from his bag.

"Did you need me to watch you put on a sweater? Is that part of the … deal? Is that something girlfriends do nowadays?" I whisper.

Theo chuckles, the sound rich and velvety. "Stop being funny. That's my role."

He balls the sweater up the best he can, then sets it down behind me. "But no, that's not why. I didn't want you to lay your head on the grass. Figured my sweater would be more comfortable than getting bugs in your hair."

Something shifts in my heart so slightly that I nearly miss it, as I feel his kind gesture nestle itself in there. Hunter would've never done something like that. Something so small, yet entirely meaningful.

"What about you? You're not worried about bugs in your hair?" I ask, pushing the action to the back of my mind and trying not to read too much into it

"Nah, I'm good." He pulls out a RLU baseball cap from his bag, fitting it on top of his hair.

A smile lifts the corners of my lips as I slightly shake my head and lean back onto the makeshift pillow he made for me.

We're silent for the first few minutes as we watch the vivid stars above us. They're so bright, it feels like I could lift my hand up and grab one.

I find myself in awe as my gaze floats from one celestial body to the next. The stars come out every night, as they have for my entire life, yet today is the first time I think I've ever sat and truly *looked* at them.

Isn't it crazy that they even exist to begin with? That we're able to see them from this distance?

"How was your day?" Theo asks from his spot beside me, snapping me out of my daze.

"It was good, and yours?" I say, in the most unconvincing way possible.

"Hey," he says softly, "Talk to me, what's wrong?"

"My mom texted me today. She wants you to come over for dinner this Saturday to meet her and my stepfather."

"Isn't that a good thing …?"

"I mean, isn't this more than you signed up for?" I glance at him warily.

He shrugs. "Not at all. It's going to sell the idea to your parents, which is important if they ever run into Ruby or Hunter anywhere."

"Okay, you do have a point, considering my stepdad and Hunter's dad are friends. But you're sure it's okay?"

"I'd be more than happy to meet them. What time? We have a game at eleven that morning, but I can make it any time after that," he explains, ready to make time for me in his busy schedule.

His willingness to be there makes my heart skip a beat, because Hunter would've never done that.

"Dinner is at six. Do you have any allergies or food restrictions?" I ask, wanting to make sure before my mom cooks an entire feast that he can't eat.

"I don't eat meat. Growing up on a farm made me think about animals differently," he chuckles. "But I'll eat what I can, or I can bring something vegetarian with me."

"Oh no, my mom will be offended if you do that. I'll just let her know and she'll adjust the menu. A lot of Costa Rican food can easily be made vegetarian if it's not already," I tell him, not wanting him to feel like a burden.

"Alright then. My stomach and I are looking forward to Saturday. What time should I come pick you up?" he asks, once again surprising me with his kindness.

"They live about twenty minutes away, so five-thirty is good."

"Perfect," he says, then adds, "Is there anything I should know that will score me some points with your parents?"

"My mom is the sweetest woman ever, so honestly just being yourself will make her like you. She's a sucker for trashy reality TV shows, and *loves* collecting salt and pepper shakers. We have so many in the cupboards from our travels over the years, and random ones she's found in antique stores."

"She sounds awesome. I'll be on the lookout for some cool shakers from now on."

I pause, not sure what to say about my stepdad. While I want to warn Theo about how he gets when he starts drinking, I am not ready to share that part of my life.

"Chris, my stepdad, only really likes to talk business. He's also into betting on horses, the stock market, and things like that."

"Sheesh, that's going to be tough since I don't know much about business. Don't you worry. I'll up the good ole Theo charm and win him over," he says reassuringly, as if it will be that easy.

I'm not worried about them having nothing in common. I'm worried about my stepdad showing his true colors.

"He can be a bit ... abrasive. Don't take it personally, okay?"

"Everything will be alright, Celly. Don't even stress about it," Theo's voice is steady and calm, unlike the tension coiling through my body. He must sense it, because his fingers gently brush against mine.

"Thank you," I say quietly as I wrap my pinky around his, breaking my own rule. But it's only our pinkies, so it's not really touching, right?

His pinky squeezes around mine. I do it back—an unspoken *we've got this* communicated in that gesture. We lie there quietly for a few minutes as we stargaze. Slowly, my entire body relaxes, the stress of Theo meeting my stepdad fading away temporarily.

"Hey, what do you think about Friday night for our first date?" Theo says, interrupting the quiet air around us.

"W-why do we need to go out Friday?" I squeak, the reality of needing to actually go on dates settling in.

"It's a tradition for the team to go out before every home game and Hunter will probably be there. It'll be the perfect opportunity to show them that you've moved on and you couldn't care less about them."

"You're right," I sigh, dreading the fact that I'll have to be around Hunter and Ruby. "Friday works. Text me a time and I'll meet you there."

"*Ah, ah, ah,*" he tsks. "What kind of a boyfriend would I be if I didn't pick you up?"

"Are you sure it's not a problem?"

Theo pauses for a moment, before turning to face me. "Did Hunter not ever pick you up for dates?"

My heart aches as memories of my relationship flood through my mind, of all the things he didn't do for me that I wish he had.

"When we first started dating in high school, Hunter made an effort. But once we went to different colleges, things started to change. I was the only one making the trip to see him, and when I would get there, we usually only hung out with his friends. Dates slowly stopped happening," I press my lips together as the realization sets in on how crappy of a boyfriend he was. "You know, I always wished he'd get me flowers. But he never did. Not even for Valentine's Day, because he thought it was *forced*."

I look over to see Theo staring at me with a mixture of sadness and anger.

"Sorry, I'm oversharing."

"Don't apologize for that, I love listening to you talk. Especially when it helps me understand you better, okay?" His voice is so gentle, it makes my chest squeeze and I nod.

"I'm sorry he treated you that way. He's an idiot. You deserve the world. You know that, right? Never settle for anything less. *Ever*," he says.

I move to unlock my pinky from his, but quickly note a sense of alarm on his face. I don't move, keeping my hand in his. His brief panic turns into a smile, his dimple popping out. He knows me, without having to say a word.

One of the things I'm beginning to love about our friendship is how easily he understands me.

I've never had that kind of connection with anyone.

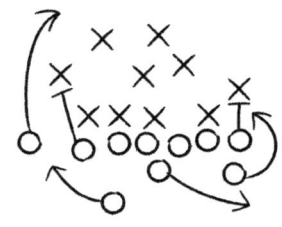

Chapter 13
Theo

I park my dad's old, white Chevy truck outside of Marcela's apartment complex in the parking lot, and send her a quick text to let her know that I'm here.

Marcela exits the building, stealing the breath right from my lungs. She's in a jean skirt that's molded to her body, making my mouth fucking water. And then there's the pink tank top she's wearing underneath her cardigan, with her tits nearly spilling out of it.

Is she trying to kill me?

I get out of my car, rounding the front to open the door for her.

"There's no one around, so you don't have to do that," she stares at me.

"I don't care, fake dating or not, I'm always going to open the door for you," I smile, gesturing for her to hop in.

I smirk when I see the look of shock on her face at the roses sitting between us.

"Theo, you didn't need to get me flowers," she shakes her head.

"You like flowers, right?" Marcela nods. "Then you'll get flowers every time we go on a date."

"Is this because you pity me? And because of what I went through?" she asks.

Shit. That wasn't my intention at all. I just wanted to spoil her and show her that it's easy to give her what she wants. That it's a privilege to do so.

"No, Celly, it's not. I got you flowers because I want to show you how easy it is to do, and why you shouldn't settle for anything less. Flowers, to me, are the bare minimum. Don't stress about it, please," I plead, hoping she's not offended.

Marcela brings the flowers up to her face, breathing them in with a soft smile on her lips. "Thank you. They really are beautiful."

Keeping my eyes on her, I say, "They really are."

I watch as her cheeks tinge red, making her freckles more prominent. She's fucking adorable.

Without another word, I pull onto the road and head towards the bar. It's only a two-minute drive, but with the way the temperature drops at night, I wanted to be able to drive her home.

We're silent on the short ride, until I put the truck into park and Marcela turns to me.

"Alright, how do we fake this?"

I stare at her for a beat, lost for words. "Uh …" I grip the back of my neck. "We do what people do on dates."

"I know I should know these things, but I'm kind of stressed right now. I need to know what to expect and what our roles are." Her voice is frantic, as if we're about to embark on something a lot scarier than hanging out at the local bar.

I take her hand in mine. "There are no expectations. I'll be myself, and you'll be yourself. We will make small talk with the group, I'll make some dumb comments, and you'll roll your eyes and laugh. I'll flirt with you, and you'll blush. Just the way I like," I chuckle, making her do exactly that.

"Okay," she says, still sounding slightly nervous.

"You're my girl and I'll make that very clear. All you need to do is smile, and look like you enjoy spending time with me—which you already do."

"Presumptuous, are we?" she chirps, and it makes me laugh. I love when she teases me.

"Ready?" I ask as I turn my truck off.

"I guess we'll find out," she mutters as I get out and round the hood to open her door.

Once we're inside, keep my hand on the small of her back as we make our way over to where my teammates are seated.

I pull out a chair for Marcela, and introduce her.

"Everyone, this is Marcela, my girlfriend. Marcela, this is … well, everyone." I chuckle, because there are way too many to introduce them individually. I'm sure she will learn their names as we talk with people tonight.

"Hi, everyone," she says quietly, giving them a small wave.

Dale is the only one to introduce himself, his hand outstretched toward Marcela. "I'm Dale."

She takes his hand, saying hi back.

"And this here is Robin," he adds, introducing his girlfriend.

Marcela and Robin hit it off while Dale and I fall into conversation about football, much to my distaste. We have a game tomorrow so the conversation should be expected.

Yet I still loathe every second of it.

I'm so lost in conversation with my teammates that an hour flies by before I know it. I'm beginning to think Hunter and Ruby are going to be no-shows—but then they walk in the door, as if I thought them into existence.

They make their way across the bar, and of course the only two empty seats are directly across from us. I sense Marcela stiffen beside me, so I lock my pinky with hers once again letting her know it'll be alright.

We knew they would be here, and it's why we're doing this in the first place. Although I imagine it is still difficult for Marcela to be across from the two people that hurt her most.

"There's the happy couple," Hunter grins crookedly at us as he wraps his arm around Ruby's shoulder, pulling her into him.

"Looks like we can say the same," I say dryly. I'm tempted to pull Marcela into me, but I don't want it to seem like I'm only doing it because he did. I have to wait for the perfect timing.

"Marcie," Ruby drawls, a conniving look on her face. "I told you everything would work out. Look at us. It's like old times."

Marcela reaches for my hand between us, wrapping her fingers with mine and resting them on her lap where they can see. "It's better than old times," Marcela responds nonchalantly, and I'm proud of her for not letting Ruby see how it's affecting her.

I don't miss the subtle flex of Hunter's jaw in irritation, and it makes me want to punch him right there. He has no right to be jealous or annoyed about her moving on.

"How did you two meet anyway?" Hunter asks, trying to seem uninterested in his tone, but his body tells a different story. He leans forward on his elbows, ready to listen.

We didn't prepare for this question, and by the squeeze she gives my hand, it's clear that she's nervous, so I take the lead.

"We met freshman year. We didn't talk much until this past summer, when Marcela gained *real* friends—who happened to be my friends. We started spending a lot of time together, and quickly realized our chemistry was too strong to ignore. The rest is history," I supply, not entirely lying.

"That seems fast for you, Marcie. I'm surprised," Ruby points out as she skims the menu. "Do they have anything that tastes good with zero calories or no sugar?"

"Oh, yeah. The water is phenomenal here. I highly recommend it," I say sarcastically, making Marcela chuckle beside me.

"Excuse me for trying to be healthy," Ruby rolls her eyes.

I put my hand over my chest. "And excuse me for trying to be friendly and joke around with you. Some people are so sensitive, huh, Celly?"

"Celly?" Hunter repeats my nickname for her. "As in what we do when we score?"

"It's not really your business why he calls me that," Marcela interjects, making all three of us go quiet. It's not her style to call people out—other than me.

I watch as surprise falls over Hunter's and Ruby's faces, followed by Hunter's brows narrowing in annoyance. "Whatever."

"What made you transfer?" I ask, switching the topic. I've been dying to know the real reason, though it's not likely he'll tell me, I figure it's worth a shot.

"To be with me," Ruby quickly answers as her hand grips his chin and she kisses him. I feel Marcela tense under our joined hands, and it makes me wonder if she has underlying feelings for him.

"You've got that right, babe. And like Coach Davis said, I've been wanting to try a new position, so this made sense for me and my career," Hunter replies almost robotically, as if it's a practiced answer.

I don't believe him for a second.

The server comes to our table to take our orders, interrupting the brewing tension.

I use this moment to wrap my free arm around Marcela, pulling her into my chest. I whisper against her ear, "You okay?"

"Yes," she says back quietly, nuzzling into me.

"We can go whenever you want," I remind her. "Or we can stay and torment the hell out of them."

That earns me a soft giggle that has me laughing along with her. Out of my peripheral vision, I notice Hunter and Ruby watching us with a sour look on their faces. To piss them off even more, I kiss her forehead, lingering for a beat before pulling away.

Marcela smiles at me, making my blood heat and my pulse quicken. I want to kiss her so fucking badly, but because of her rule, I won't. Not unless she kisses me first.

"You two are adorable together," Robin comments, earning an eye roll from Hunter.

"Thank you. She's pretty amazing," I say.

"Babe, tell them what you love about me," Ruby says in a baby-like voice. God, she's annoying.

"I … um," Hunter fumbles over his words.

Ruby's face morphs into anger. "Seriously? Not one thing you can think of?"

"No, there's just so many reasons, it's hard to pick one. You know I love it when you …" he trails off, shooting a knowing look right at Marcela.

"Shut the fuck up already, would you?" I shout, done with his antics to clearly hurt Marcela.

"You got a problem with me telling everyone what I love about *my* girlfriend?" Hunter sneers.

"I have a problem with you making *my* girl uncomfortable."

"No, it's okay," Marcela speaks up, her voice strong but quiet. "It doesn't bother me. I'd have to care about either of them for that to happen."

That's my fucking girl.

"Let's get out of here, Celly. I'm ready to watch a movie, cuddle, and fall asleep with you snuggled in my arms," I lie, purely to piss Hunter off. I know what I said moments before, but I needed to get one last jab in.

And boy does it work. Hunter's jaw tightens, as does his hand on the drink that was put in front of him mere seconds ago.

Fuck. Him.

He wronged the most beautiful, kind, and loving girl I know and now he gets to pay for it. Especially after he parades around with her former best friend and shoves that hurt in her face.

"Well, I can think of one more thing we need to do first," she chuckles, her cheeks flushing.

Oh, hell yeah. I like flirty Marcela. Even if it's fake.

"Yup, time to go," I say as I hold my hand out and help her out of her seat. With my free hand, I wave to the group. "See y'all tomorrow."

Once we're in the safety of my truck, I ask, "Are you okay? They were being idiots. I'm so sorry."

"Why would you be sorry?" Marcela looks at me with her brows furrowed.

"Because I feel bad for making us do this tonight. If I knew they were going to pull that crap, I would've suggested another way to show off in public."

Marcela shakes her head as she stares at the ring she's twirling around on her middle finger. "No, this is exactly what I expected to happen. It shows me their true characters, and it's another reminder that I'm truly better off without them."

I take in what she said, and can't hold back what I'm about to ask.

"Do you still have feelings for him?"

"No," she says easily. "I was only bothered because they hurt me, and seeing it up close and personal was … interesting. But in no way do I miss or love him. Not one bit."

"Honestly … those two are perfect for each other. Two vicious people. Couldn't be a better match," my voice drips with disdain.

That earns me a small laugh from her.

"Did I do okay tonight?" she asks, her honey-brown eyes locking at me with so much vulnerability in them.

"You were perfect. You always are."

That earns me an eye roll with a smile, which is exactly what I wanted. For her to stop being in her head and laugh a little.

"I am not, but thank you. You were great."

"There's a reason everyone loves the Theo charm. It works every time," I joke as I turn the key in the ignition, making my truck rumble to life.

"Robin and Dale seem nice," Marcela comments as we begin the quick drive to her place.

"They're some of the best people I know, aside from the squad of course. Dale and I have gotten closer over the years."

"I like them. I'm glad I met them tonight."

"Maybe we can have a double date sometime," I say, not even thinking twice about it.

"Theo … we only need to go on dates where Hunter and Ruby will be," she replies, her words careful.

My chest deflates as I'm brought back to reality. To the fact that none of this is real.

"Oh, right, duh." I wave her off, acting as if her words didn't sting.

"I know we need to keep up appearances for the general public, of course. But I don't think going out on dates with Dale and Robin benefits the purpose of our arrangement. That's all," she explains, with the underlying notion that we don't want to blur the lines we so clearly drew out.

I put the truck into park, doing my best to remind myself that I'm doing this for her. Not for my own personal gain, but for her.

"I agree," I say. "I would say we could actually watch a movie, but I do need to get home and get ready for bed. I have to be at the stadium early tomorrow."

"That's okay. I want to catch up on some reading anyway. Thanks for the ride," she says, giving me a smile before hopping out of my truck. I watch her until she's in the safety of her complex, and only then do I begin to back up and pull out of the parking lot.

The ride back to my house is consumed by thoughts of her, much like any other day. But today, they feel different. While I've always been into Marcela, and now that I'm beginning to get to know her and have the opportunity to be close to her, it's changed things.

It's much, much worse now. Because I'm not simply into her, I like her. A lot.

And she can never, ever know. Not if this is going to work.

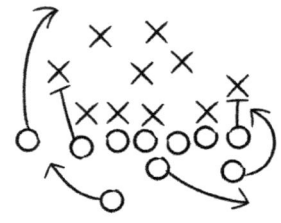

Chapter 14

Theo

"Flowers again?" Marcela looks stunned as she takes in the bouquet of lilies, roses, and daisies.

"Yes. Deal with it, woman," I chuckle as I punch her parents' address into my phone. When I look back up at her, I notice the sadness on her face and it guts me.

"What's wrong?" I ask softly, turning down the music in my truck.

"We've been fake dating for over a week, and you've gifted me more flowers than Hunter ever did."

"Celly," I say her name on breath. "I want to be respectful of that time period in your life, but what the hell were you thinking?"

She chuckles softly. "That's okay. I get it. I've been asking myself that since the breakup. It's like the rose-colored glasses finally came off. I didn't realize how murky things were between us before that."

"Understandable. So, if he never opened the door or bought you flowers, what did he do?" I ask, my curiosity getting the best of me.

"Um," she pauses, then starts again. "In the beginning, he was very sweet. He would do all the right things. He'd text me a lot, he made me laugh and told me I was pretty, and he would take me out on dates to the movies or bowling. Then after a while, he just stopped trying, maybe because he thought he had me, so why keep trying? But I needed that, wanted it. I wanted someone to buy me flowers, even if we've been together for ten years, because they know it makes me smile. I wanted someone who's going to open my damn door, or bring me my favorite soup when I'm sick without me having to ask. I wanted someone who's never going to stop showing me their love, instead of merely saying it without the actions to back it up."

With my eyes on the road in front of me, I tell her "You deserve to be loved exactly how you want to be loved."

"Thank you," she says quietly. "How was your game today? I'm sorry I couldn't make it. I had a bunch of stuff I needed to get done for my classes."

"All good, Celly. Always take care of yourself first," I tell her, not wanting her to end up like me, overworked and overtired from trying to please everyone. "We won though, 28-12 against the University of California."

"That's awesome. How did you play?"

"I threw a touchdown and had some great passes. All in all, a good game for me."

Which made my dad very happy, as reported in his usual post-game phone call.

But of course, he had a long list of things I could do better and how he would've acted in certain plays. It was exhausting to listen to, and I've been tired of it since I started playing. I wonder how long it'll take him to realize I'm human and not perfect. I'm going to make mistakes. Hell, who doesn't?

"Did you have fun?" her voice trails off, letting me read between the lines.

We haven't talked about me hating football since I first told her, and now that we've grown closer, I don't blame her for checking in.

"Nope," I say bluntly. "I act hype with the guys. And yeah, it feels good to make a good play, but more than anything I'm anxious and annoyed the entire time, because I feel like I'm wasting my time."

"I'm guessing quitting isn't an option for you?" she infers.

"Ding, ding, ding, we have a winner," I attempt some humor, but Marcela has none of it.

"Don't do that," she mocks the words I once said to her. "Don't cover up something serious with a joke. You can talk to me about it. If you want to, that is."

I inhale and exhale, then clear my throat.

"No, it's not. My dad's already lost so much, I can't take this away from him too."

Marcela nods, not prying for more information. We continue our drive in silence, other than the soft melodies coming from the radio.

It leaves me to think about the life I wish I could have, but never will.

Marcela's childhood home is massive.

The three-level home has a white-and-grey brick exterior that screams money. Even their lawn is perfectly manicured.

So far, her parents have been courteous, but her mom wins the award for being the sweetest person I've ever met. I can so easily see the love she and Marcela have for one another. It's refreshing despite the little twinge of jealousy I feel.

It's what I wish I had with my dad, and will never get with my mom.

The moment we arrived and her stepdad greeted us at the door, I noticed a shift in Marcela. Her voice was quieter than normal, and each word was said carefully, as if she was scared of saying the wrong thing. And throughout the evening, I noticed Marcela would tense every time her stepdad spoke to her or put his hand on her shoulder in passing. I also didn't miss how the guy was never without a small glass of whiskey in hand.

It has me on edge, unsure of what exactly she meant when she said he was abrasive.

We're currently sitting around the grand, oakwood dining room table with a large spread of various foods between us.

"Mrs. Bass, these tamales are to die for," I tell Marcela's mother, cleaning my plate after my third helping. The tamales are wrapped in banana leaves and stuffed with chicken, potatoes, rice, and a mix of spices. Her mom made special ones for me without meat, and I'm grateful that she was so kind to do that. They're delicious, and I don't think I've eaten so well since … well, I can't even remember. I'm on a pretty strict meal plan, and even when I go home, my dad never cooks anything he deems unhealthy.

"Theo, please call me Alana. But I'm happy you like it." She smiles at me, plating some of the ceviche into her bowl.

"She's an amazing cook. It's what made me fall for her," Chris, her stepdad, says.

"He's the sweetest, isn't he?" Her mom giggles, sipping on water.

I smile and look at Marcela, who gives the most unconvincing smile I've ever seen. Now I'm really getting concerned. Something has to have happened ... because Marcela does not seem to like him much.

Chris drains his glass of whiskey, then sets his eyes on me. "What made you fall for Marcela?"

"Don't feel like you have to answer," Marcela whispers to me.

I wink at her with a goofy grin, letting her know I've got this. It's not like it's a hard question to answer, so I go with the truth.

"Other than the fact that she's the most beautiful girl I've laid eyes on," I start, placing my hand on top of Marcela's on the table. "She's kind, caring, smart and funny. That last one took me by surprise, because usually, I'm the funniest person in the room. It's nice having someone put a smile on my face instead of the other way around for once. Simply put, she's my peace in this crazy life."

"Oh, Marcie, I think you got a good one." Alana smiles at her daughter.

Marcela's eyes are fixed on me, lips parted slightly as if she's shocked by my response.

"Yeah, I do," she says softly.

Chris clears his throat. "That's nice and all, but if you distract her away from school during her most important year, I will not be happy."

"*Mi amor*," Alana chides. "Marcela is a smart girl, she knows how to prioritize. School was never a problem for her when she was with Hunter."

I like her mom. I like her a lot for sticking up for Marcela the way she did just now.

"School is a big focus for me too. As much as I enjoy being with Marcela, we know our education comes first," I reassure him.

"Speaking of Hunter," Chris says, ignoring me. "I heard he's at RLU this year. Is there no chance of you guys getting back together?"

Marcela's spoon clatters against her plate, and the table goes silent for a beat. I've gone from being uneasy about the guy, to wanting to shove my fist into his jaw.

"No, Dad, there's not. He cheated on me with my best friend, and they're happily together now. And even if they weren't, I'm happy with Theo," Marcela says, treading carefully with her words, as if she's trying to not upset him.

Chris sighs loudly as another glass is placed in front of him. Of course, they have a wait staff. "All I'm saying is people make mistakes, and I liked him a lot. We come from a similar background."

"I don't want to date someone similar," Marcela says under her breath, causing Chris to pause his drink halfway to his mouth.

"What was that?" he scoffs, making the tension in the air more taut than before.

"Nothing," she says louder this time.

Chris takes a swig of his drink, slamming it back on the table. "Now are you going to answer me? Why can't you give him a second chance?"

"That wasn't a mistake, that was a choice. One he can never take back, and one I'll never forgive. I'm sorry," Marcela replies.

"You have nothing to apologize for." The words are out of my mouth before I can stop them.

"And you have no reason to be speaking," Chris fires back, his eyes full of venom. With every drink, he transforms into someone entirely different from the person we met when we first showed up. It's scary to witness up close the effects alcohol can truly have on a person.

"Why don't we get the dessert out? I made tres leches," Alana tries to ease the growing tension.

Chris downs his drink in record time.

I feel Marcela tense beside me. I'm about to tell her we should leave when he opens his mouth. "She can apologize for being a lazy little shit. All her life she's never had to work for a dime. It all came from my paycheck."

"Chris," her mom cuts in, her tone placating.

"It's the truth," he signals to the staff for another drink.

"Maybe you should slow down," Alana says softly. "We have a guest for dinner."

Chris slams his fist down on the table, making the glass plates shake. "Don't tell me what to fucking do. This is my house that I pay for, and all of you live in for free. I'll do what I fucking please in it."

I'm about to intervene when Marcela's hand lands on my thigh, squeezing. I focus on taking a deep breath instead, before I say or do something to make matters worse.

"All she and her fucking sister did growing up was sit around and take from me. Not once did they have to lift a finger," he remarks, getting angrier with each word.

"You wanted us to focus on our studies …" Marcela's voice trembles.

"Are you talking back to me?" he growls, the vein in his head throbbing. "You know better than to interrupt people, and I wasn't finished."

"No," she shakes her head adamantly.

"That's what I fucking thought," he raises his voice, just as another drink is placed in front of him.

I've had enough of his verbal abuse towards her. We need to get out of here before I do something I shouldn't.

"It's a long drive back, so we better go," I push my chair back and stand while pulling Marcela up with me. "It was so nice to meet you, Alana."

I purposely ignore her stepdad, and so does Marcela as she says a quick goodbye to her mother.

Alana attempts to follow us out, but Chris calls for her. "Alana, dear, come look at this house for our trip next month," his tone is a complete one-eighty from the way he was just talking. It's staggering how fast he can change.

"I'm sorry," she mouths, giving us a small smile before turning back to her husband.

We make our way down the hallway and grab our jackets from the foyer, not bothering to put them on to get out of here as quickly as possible.

Once we're inside my truck, I notice Marcela's teeth chattering from how hard she's shaking. With the truck being old, the entire front seat is a connected bench, it allows me to scoot right over to her.

My fingers gently brush a brown wave out of her face. "Talk to me," I say, my voice barely above a whisper.

I'm surprised when she rests her head on my chest, nestling herself there. I stroke her hair, trying to bring her any semblance of comfort as she stays silent.

"I-I hate leaving her when he's like this," she finally says.

"We can go back in there if you want," I offer even though it'll kill me to keep quiet. It's never been my forte.

"I can't be in there. I want to crawl out of my skin when he's like that. He won't physically harm her, but he'll say really mean things and pass out soon. Like he always does." She sighs in defeat, which tells me that this has happened multiple times.

The thought makes my stomach churn, knowing she's grown up like this.

"I still don't like it."

"Neither do I," she sighs. "I wish she would leave him. How can she stay when he hurts us all like this? I know there was love there once ... but I don't know."

"Not everything is as easy as we think it is."

"I mean, she's never left him or even talked about it. There must be something holding her back. I'm just hoping that whatever it is, we'll be able to overcome it."

I don't say anything, and instead, I kiss her forehead.

I expect her to tell me not to do that again, but when her honey-brown eyes look up to mine, a small smile on her lips, I know she didn't mind it.

"Thank you for being here with me," she says.

"Always," I tell her, sliding back into the driver's seat. I turn the radio on, and we settle into a comfortable silence as I drive back to campus.

"I think we need to go on another fake date," Marcela blurts suddenly.

"You want to take me out, huh? I don't blame you. I'm quite the catch," I tease her.

Marcela groans, but I don't miss her tiny smile. "So cocky."

"What brought this idea on?" I ask as I switch lanes.

"Hunter and I started dating when we were in high school. Dating as an adult seems so different from those days, and I guess I want to practice being out with you in public. So it looks natural between us. Does that make sense?"

"It does." I nod, resting one hand on the wheel. "I mean, dating is pretty much like being friends. I would like to think our friendship is already natural."

"Please don't say all relationships are like friendships. I may never be able to trust a guy with a girl for a friend again, after what happened between Ruby and Hunter. Especially considering they told me they were just friends."

"I get where you're coming from, Celly, but there needs to be an aspect of friendship in every relationship for it to work. That's all I meant. I'm friends with Aurora, Jasmine, and Camille, but that doesn't mean I want to be with them."

She's silent for a few moments, as if she's processing what I just said.

"Friendships with the opposite sex can be tough to navigate when you're in a relationship. It requires honesty, boundaries, and trust," I add, in aim that this gives her the reassurance she needs. I hope she can grow to be okay with it if things work out between us in the future, because I couldn't imagine my life without the girls in it. Hell, Aurora was my first real friend here, besides Ryker of course.

"You're right, it'll take me time to adjust. That's all," she says quietly.

"It will, and that's okay. The right partner will never make you doubt that, and will reassure you when you need it."

"I hope so," she murmurs, her tone sad.

"Since we didn't have dessert, where do you wanna go to get some?" I ask her, desperate to put a smile back on her face.

"Theo, we don't have to pretend anymore. You don't need to do that," she shakes her head.

"Pffft, this isn't because you're my fake girlfriend. This is because my dessert belly is starving, and you're my friend. Put those two things together and it means we must get dessert."

She chuckles at that, making my heart feel lighter than it was when we left her mom's house. Seeing her happy is my favorite fucking thing.

"Is Wendy's okay? I could really go for a Frosty."

"Why wouldn't it be okay?"

"Hunter was always on a diet. If he did let himself have a treat, he always thought Wendy's was below him,'" she says, her tone full of disdain.

"God, he is more of an idiot than I thought," I groan, not sure how I'll ever look at him again without wanting to punch him. "But yes, we can get them as long as we split some fries for dipping."

Marcela sighs with relief. "Thank goodness you do that too. I didn't want to be weird."

"That is a childhood staple. If anyone says it's weird, they're just jealous because they never got to try it."

"Exactly," she chuckles, warming up the truck with her aura.

Nothing feels as good as being around her, it makes a part of me light up that's been dark before this. It stays that way as we get our two chocolate Frostys and fries, eat them in my truck in the parking lot of Wendy's, and when I drop her off back at her apartment.

It's not until I'm tucked into bed that I'm hit with the anxiety of my fucking to do list for tomorrow. As I try to fall asleep, I realize that I need to figure out what's more important to me.

Finding a passion that makes me feel as good as Marcela does, or continue to suffer just to please my father.

Chapter 15
Marcela

I don't think I've ever had this hard of a time choosing an outfit. Theo's picking me up for our fake date, and I'm panicking over what to wear as if this is an actual date. Despite it being our second, this is the first time it will be just us.

I whip my gray sweater off and onto the floor, along with the other clothes that I deemed unworthy.

Deep breath, I tell myself. It's just Theo. Two friends hanging out.

Except we'll be acting like a couple.

And honestly, what does that even entail? Are we going to hold hands? Or try different ways for his arm to wrap around my waist?

Kiss?

I shake the ridiculous, fleeting suggestion and keep looking through my closet. I know this was my idea in the first place, but now I'm overthinking it and questioning why I'm doing this to myself. Someone who was in a serious relationship for nearly eight years shouldn't need to practice how to date. I guess that says a lot about how awful my previous relationship really was.

With a sigh, I return to my dresser and pull out another stack of tops to go through.

I debate FaceTiming one of the girls, but I don't want to bother them. Aurora is probably training, and Jasmine is working hard on getting her café up and running, while Camille is in Detroit with Ryker.

After a few more minutes of excruciating decision-making, I finally decide on a pink tank top and white pleated skirt that I pair with my white canvas shoes and a matching pink cardigan.

My hair's up in a ponytail, my curtain bangs styled in slight waves, framing my face. I keep my makeup simple, not wanting to overdo it.

Theo was tipped off by a guy on his team that Hunter and Ruby would be at Fall Fest, a campus party featuring different food vendors and activities like bobbing for apples, pie-eating contests, and more. So I think I'll be dressed perfectly.

I'm dousing myself with perfume when my phone buzzes with a text.

> **Theo**
> I'm outside, come down when you're ready, Celly. It's time to fake the hell out of dating you.

> **Me**
> I'll be down in two minutes.

I throw my phone into my tote bag as nerves begin to swirl in my stomach. It's not nerves from being with Theo, because I feel comfortable with him. It's more from not wanting to mess up while we're pretending today.

Sure, I went to his football game, but it's not like we spent time together there. He was playing and I was watching. And then our date last weekend at Beers 'n' Cheers felt more like a hangout with friends. But going out on campus just the two of us, for everyone to see? It's a completely different story.

As I exit my building, I come to a halt when I see Theo standing outside with a bouquet of roses.

Before I can process the words, he says, "I told you. Every date."

Knowing Theo like I do now, it's pointless to argue about it.

"Thank you for these. I'm going to run these back upstairs quickly."

I do just that, and within a minute, I'm back down and walking beside Theo as we head to the center campus quad where the festivities will be held.

We're silent for a few minutes, walking side by side. My eyes roam over piles of yellow, orange, and red leaves, the sun dipping low on the horizon much earlier than it did all summer.

I'm used to silence—and actually, quite enjoy it—but since we're practicing how to date each other, it makes me nervous because Hunter always assumed I was upset when I was quiet.

"So, uh," I start, fumbling over my words.

"Why do you sound nervous? Tell me what's going on in your head," Theo says calmly, not an ounce of annoyance in his tone.

"Well, we're supposed to be practicing dating each other and I haven't said a single word in a whole five minutes. I'm worried you're going to be mad at me or think I'm awkward. And now you're probably thinking that I think too much, and to that, I would say I agree," I ramble.

Theo laughs, and the sound stops my anxious words from tumbling out further.

"Celly, you're good. Be as quiet as you want. I'm enjoying a nice walk with you whether we talk or not. There doesn't always need to be conversation."

"But you love to talk," I point out.

"I do, but I know that you're a quiet person, which is fine. There's nothing wrong with that. So I won't force you to talk all the time," he explains, easing my worries.

"I like talking to you." The words slip out of my mouth before I can stop them.

"I like talking to you too," he says, lacing our fingers together, pulling me to walk closer to him.

My heart races at the gesture, but I quickly remember that this is a role we're playing. I need to get used to it. If he touches me and I look uncomfortable, people will notice, which won't work very well for the purpose of our plan.

We hold hands in comfortable silence the rest of the way, with Theo saying hi to nearly everyone we pass, seeming to know everyone on campus—which honestly makes sense.

After all, he is friendly and popular.

What surprises me is that these people say hi to me too. I usually get through campus without so much a word from anyone, but now that I'm on Theo's arm, everyone sees me.

It's an odd feeling. There's something to be said about the power of connection between strangers, of how a simple hello or kind gesture can boost someone's mood.

As we approach the quad, which is louder than usual, with his hand in mine, he guides us through the crowd. Even though it's all for show, I can't help but think about how I never thought I cared about small things like that until Theo came into my life.

"Where do you think they are?" I ask.

Theo looks down at me as he shrugs a shoulder. "I'm not sure. Let's have some fun. I bet we'll run into them at some point."

And that's exactly what we do. We drink apple cider and navigate through the maze, laughing the entire time. Although we totally get lost, we eventually make our way out. I crush him when we bob for apples, but he retaliates when we challenge each other at a game of ring toss.

Time flies as we move from one activity to the other, lost in our own little bubble.

It's the happiest I've felt in a long time.

All my nerves are gone, replaced with a sense of contentment. Everything between Theo and me is so natural that my usual overthinking self never rears her head. The way his hand reaches for mine effortlessly, or how I'll lean into his body whenever he kisses my forehead, feels like home.

As if we've been doing this much longer than we actually have.

Since we're both starving by the end of the festivities, we order from a food truck and make our way to an area full of picnic benches. Once we're settled with our tacos and nachos, I ask, "Okay, what's our next lesson?"

Theo looks up from his food, his light-blue eyes gleaming with delight. Then he's sliding out from his side of the picnic table, and sliding next to me, pressing his thigh against mine.

"For starters, we need to be closer. Show people that we're so in love we can't even sit across from each other because it's far too much distance to handle," he says with a wink.

I hold two fingers up, nearly pinching them together. "That's a tad cheesy."

Theo wraps his arm around my shoulder, dropping a kiss to my forehead. "I'm a cheesy guy. You'll have to live with it as long as you're my girl."

I'm surprised at how comfortable I feel wrapped under Theo's arm in a public place as we talk about random things. I find myself even enjoying our date, almost forgetting that we're supposed to be practicing.

Until Ruby and Hunter sit themselves at the picnic bench right next to ours.

Oh, no—

No, I cut off the thought. This is exactly *why* we're here.

To my surprise, Hunter merely nods at us, while Ruby doesn't bother acknowledging our presence.

Relief washes through me knowing it won't be another pissing match between everyone this time. I focus on Ruby as my brain tries, once again, to process how she did this to me.

A press of lips to my cheek draws my attention back to Theo.

"Eyes on me, Celly," he whispers into my ear, his lips brushing against the shell of my ear.

"Didn't we say no kissing?" My words come out breathy as my cheek still tingles from his lips.

"I've always been a rule follower, but it was a dire situation."

"Dire?"

"You were in your head and staring at them, who aren't worthy of even breathing the same air as you. So, yes, it was *dire*," he states, making me blush and look away.

"Theo, you don't need to say things like that. No one is listening."

"Exactly. If I'm saying it now, it's because it's real. Not for show," his voice is so sure yet soft, and it draws my gaze back up to his.

"But—"

"But nothing," he cuts me off, kissing my forehead. "I know what you're thinking, and I only said it because I care about you as a friend. Relax, Celly."

I peer up at him, suddenly noticing how close we are. How close our lips are. If we move even an inch, we could be kissing. The thought startles me.

Do I want to kiss him?

No.

No, I don't want to kiss Theo.

I was merely acknowledging that we could, that's all.

My mind is about to spiral, so instead, I pick up a taco and shove it into Theo's mouth. Theo's eyes widen for a fraction of a second and then he shrugs and begins chewing on it.

"Ahh, you want to be the couple that feeds each other. I got you," he rubs his hands together as I laugh, then takes a nacho chip dipped in salsa from his plate and holds it up to my mouth.

I open it and Theo hums. "That's my girl. Open up for me."

Thankfully, he puts the chip into my mouth before I can think about how those words made my core warm. That never happened when I was with Hunter.

As I chew and swallow, his eyes never leave mine, watching me with an odd admiration that I find myself wanting more of.

In the quiet moment we're having, I overhear Ruby hissing at Hunter. "Why won't you come sit next to me?"

"Because it's too tight. I like my space," he says, sounding frustrated.

"Oh, you want space, huh? I'll give you plenty." Ruby sneers as she pushes up from the table and storms off.

I watch as Hunter rolls his eyes and begins texting on his phone, making me avert my attention back to Theo.

"Awkward …" he says with his eyes wide and his lips pressed together.

That makes me laugh, and soon we're both giggling. The sound of a hand slamming on the table nearly makes me jump out of my seat. I turn to see Hunter, his fist clenched tightly, pushing away from the table and walking away.

"Think we upset him?" Theo raises an eyebrow at me.

"I think we did. Is it bad that I feel good about that?"

He smirks at me. "Not at all. I think that's rather healthy."

We finish the rest of our food, continuing the date even though Evil Thing One and Two are gone.

"I'm buying our next dinner," I tell him, determined to be fair.

"Ooh, so you think this went well enough for a second date, huh?" he teases.

I nudge him playfully with my shoulder as I attempt to wiggle my hand out of his, but he holds it firmly.

"You can take me on a fake date anytime," Theo assures me, hitting me with a smile so big I swear his dimple is going to indent his cheek forever.

"Agreed, this was a lot of fun." I smile back at him.

Theo holds his hand out to me, and I take it, letting him guide me as we stand and make our way back to my apartment. I can feel a set of eyes on me as we walk out, but I don't dare look back.

I only keep my eyes ahead, smiling at my best friend who treats me better than anyone in my life ever has.

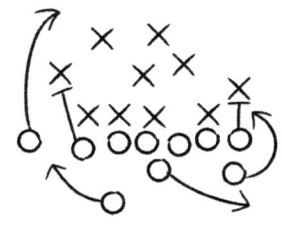

Chapter 16
Theo

"Jay bay bay!" I yell, cupping my hands around my mouth to project my voice as Marcela and I reach Jasmine's brand new café and bakery, Minniebakes.

Elio, Aurora, Cameron, Camille, and Ryker are all outside the front doors, waiting for Jasmine to open for the first time. Today is open strictly to family and friends, to prepare for tomorrow's grand opening to the public.

"Here we go," Elio shakes his head, but I don't miss the smile on his face.

I wrap Jasmine in a hug. "I can't wait to try everything you've got in there."

"Aren't you on a strict diet for football?" She raises a brow at me once we part.

"Celebratory calories don't count. You've never heard that?"

"They absolutely do," Ryker mutters.

"You grumpy asshole. I missed you, Ry Guy," I pull him into a hug, one that he will deny he enjoys, but I know he secretly loves.

"He'll never admit it, but he's missed you too," Camille says, wrapping her arms around me for a hug after I let go of Ryker.

"Theo Miller!" Aurora shouts.

I swivel around to face her, finding her with her hands on her hips and a look of dismay on her face.

"AV baby!" I shout, about to hug her, but she stops me.

"I was your very first friend at RLU and I'm nearly the last person you greet?"

"I'm sorry—"

Aurora giggles, and her entire demeanor changes. "Pretending to be as dramatic as you is so much fun. Come here." She smiles before hugging me.

"She's been waiting to do that for awhile," Cameron adds in, attempting to shake my hand.

I gently push his hand away. "Ronnie boy, we're huggers here. Get in here."

After we hug, I turn to Elio who's looking at me with narrowed eyes.

"Miller, if you even think of hugging me, I'll punch you," he grumbles, folding his arms over his chest.

"Well, it makes sense that you're the oldest and least fun one—your age is really showing, Eli Oldi," I tease, offering him a fist bump instead.

When I look over my shoulder, I find Marcela and the girls talking animatedly, hugging and laughing.

It does something to me to see her as a part of our friend group, knowing that my friends like Marcela as much as I do. Especially when her friend was so shitty to her, I'm happy that these girls treat her better than Ruby ever did.

Elio walks over to Jasmine, wrapping his arms around her waist as he says, "I hate to break up girl time, but let's get started. Camille and Ryker have to fly back tonight for a playoff game tomorrow."

"You're right, we'll catch up inside," Jasmine says to the girls before walking to the front doors.

"Here goes nothing," her voice is riddled with sarcasm as she pulls the key out of her pocket.

We all clap and cheer as she puts the key in the lock, and opens the doors for the first time.

"So proud of you, *dolcezza*," Elio tells Jasmine, pressing a chaste kiss to her lips before they head inside.

We all follow suit, walking inside to the stunning café. Every detail of this place screams Jasmine, and I love it.

There's a wall filled with hearts in many shades of orange. The counters are a bright white, and the displays are filled with various treats that all look so good. The brick wall across from the display counter adds a touch of coziness, along with the bookshelf that sits against it.

"It turned out perfect, Minnie," Aurora squeals, wrapping her arm around Jasmine.

"I'm taking pictures to post immediately," Camille says, pulling her phone out to snap some photos.

"This is amazing," Marcela remarks as her eyes move around the room.

I go to reach for her hand, but she stops me. "No one's around that we have to pretend in front of."

My heart pinches painfully at her comment, but I do my best not to show it on my face. "Yeah, you're right."

And she is. We're only pretending to date, and our friends are all in on the secret. There's technically no need for me to hold her hand right now, despite how much I wish I could.

Which is another problem in itself, but I'll deal with that another time.

Once we're done marveling at the interior, we all line up to buy some baked goods that we bring to a table we all crowd around and catch up.

It's the first time in a while that we're all in the same room, and I have to admit, it feels like a part of myself has finally returned to my body. These people are my family, and every time we're together, I feel better than ever.

Unsurprisingly, Marcela sits with the girls, probably wanting to be close to them since we don't see them often. While I love that for her, there's a part of me that realizes she's putting distance between us right now, because it's the first time she can. At campus, we're always *on* in case someone is watching. But here, she gets to drop the act and I hate it.

I crave a distraction, so I peel the wrapper off my mini apple crumble with a maple glaze. I let out an audible moan as the flavors hit my tongue. "This is delicious," I say through a mouthful.

"Seriously, Jasmine. This lavender and honey donut is divine," Camille swoons, giving her own stamp of approval.

"I'm in love with this pumpkin muffin," Marcela adds.

"Our girl is good at what she does, huh?" Camille nudges Marcela's shoulder with her own, making them both chuckle as she nods in agreement.

I wish I could take a picture of her right now. Watching her smile light up, a genuine one at that, with her head craned backwards, her eyes shut. I could put it under the word bliss in the dictionary and it'd be a fitting description.

"How's football going?" Elio asks, making me turn my attention to him as he takes a bite of his raspberry scone.

Dread seeps into my body, taking over the elated feeling I've been having all day. "We're undefeated so far," I tell him, sticking to facts.

"That's great! Congrats," Camille cheers.

I feel Marcela's eyes on me, and I look to her for a beat. There's a look of understanding in her eyes, like she can tell how much I hate talking about this. She gives me a sympathetic smile from across the table.

"Yeah, it's pretty cool or whatever," I laugh, wanting to try and sound happy about it.

Ryker glares at me, his hands folded under his chin. "Why don't you seem more excited about that?"

My heart begins to pound erratically, like it always does whenever someone questions my enthusiasm for football. It doesn't happen often, yet when it does, it scares the shit out of me that someone might know my secret.

"I'm just tired, Ry Guy. Between classes, studying, and extra workouts on top of the team ones, you could say I'm running on empty," I admit, shoving the last bite of the delicious dessert into my mouth.

"Theo," Aurora says my name with far more pity than I'd like to hear. "You need to take care of yourself. Do you remember what happened to me senior year?"

I do. She pushed herself harder than ever and ended up in the hospital. Aurora almost played a game of volleyball after her concussion, not wanting to miss the scouts at the game, but with Cameron's help, she was able to realize her health was more important than anything.

Cameron brings Aurora's hand to his lips, closing his eyes and likely thinking back on that time.

"I know, AV. I'm doing my best to rest in between it all," I reassure her.

"What do you mean by extra workouts?" Ryker questions me.

"My dad hired a personal trainer that I see a couple days a week. He doesn't think the football program offers enough for me."

This time Elio speaks up, "That's insane, and this is coming from a guy who used to play professional hockey. Your body needs a break or it *will* break. Trust me."

Elio used to be an NHL legend until he suffered a career-ending injury. He now coaches the RLU hockey team alongside Jasmine's dad.

Not wanting to be serious any longer, I turn up the classic Theo silliness. "Pffft, that's because you're an old man, Elio."

"How has it been working together?" Marcela's quiet voice filters into the group, drawing everyone's attention away from me as she talks to Camille and Ryker.

I couldn't be more thankful for her intervention, especially knowing she did it on purpose to help me out of a conversation I wanted no part in.

"It's okay," Ryker shrugs, making Camille's mouth pop open. "I'm kidding, baby, it's the best."

"He especially likes it because we get to fuck on company time," Camille says nonchalantly.

"Jesus," Cameron sputters, nearly spitting out his cookies 'n cream cookie.

"Risky, I like it," Jasmine hums, making the group laugh.

Our visit isn't long as we all have other obligations to get back to, but we make plans to get together again for Aurora's birthday next month since it'll be the long Thanksgiving weekend.

On the drive back to campus, Marcela is quiet as we listen to the radio, but I find myself itching for a conversation with her. She's easily my favorite person to talk to.

"I'm so proud of her," I say, breaking the quiet. "And it was nice that her parents showed up as we were leaving."

"It was, and I know Jasmine must be thrilled, because her parents weren't always supportive of her choice," she says.

"What about your mom? Does she support you wanting to work at a publishing house?" I ask, turning the volume on the radio down.

Marcela hesitates for a few moments before answering my question. "The plan after graduation has always been to work for my stepdad for a few years since he paid for my tuition. But my goal is to get my master's in English literature while I work for him. Then, I'm going to leave Bass Hotels for a publishing house. I love books, and I think I'd enjoy working in that world a lot more. I'm hoping at that point she'll understand my need to separate myself from him."

"I know she will. I could clearly see the love she has for you." I do my best to reassure her. It's a tough situation, and there's not much I can say about it.

Families are tricky, and I know that all too well.

I leave my hand out in the middle console. An invitation.

She accepts it, lacing her hand in mine the entire ride back. It feels like a win, especially after feeling set back with our friends today. I want to ask her about that, but I already know why. And she's not wrong.

I'd be smart to do the same thing and back off when we're alone, yet I can't help myself around her. Marcela pulls me in like nothing else has in my life.

If I wasn't put on this earth to be in her orbit, then I don't know what else it was for.

Marcela has been oddly quiet since we left our friends, more than usual. During our entire ride home, I've tried my best to make her smile or laugh, but nothing's worked.

It felt like she was slowly pulling away, and I couldn't figure out why.

I pull my truck into the lot, shifting into park as I turn the radio off. Rain hits my windshield, the soft pattering providing background noise to the silence.

"Is everything okay? Did I do something wrong?" I ask her, wanting to know what changed in the last half hour.

"No, it's not you at all," she says quietly, looking at me apologetically.

"Tell me what's going on, please. I hate seeing you look so sad."

There are many undesirable tasks that I'd do in a heartbeat, if it would stop her looking like this.

The rain begins to hit off the windshield a bit harder as she takes a moment before speaking. "Tomorrow would have been my dad's fiftieth birthday," Marcela's voice cracks at the end of her sentence.

"You must miss him a lot," I say gently.

"He had a heart attack before I was born. I never got the chance to meet him, yet I grieve him all the same. Every year on his birthday, I think about what life would be like if he was still here, you know? All I have are stories my mom has told me, and a photo of them while she was pregnant. That's all I will ever have." She looks at me, her voice filled with pain as a tear slides down her cheek.

In an instant, I'm sliding across the bench seat and pulling her into my arms. I clutch her to me, trying my best to give her all the support and comfort she needs right now. Marcela's body quakes in my arms as she lets her feelings out, while her hands fist the back of my sweater.

It breaks my heart a little that she's been dealing with a pain similar to mine, because I know all too well what it's like to miss someone you never knew.

Once her breathing evens out and she settles in my arms, I begin to play with her hair while I speak softly.

"Not knowing who you're grieving, but feeling that pain is an odd, yet torturous, feeling."

Marcela pulls her head from my chest and looks at me in question, so I fill her in without as she moves back to her spot.

"My mom passed away from breast cancer when I was four," I start, swallowing the lump in my throat. Her pinky rubs against mine as our hands rest in the space between us, before she wraps hers gently around mine, giving it a squeeze.

"It fucking stings not having her here, but I think what drives me mad is not having known her. I don't know who I'm missing and grieving. My sister has told me stories, because she was much older when it happened, but it's not the same. I wish I could remember her."

She unwraps her pinky from mine, and instead intertwines our hands together.

"I'm so sorry," she sniffles as a tear strolls down her cheek. "I know exactly how you feel, and it sucks not knowing or remembering them."

"You've got that right," I say as I blink rapidly, trying my best to keep the tears at bay.

"How did your dad handle that?" she asks quietly, rubbing her thumb along the top of my hand.

"Not well. He had just retired from the NFL a year prior due to an injury, and was getting used to working at the farm full-time. He was already in a shitty head space, and then that crushed him. He threw himself into work and truly did everything he could to provide for us. But I wish he had more time to be a dad, you know what I mean? He was already so withdrawn from losing his career that I barely got time with him, and then after Mom died, the only quality time we spent together was him training me to finish what he couldn't."

What I don't say out loud is that the biggest reason I won't quit football is because I can't take anything else away from him. Not when he lost his dream and the love of his life in such a short amount of time. I refuse to add to his pain, even if it creates my own kind of hell.

"That's so tough … I couldn't imagine what your dad went through. Or you, basically losing two parents. I'm sorry," she says, her cheeks wet with tears once again.

I raise my free and gently swipe under her eyes, and it's not until her hand comes up to do the same to me, that I realize I'm crying too.

"Fuck." I sniff, trying to reel them in.

"Don't run from your feelings. It only gives them more power," she says, still wiping at the tears I can't seem to stop.

"I … I …" I struggle to catch my breath as the beginning of a panic attack sets in. My hand on her face begins to shake and she notices. She pulls me into her arms, hugging me tightly.

"It's okay. Let it out," she says as she rubs soothing circles on my back with the tips of her fingers, while I try to center my breathing and focus instead on her scent of mint chocolate.

I struggle to take deep breaths at first, but with her sweet voice in my ear and her fingers on my back, it allows me to eventually shift my focus to her touch and my breathing.

While I inhale and exhale deeply for a few breaths, I bring my hand up to her hip, squeezing her there to ground myself. We stay like that for a few more minutes, and once my breathing evens out into a steady rhythm, I slowly lift my head from her neck.

I wipe my eyes as I say, "Thank you for that."

"No need to thank me. I think we both needed this," she responds softly.

"I oddly feel somewhat better," I tell her, and it's true.

The weight on my shoulders feels a little less heavy after letting myself feel what I've been ignoring for a long time—that I miss my mom a lot, and that I not only grieve the life I've had to live without her, but also one where my dad isn't the way he is now.

Knowing Marcela and I share a similar pain, along with wanting to be there for each other during vulnerable moments, has changed something in our dynamic.

And I don't think I ever want to go back.

"Usually you feel better when you allow yourself to acknowledge your emotions, then let it go and try to move on to a better feeling. At least that's what a therapist told me once." She chuckles, making me smirk.

My therapist has changed my life by giving me the mindfulness practices and tools that I now incorporate into my daily routine. We're still working on the whole communicating my feelings thing with my dad though.

"I should get going. I want to read before bed," Marcela says, undoing her seatbelt.

I could stay out here all night with her, baring my soul, because with her by my side, it feels easy.

"I'll be expecting an update on what happens to Selena and Cole," I say, referencing the characters in the book she's reading.

That finally manages to pull a smile from her. "I will. Get home safe and text me when you do."

I give her a captain's salute. "Will do."

She exits my truck with a wave, and I wave back, watching as she runs inside her building to avoid getting drenched in the rain.

On my short drive home, and in my bed later that night, all I can think is how if it was that easy to talk to Marcela, maybe in time, I'll be comfortable to talk to my dad about everything.

And that tiny piece of hope allows me to get the best sleep I've gotten in a while.

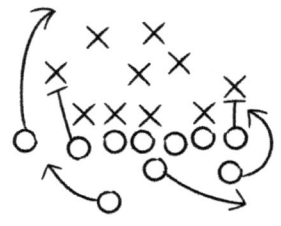

Chapter 17
Theo

Things have been going well, almost *too* well.

Of course, my dad has been calling to pick apart everything I do and football is as dreadful as ever, yet I find myself focusing my attention on one thing.

Marcela.

I love being able to put my arm around her in public or hold her hand whenever I want to. Not to mention all of the time we've been spending together studying at the library, having dinners at her work, or when we walk home from class together.

I've loved every second of it, because despite us not really dating, I get to spend time with her and get to know her more. The cherry on top? Pissing Hunter and Ruby off every time they see us together.

They never said anything to us after that first dinner we spent together, only giving us the occasional eye roll and muttering under their breath.

We're going to our first big party as a fake couple tonight for the annual Pumpkin Party at the football house. It's a tradition that started about ten years ago, and happens on the first weekend in November. It's your typical college party, except everyone—minus us players—brings a decorated pumpkin that we then judge when we're all drunk. The winner gets a cooler full of alcohol.

I was shocked when Marcela agreed to come, because she doesn't love big social settings like this. When I asked her why she said yes, she said she needed to get out of the house for a bit. Whatever the reason is, I'm glad for it, because it means another night I get to spend with her.

I spend the afternoon getting the house ready with Dale, Will, and some of the other guys from the team. We pushed the couches aside, leaving space for a dance floor in the middle. There's multiple tables set up for beer pong, a large speaker standing between the kitchen and living room so that everyone can hear it, and there's a bunch of alcohol on the kitchen island, along with some chips and dips.

The best part of it all? The fall decorations. We went all out this year, and if you look anywhere in this house, you'll see some sort of pumpkin-themed item.

I shower quickly once we're finished and change into black sweats, a burnt orange sweater and my UGG slippers. Before I know it, our place is flooded with people and the backyard is filled with decorated pumpkins.

The music is blasting through the speaker and the guests are laughing and drinking, which means the party is already off to a good start. I don't like to drink much during the season, but it's a special night, so I decide to treat myself to two beers. I'm about to grab my first from the fridge when it dawns on me that Marcela still hasn't shown up and the party's been going on for about two hours.

I pull out my phone and shoot her a text.

Me

CARLIE JEAN

> Celllyyyy, you better not be leaving me hanging over here.

My girl
> Sorry, got caught up with something. I'm driving over now.

Me
> Drive safe and come right on in, don't worry about knocking.

I pocket my phone when I see the front door open, and fucking Hunter and Ruby walk in, arm in arm. My jaw tightens as I grit my teeth, already on the defensive for my girl.

They've been quiet recently, but at a big party with alcohol involved? Yeah, I'm worried about what might happen.

"He's allowed to be here," Dale reminds me. He's aware of why I hate Hunter, since Marcela gave me permission to tell Dale what happened.

"I know," I grunt.

"Look, this house is massive and filled with people. I doubt you'll even run into each other," Dale says, doing his best to be positive.

"It's not me I'm worried about," I mutter, cracking open my beer and taking a large sip. "Is Robin coming tonight?"

Dale's face crumples at my question. "It's been hard on her. The first trimester morning sickness has been nonstop. She's coming though—she should be here any second."

"When my sister was pregnant, she had the same problem. During your next appointment, tell the doctor and he'll get her some meds to help with it."

"I hope so. I hate seeing her like this," Dale sighs, looking tormented.

Dale and I stay by the fridge where we can see the door clearly, waiting for our girls to arrive as we talk about the upcoming game next weekend. Minutes later, the door opens to Robin and Marcela with their pumpkins in hand, laughing as they arrive.

The sight makes me smile.

Dale waves, signaling them to come over to us. Robin takes Marcela's, and my chest goes tight at the sight of her.

She's always pretty, and seeing her in her pink sweats and matching sweater confirms that she looks good in anything.

"Hey, baby. How are you feeling?" Dale asks, pulling Robin into his side as he kisses her forehead.

"There's my girl." I smile, pulling Marcela into my side for a hug. She hugs me back, resting her head on my chest for a beat before pulling away.

"I'm not very artistic, so …" She holds out her pumpkin to me, and I bark out a laugh.

"This is fucking amazing, are you kidding me?" I gesture to her pumpkin that she painted as a green olive with red on the top, as if it's stuffed with red pepper—my favorite kind of olive.

"I won't be winning the contest, but I hoped you would like it." Her smile is shy.

"I love it," I reassure her, kissing the top of her head.

"You did not paint him an olive pumpkin," Dale says in disbelief.

Robin lays her hand on his chest. "Hey, be nice. It's cute. She did a great job."

"Thank you," Marcela says quietly.

"Oh no, it's great. Good job," Dale back tracks. "It's a joke between us. I make fun of him for eating olives, and he makes fun of me for eating meat."

"Well, I painted mine as a donut, because that's all I've been craving for the past month." Robin shrugs, showing us her pink sprinkle donut pumpkin.

"Whatever my babies want, my babies get." Dale smirks, pointing to the tray of pink sprinkle donuts he picked up today.

Tears prick the corners of Robin's eyes. "God, I hate being pregnant already. I'm really about to cry over some fucking donuts?"

We all laugh at that, and then she and Dale take off for the donuts, leaving Marcela and me alone.

That man is so in love, and God, I'm jealous.

What would it be like to fall in love like that? Where their hurt becomes your hurt, their joy becomes your joy, and you can live your lives together knowing your love is there for you at the end of any hard day.

I hope I find out.

"How far along is she?" she asks, leaning into me.

"Six weeks. They're happy but scared. It wasn't supposed to happen this early."

Marcela watches the two of them, a soft smile on her face. "I think they'll be just fine."

"I think so too," I say with a smile, looking down at her. "How are *you* feeling? I know parties aren't your thing, so I appreciate you coming." I take her hand in mine because I may never get the chance to do it again once this is over. I'm going to enjoy it every chance I get.

"It's a little overwhelming, but I feel better being close to you," she peers up at me, and I nearly lose myself in her honey-brown eyes.

"Good. Then stick with me all night, okay?"

"Really? Hunter used to hate it when I did that. He said I was too clingy, and would get mad at me for being quiet all night and not socializing much."

"He's a goddamn idiot. It's not clingy. You're uncomfortable in social settings, and if being near me helps you, then you can cling to me all you want. And if you don't utter a word to anyone, I won't care. All I want is for you to have fun and be comfortable."

Marcela looks at me with wide eyes, her lips parting for a moment before she speaks. "Really?"

"Yeah, really." I nod, my fingers toying with the ends of her hair. "I should let you know though—he is here. Ruby too."

The color drains from her face and she freezes.

"Ruby and alcohol don't mix well," she murmurs.

"Hey, look at me," I demand gently as I grab her chin between my thumb and forefinger to tilt her head up. "I'll do my best to make sure that we stay away from them. But remember, you have me. I won't let anything happen."

Marcela intertwines her small hand in mine. "Okay, let's do this," her voice wobbles slightly, but physically she stands taller, ready to take on the night.

"That's my girl."

The party has been a blast so far.

Dale and I dominated at beer pong, and Robin's pumpkin won the contest. As for Hunter and Ruby, they have been out of our sight all night.

And best of all? Marcela has been by my side the entire time. Though quiet, she stood by and watched me play beer pong and laughed along with my friends. She even made small talk with Robin from time to time.

I don't understand how Hunter could get mad at her for that. Who cares if she's quiet and doesn't socialize? Trying to wrap my head around the way he thinks makes my brain fucking hurt.

We're standing outside around the fire pit, soaking in the warmth on this chilly fall night as people roast s'mores. The sliding door opens, and my head snaps that way to see Hunter and Ruby making their way towards the bonfire.

Technically, it's a free world and they can be wherever they want. But God, I wish they'd just go home already.

Marcela stiffens beside me, noticing them approaching. My hand slides around her waist pulling her in closer. I feel her body melt into mine, and I revel in the fact that she's comfortable with me, because even though this is all pretend, she can't fake that.

"Miller," Hunter drawls.

I nod at him in greeting.

"Hi, Marcie," Ruby giggles, clearly drunk.

"Hey," Marcela says politely, though I imagine she is swallowing down what she really wants to say.

"Beautiful night, isn't it?" Hunter comments. No one responds, all too absorbed in their own conversations.

I ignore him, whispering into Marcela's ear. "Do you want to go?"

She shakes her head. "No. Let's sit down though." She gestures towards the open chair by the fire.

With her hand in mine, I lead us to the chair and sit before pulling her onto my lap. Her legs rest over mine, her back against the arm of the chair.

We fit together so perfectly that it breaks a part of me in that moment, knowing none of it is real.

She lays her head on my shoulder, and I kiss the top of her head. I rest my chin there as we snuggle into one another, with my free hand resting on her leg.

Not trying to be quiet, Ruby stands on her toes to speak in Hunter's ear. "I can't wait for you to take me home and fuck me."

I cringe, because who the hell says that shit out loud for everyone to hear? Someone clearly trying to stir up jealousy.

Well, two can play that game.

I start trailing my hand slowly up Marcela's leg.

She lifts her head and whispers into my ear, "What are you doing?"

"Trust me?" I whisper back, my hand halting on her knee.

She takes a few seconds to think. "Okay. Just … not *too* high."

I chuckle softly. "Don't worry, Celly. I'm not into letting people watch when I make my girl feel good. That's for my eyes only."

Marcela blushes and ducks her head back into my chest. I trail my hand around her knee in a circle before moving it up her thigh, giving it a squeeze.

She rocks against me, her ass rubbing on my thigh.

"We might be fake dating, but I am still a man who finds you very attractive. If you rub your ass against me, I can't control my body's reaction," I whisper through gritted teeth, trying to control my cock.

"Sorry," she squeaks.

"Don't be," I kiss her forehead, not missing the glares from Hunter and Ruby.

I move my lips to Marcela's cheek, pressing a few kisses there before whispering in her ear, "Is this okay? Can I go lower?"

"Yes," is her breathy response as she melts further into me.

I lock eyes with Hunter for a brief second, noting the snarl on his lips, then focus as I trail kisses from her cheek, down to her jaw and finally her neck. I close my eyes, reveling in the feel of my lips on the soft skin of her neck for the first time.

And fuck, I want to lose it at the small moan that escapes her lips as I kiss along her neck, while inhaling her sweet minty scent. It reminds me of mint chocolate chip ice cream. My new favorite flavor.

Marcela's hand comes up, her fingers fisting in my hair as I continue to ravish her neck. Then to my surprise, she turns her head slightly and angles my head to press her lips against mine.

It takes a moment before I process that Marcela fucking Bass is kissing me.

My heart rate speeds up, and before I can overthink it, I grip her chin and take control of the kiss. My lips are gentle yet demanding as I devour her the way I've been dreaming about for the last three years.

I know this is just for show, but I'm going to enjoy every second of it.

She whimpers into my mouth, and I nip on her bottom lip before sucking on it.

Dale whistles, causing us to break apart. "Get a room, you two," he chuckles.

Our eyes are locked on one another, our breaths labored as we exist in our own world—one that is changed forever. Because now that I know how her lips fit perfectly with mine, there's no going back.

With my hand on her chin, I take my thumb and gently brush it across her swollen bottom lip, causing her to shiver in my arms.

"Be careful, unless you want to end up like me," Robin gestures to her barely-there bump, causing reality to drift back in.

Marcela pulls her head back as we both laugh, and my hand falls from her face. I bring it to the back of my neck, giving it a grip, as I try to process what just happened.

Marcela kissed me. And then I kissed her back. We were kissing *each other*.

We're supposed to be fake dating, and we're *definitely* not supposed to be kissing. I like her more than I should, considering our predicament. I'm screwed.

Because now I know there's a physical chemistry between us. The way her body melted against mine. The way she whimpered from just a kiss. Or how when we broke apart, her eyes were filled with lust and longing. I'd never seen her look at me like that before.

Fake or not, she can't deny what just transpired between us. I felt it, and there was no fucking way she couldn't. Right?

Hunter throws his hand up to everyone. "See you guys later," he growls, stomping away with Ruby trailing after him.

I know what we did was probably immature—kissing Marcela's neck to make him jealous—but it was worth it just to see that look on his face after what he did to my girl.

Conversations begin to flow around us, yet I can't seem to join any of it. My brain is failing to do anything but fixate on that kiss. It's on a never-ending loop in my brain, and I actually might be okay with that.

"I, uh, need to go to the bathroom," Marcela says quietly as she gets off of me, then dashes up the back patio steps and through the sliding door.

I debate whether to give her some space to process it all, because I'm trying to do it myself too, but I decide against it.

Why not figure it out together instead of freaking out alone?

I follow her into the now empty house, and upstairs to my personal bathroom that I told her she could use earlier today.

My back rests against the wall opposite the bathroom door as I wait for her, replaying over and over in my mind how good her lips felt against mine.

The door flies open, and Marcela's eyes widen as she yelps, a hand flying to her chest.

"I was not expecting you to be right there," she breathes heavily.

"Sorry."

Marcela's eyes travel down to my lips, making my entire body heat. The urge to kiss her again washes over me.

When her gaze lifts back to mine, she must see the desire in them because she suddenly snaps out of the moment.

"I need to go," her voice is high pitched as she attempts to get by me.

I block her path, shaking my finger in front of me. "We need to talk about what happened outside."

"Nothing happened," she mumbles, looking anywhere but at me.

"Celly," I call her name softly, slowly drawing her attention up to me, and when her eyes meet mine again, I see the fear etched on her face.

"Why do you look scared right now?"

"I'm not scared," she says defensively. "I'm just ... not sure what happened, exactly. One minute, we were putting on a show for Hunter and Ruby, and the next ..."

"And the next ...?" My voice trails off while my heart inflates with a sense of hope.

"It was a mistake. Friends don't kiss each other like that."

And my heart instantly deflates.

I want to tell her I don't agree. That it's bullshit, because yeah, friends don't kiss with that much passion, but it's not what she wants to hear right now. If I say that, I'm afraid she'll call this whole thing off and walk away from me.

"I would say I'm sorry, but you did kiss me first," I tease, trying to lighten my own mood so she doesn't see how much her words have bruised me.

"I was caught up in the moment, and I really wanted to sell it. I'm sorry for confusing you. It didn't mean anything, and it won't happen again. I promise."

Each word is another shot to my heart, because how the hell can she say that? Was it seriously one-sided? I refuse to believe it, even though that's what she's trying to tell me right now. For the sake of our friendship, I bottle down what I really want to say.

"It won't, unless you decide to kiss me again." I chuckle, earning me a strained smile as she shakes her head.

"Goodnight, Theo," she says, walking past me. I follow her down the stairs to her parked car on the street.

"Did you have fun tonight?" I ask, before closing her door as she rolls her window down.

"I did, even if I was quiet for a majority of it."

"I'm happy you enjoyed yourself," I smile, giving her a wink as I tap the roof of her car. "Text me when you get home safe."

"I will." She smiles back and I step away, allowing her to pull away from the curb and drive off.

And I stand there watching until her car turns out of sight, smiling to myself because I kissed the girl of my fucking dreams tonight. More than that, I'm elated, because despite what she said, I know she feels the same way. That there's more between us than she wants to admit.

I've got until the end of the school year to prove that to her, and I'm going to try with all I've got to make it happen.

Chapter 18
Marcela

"She shouldn't be here," I mutter to myself, watching the purple-and-blue scales of her tail sparkle as she swims by.

I hear the door to my secret cove open and close, not turning around to give her the privacy needed so she can do the spell to dress herself.

"Dom," she croaks, and the need in her voice has me turning to face her.

I open my mouth to say something, but her long black hair sways and I realize that she's naked.

I quickly look away. "Mari, you didn't cover up." I'm about to cast the spell myself when she cuts me off.

She closes the distance between us. "Dom, I need you to do something for me." Her voice is pleading, her dark-purple eyes widening as she peers up at me.

"Anything," I tell her, because it's true. She might be the daughter of my family's enemy, and set to be married in ten days, but I'd do anything for her. They say hate is close to love, and I'm beginning to realize my enemy might very well be the love of my life.

"I want you to be my first everything. I know we've hated each other for years, but since the day you saved me from the attack, I've never felt safer with anyone as I have with you," she says softly as her hand reaches to grab mine.

My mind goes back to that moment when I was swimming by the outskirts of my family's palace and I saw her being chased by our guards.

I should've turned away. It wasn't my business, and she shouldn't have been so close to our kingdom. But I went anyway.

I took out three of my own people just to save her, because the second I saw them pull a knife on her, I realized how much I didn't want anything to happen to her.

My free hand lifts, gently caressing her cheek. "Is this really what you want? Because once I take what's mine, there's no going back."

She nods fervently. "Please."

With her confirmation, I crash my lips against hers. Her lips are soft and fucking perfect for mine.

I stare at my last paragraph on the screen, reading it over again as I try to continue the scene with Marissa's and Dom's first time. I only got this far the night I kissed Theo. My brain was running a mile a minute with ideas when I came home, and the need to write had never been stronger.

It was as if kissing Theo removed the mental block in my mind, allowing me to finally get to this scene. But now that my characters are ready to progress to the next step intimately, I find myself unable to do it.

Maybe it's because my sexual experience wasn't all that great, and I don't authentically know how to write a scene like that. I reread the scene again while the image of kissing Theo replays in my head.

I still can't believe *I* did that.

In the heat of the moment—wanting to prove to Hunter and Ruby how happy I am without them in my life, and with Theo's lips pressing against the soft spot on my neck—I lost control.

And the kiss was ... unlike any I've ever experienced before. I thought getting chills and feeling it down to your toes from a simple kiss could only be experienced in books.

Until I kissed Theo.

That notion terrified me, which is why I pulled away and told him it was a mistake. And it was, because if our kisses feel like that, we definitely shouldn't kiss again—we're just friends. That's it.

Theo has given me the space I need, but we have class together tonight.

Which means I'll have to face him for the first time since Saturday night.

I expect nerves to flare in my stomach, but they never come. Probably because Theo is the kindest person I've met. He's not going to bring it up or act differently. He's just going to be Theo.

To avoid thinking about it further, I set my laptop on my bed and walk to my small kitchen, placing the kettle on the burner. Tea always makes me feel better, and with the stress of over this next chapter up and posted, I need it now more than ever.

I've been publishing a chapter at a time of my romantic fantasy, *Under Water*, once every two weeks to keep up with the demands of my readers. I'm already twenty chapters in, and with every new chapter posted, the story seems to gain more and more momentum.

It's thrilling and terrifying all at once, but with the amount of love I'm receiving from readers, it makes it all worth the feelings that come with putting your words out there for everyone to see.

Writing is what drives me forward, a way out from my stepdad's control. It's the one thing he doesn't know about, the one thing his hateful words can't tarnish.

It's the future I dare to dream of, where I can say and do what I want.

The kettle whistles, pulling me back to the present. I turn the burner off and pour the hot water into my pink mug. I place a chamomile bag in the mug, grab a banana, and head back to my bed to settle in.

I scroll through the romance section on Netflix, feeling the need to be inspired to finish writing this scene. *Fifty Shades of Grey* catches my eye, and I decide a rewatch won't hurt until I need to get ready for class.

As I watch, it dawns on me that these actors are doing just that—acting. I bite my lip as an idea begins to form.

Despite being scared of how the kiss with Theo made me feel, I can understand the purpose it served. Even though it was a toe-curling kind of kiss, it can't ever mean anything.

And maybe—just maybe—if I can do that, we can do … *more.*

We can be like actors. I know they don't actually hook up, and it's choreographed … but the idea is the same, right? He can teach me some things, then we stop the lessons. One friend helping another friend out.

I'm more comfortable with Theo than anyone else in my life, and if he can help me get through this writing block, then I want to give it a shot.

I want to feel confident with sex before I meet *the one*, and confident enough to write about it. That's if Theo will agree to it.

Unfortunately, the only way for me to find out is to ask.

Here goes nothing.

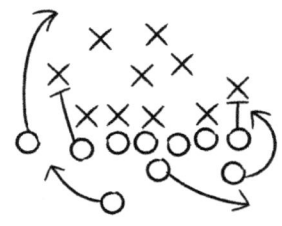

Chapter 19
Theo

"Fuck," I mutter, my shoulder in pain as I slide my backpack off and onto the floor.

I tweaked it at the away game on Saturday, and my trainers have me under intense physical therapy to get me ready to play as soon as possible.

My dad's been calling more than ever to get on me about proper nutrition, rest, and post-game recovery so that this doesn't happen again. I do all of that already, yet it still happened. I'm a human being, and shit happens. I know he doesn't want me to have a career-ending injury like he did, but he'd be disappointed to know that I wished for one.

I'd love to have a reason to never play again.

"You okay?" Marcela whispers beside me as she sets up her desk for the lecture.

"Yeah, just sore." I shrug, not wanting her to worry. "How was the rest of your weekend?"

"It was good. I got a lot of reading done," she says happily.

I'm about to ask what happened in the book she's been telling me about, when Professor Grum enters the room.

"Hello, my lovely earthlings. I hope everyone is ready for another night under the stars. Bundle up in your jackets and let's get a move on before we miss the meteor shower." She motions for us to stand, looking more excited than ever.

Everyone grumbles as they don their jackets. It's a chilly fall night, the kind where you don't want to be outside for too long.

Marcela and I walk side by side as we follow Professor Grum and the other students outside the building and up the hill to our spot.

Once we're at the top, spread out onto the hill in pairings, and I slide my backpack off and onto the ground. I hiss under my breath as pain radiates throughout my deltoid, which is feeling so tender right now.

"It seems like it's more than just sore. What happened?" she asks.

We're standing close to one another, staring up at the sky as we wait for the meteor shower to begin.

"I pulled a muscle in my shoulder at the game on Saturday. It hurts right now from all the massages and exercises the team trainer has had me doing. They're seeing me everyday, and on Friday, they'll make the call about if I'm able to play in the next game. But it's looking like I'm going to have to." I sigh dramatically, trying to make fun of my situation.

Marcela's lips press together, her expression sad. "I'm sorry."

"Don't be. It's my crap to figure out." I brush it off, not wanting to talk about it.

"Tell me something good, then," she says with a soft smile, and I love that she's trying to change the focus of our conversation.

"Hmmm," I tap my finger against my chin. "Hunter has been avoiding me like the plague. I think our plan is working, which is good."

"Really?" She sounds surprised.

"He's definitely kicking himself for what he's lost, but he's never getting it back now." I pause, looking to Marcela who's staring up at the stars. "Right?"

Her eyes cut quickly to mine. "Do you really think I'd ever want him back?"

I shrug. "I'd hope not, because you deserve way more than he ever gave you, but I just want to be sure. People have been known to do crazy things."

Her face drops, and a sad smile curves her lips. "I'm beginning to realize that now—that I deserved more. No need to worry though, I'm pretty predictable and boring."

"What?" I nearly shout. "Who the hell has ever said that to you? Wait, don't even tell me, because my patience with those two is already running very thin."

"I mean, I've always followed the rules and I love staying home. None of that makes me very exciting."

I shoot her a look. "You are far from boring. Getting to know you more is all I want. You intrigue me. And even when I figure you all out, I'll still think you are the most fascinating person I know."

My heart hammers in my chest when she brightens and a laugh bubbles out of her. "You are *really* cheesy."

"And don't forget that." I wink as she shakes her head and turns to face the night sky.

I do the same, but I'd rather be watching her. I find her far more beautiful than anything in nature.

We stand in silence for a while, watching with excitement as the meteor shower begins. Flashes of white streak across the sky, and my lips part in awe as I watch.

Suddenly, Marcela's pinky wraps around mine.

"There is something you don't know about me." She swallows.

"I'm all ears. No judgement whatsoever," I tell her, my voice serious yet gentle.

I watch as she takes a deep breath, then says, "I love writing. As in, books. I'm writing a book right now, putting chapters up every few weeks on a platform online."

As if I couldn't be more into this girl, she goes and tells me she's a secret author? Goddamn.

"Celly, that's fucking amazing. Do you have any idea how cool that is? What's it about?"

"It's a romantasy novel set under the sea with two royal mermaid families at odds. It's an ode to *Romeo and Juliet*, except my ending will be a happy one," she explains, her eyes lighting with a passion I've never seen before.

"Can I read it once you're done?" I ask excitedly.

"Well, I kind of need your help with it now ..." she trails off as she finally turns towards me, biting on her lip.

Unsure of what she means, I tilt my head in confusion.

"*My* help?" I ask, wondering what she would need help with. "Are the mermaids in your book playing football somehow? 'Cause I can do that," I add, excited about her needing me in any way.

"Um, no." She chuckles nervously.

"What is it?" I ask, confused by her reaction. I don't know what made her so nervous about asking for my help, so I gently pull us farther away from the class.

"No, I need help with something else." She pauses, swallowing harshly and looking uncomfortable. "I'm ... dealing with a mental block."

"I'm sure that's normal, so how can I help?"

Marcela closes her eyes for a beat, and I've never seen her more vulnerable. She opens them again and gives me an earnest look. "If it's too much or it will make things weird, I get it. You can say no."

Now she's making *me* nervous.

"It won't be. Just say it, Celly."

She blows out a breath, and then ever so quietly says, "I need you to teach me about sex."

My eyes nearly bulge out of my head as her words sink in.

I need you to teach me about sex.

"What?" I ask, thinking I must have misheard her. "Did you and Hunter never …?"

"No, no, we did. But there's a lot we never did … and things I never got to experience. Now that I'm getting to writing the spicy scenes in my book, I can't do it. I have anxiety around sex, after Hunter said I was bad at it."

Anger pumps through my veins, unlike anything I've ever felt before. He fucking said that to her? She's the sexiest woman I've ever laid eyes on. What a fucking prick.

"Marcela," I grit. "I'm so sorry you ever dealt with such a lowlife of a human." Taking a breath to calm the storm within me, I calmly ask, "What exactly do you need? It's been a while for me, but I can try to do my best."

Her head tilts at that. "Really?"

"I told you, I haven't been with anyone since I started at RLU. In high school, I tried to live up to the playboy image of being the hotshot quarterback, but I got sick of it quickly. I craved something deeper than just meaningless sex."

"Oh, wow," she murmurs.

"What do you need?" I ask again as I step closer to her, and bring our joined pinkies to my chest, needing more clarity.

She visibly gulps, and with her eyes closed she says, "I want to explore the things I missed out on with him. I feel comfortable with you, and we clearly have chemistry. I figured if we're already pretending to date, why not enjoy the benefits?"

Someone call 9-1-1, because I'm pretty sure my heart and brain are malfunctioning.

Did Marcela really say she wants me to teach her about sex? That she wants to hook up with me?

"I know it could make things weird, but because we started as friends, I figured it would be easy to go back to that. Almost like an experiment, and when it's done we go back to normal. That way, I can get over this mental block to write these scenes, and in the future, I won't be so nervous when it comes to sex."

My mind swirls at what she's saying, unsure what I'm feeling. On one hand, I'm in awe that she feels comfortable enough with me to even ask that, and to want me to be the one she explores her sexuality with. On the other hand, I'm devastated at the idea of me being an experiment, and her moving on to the next guy.

I want to say no, because that one kiss fucked me up more than I'd like to admit. It's all I think about and crave. What the hell will happen if we have sex? I don't know what the aftermath of that situation looks like for me, and that scares me.

But I've never been able to say no to this girl and I don't see that changing. No matter how much more this is going to make fake breaking up at the end of the year hurt.

"I mean, that's if you're even attracted to me. And if you want to, of course," she mumbles, her eyes still closed.

If I'm even attracted to her? Is she serious? More than half of my showers are spent with my hand on my cock, thinking of her naked in my bed with her legs spread as I feast on her.

That reminder alone, of how I get off to thoughts of her, has me getting hard.

"Look at me," I demand softly, and she does as she's told. "It took me a minute to process what you're asking me, that's all," I begin, licking my lips as I lean in to whisper in her ear. I use my free hand to grab hers, placing it on my hardening cock. "Don't ever question if I'm attracted to you. Got that, pretty girl?"

Her bottom lip drops open, and I'm tempted to take it between my teeth but I restrain myself. "Y-yes."

"Use me however you want me. I'm yours."

She shakes her head slightly. "I need *you* to use me, show me how good it can be. How good I can be at this."

I smirk at that and press a quick kiss to her jaw. "You want to learn how to be a good girl for me, huh?"

"Yes," she responds instantly, almost desperately.

It turns me on like nothing ever has before.

I slightly pull away from her. "You let me know when and where, and I'll be there."

"How about tonight? Do you want to come in after you walk me home?"

Am I actually about to go home with Marcela and teach her a sexual lesson? I'm not even sure what that is exactly, but I'm sure as hell up for it. Quite literally.

Never did I think any of our time spent together would lead to this, but I can't say I'm mad about it.

I'm slightly nervous about the repercussions, but the need to make Marcela happy outweighs any of my personal concerns.

"If you're ready, yes."

"I am." She nods. "We can call it lesson number one."

"How many lessons are there in total?" I tease.

"I'm not sure." She chuckles. "But I think the first thing I need is an orgasm. I've never had one."

"Did he not go down on you? And you've never touched yourself?" I ask in disbelief. How the hell did he not want to feast on her every day? I know I fucking would—or will, now.

"No, he didn't, and I haven't. I've been too shy to try," she admits.

"I hate him, I fucking hate him," I groan, running a hand through my hair. "But I have an idea now."

"What's that?" she asks nervously.

"What fun would it be if I told you?" I wink.

"Alright," Professor Grum yells, interrupting our moment. "Class is dismissed early. Go home and write about what you saw for this week's discussion post. Remember internal or external findings, it's all a part of the journey."

Our classmates disperse from the top of the hill, while Marcela and I stay rooted to our spot, staring at one another. I have a feeling everything's about to change between us, and I don't know if I'll survive the fallout afterward.

But I'll be damned if I waste the opportunity to claim her as mine.

Chapter 20
Marcela

Nerves and excitement trickle down my spine as my fingers fumble with my key as I try to jam it in the lock.

Theo settles his hands over mine, stilling them. "We don't have to do anything you're not comfortable with." His husky voice dances across my neck as his chest presses into my back.

I crane my head, looking up at him as I say, "No, I want to. And I need to… for my book."

As soon as the words are out of my mouth, it feels cheap, as if I'm using him for my own benefit. I'm about to apologize when he interrupts me.

"Don't even think about apologizing. There's nothing wrong with taking what you want, and I'm more than willing to oblige." He chuckles, the sound so warm that it calms me instantly.

My cheeks heat and I turn away from him, this time successfully unlocking the door. I push through and hold it open for him while saying a silent prayer that my apartment isn't a mess. That would be embarrassing.

Not that Theo would care, but I would.

Catch Me

Ever since I can remember, my stepdad ingrained in me that a clean house resembles a good life, and we must always portray that we were living the good life.

Even though he's the reason it felt like hell, more often than not. Although he's never cleaned a day in his life, as we always had staff for that.

"Wow," Theo murmurs, taking in my small living room and kitchen.

"It's all I need, so it works." I shrug, kicking off my shoes.

"It's very you. I love it." He smiles, taking in my mug collection, a mix of pinks, bows, and hearts, all sitting on a shelf next to my fridge.

I lead Theo down the small hallway to my room. Once we're inside, I find myself staring at my queen-sized bed and pink comforter, realizing the weight of what we're about to do.

Theo drops his bag on my mirror-top dresser, and immediately picks up the picture frame sitting there. His lips curve into a small smile, before his eyes are on me. "Is this your dad?"

"Yeah, it was taken shortly before he died," I croak, the words burn my throat as they come out. I'll never know him, and the reminder kills every time.

"They were a beautiful couple," he remarks, placing it back where it was.

"That they were," I reply softly.

Theo moves toward me and before I can overthink what happens next, Theo has me in his arms, his chin resting on my head.

"I'm so sorry, Celly."

I melt into him and his scent of freshly-baked chocolate chip cookies, which I learned is from the cologne he wears.

Whenever Theo pulls me into him like this, there's a strange feeling in my chest that I've never had before. It's a sense of security, of safety. Like I can be myself and trust that Theo will still be there and respect me.

He's the friend I never knew I needed, and I'm so grateful we're going to be able to do *this* without it ruining anything.

At least, I hope it happens that way.

His lips press against my forehead, and the gesture is so sweet, it melts my heart. But it's not what we need. Sweet gestures will do no good for my head or heart.

I swallow down the fear telling me I'm not good at this, and just like I did at the party, I lean up on my tiptoes and kiss him.

His lips are perfect, making kissing him an easy thing to do.

Theo's hand cradles the back of my head as he takes charge of our kiss. His lips press against mine more insistently, and I respond, matching his movements as our mouths meld together.

His tongue prods at my lips, and I open willingly. I whimper when his tongue enters my mouth, tasting and taking. I tangle my tongue with his, drawing a deep groan from him that elicits a shot of warmth to my core.

I can feel my core heating up as my thighs begin to rub together, while our mouths continue to work against each other's.

Theo tears his lips away from mine, allowing me to catch my breath as he trails kisses down my jaw and to my neck. A low moan leaves my lips as he finds the spot on my neck that drives me wild, making my core tighten.

"Lay back on your bed," his voice is lower than I ever heard it before.

I follow his order, and my heart beats wildly with anticipation.

"Take off your leggings," he orders, crossing his arms over his chest.

Slightly confused, I ask, "Don't you want to do that?"

"Oh, I do." He groans, his neck cords clenching. My eyes trail down to his chest that's defined even through his long-sleeve shirt. I wish I could explore every muscle on his body, but he's in charge right now.

My eyes move lower, and it's then that I notice that massive bulge in his pants. His cock is hard and long, making his sweatpants stick out from his arousal. The sight makes my core heat up at the fact that *I* did this to him when we've only kissed.

Judging by the tension radiating off his body, he must be uncomfortable because ... wow.

He's *huge*.

"But this is about you right now. First lesson is learning how to make yourself come."

"I don't know how you could help with that," I answer honestly. *Shouldn't he be the one to make me come?*

He raises a brow at me. "Celly, have I ever failed you?"

"No."

"Then trust me. Think you can be a good girl and do that?"

As soon as the praise settles over me, I'm putty. Willing to form and be whatever he wants me to be.

"Yes," my voice is breathy as my hands skate down my body until I reach the waistband of my leggings. I lift my ass off the bed and wiggle them down and off my legs.

"Jesus," he sucks in a sharp breath, his eyes glued to my pink lace panties.

My heart skitters, slightly nervous but mostly excited. I hook my thumbs under the thin lace, slowly trailing them off my body.

Theo falls to his knees at the end of my bed, his eyes focused on my pussy, lips parted as he licks them. "So fucking pretty."

"Theo," I whimper, my body blazing with a need for him to touch me. "Take over, please."

He complies, coming to hover over me and pressing a kiss to my lips. Pulling away, his breath mingles with mine. "Open up for me," he says, his hand moving from beside my head to my thigh, giving it a squeeze.

I let my thighs fall apart as anticipation builds. I don't know what he's going to do, yet I trust that it's going to make me feel good.

Then his hand begins to trail upwards, to the hem of my sweater. He moves a single finger on the sliver of skin between my pussy and sweater, back and forth. That single touch makes my toes curl.

"Take this off," he orders, slightly pushing up the hem.

I lift my sweater over my head, throwing it to the side of my bed where my leggings are, and reach behind my back to unclasp my matching pink lace bra.

Theo's eyes darken at the sight of me completely naked and he blows out a breath as I lay back down. "You are a fucking sight, Marcela. An absolute masterpiece."

My cheeks heat at the compliment. "Thank you."

"I can't wait to taste every inch of you," he says hungrily, his eyes roaming up and down my body like he can't decide where to look.

A soft sigh escapes me at his words, my body begging for his attention.

"But first, you're going to make yourself come. You okay with me using your hand to teach you how?"

I nod, and he smirks, that dimple of his present.

Theo lifts off me and moves to sit with his back against the headboard, motioning for me to come to him.

"What are you doing?" I ask as I sit up and face him.

"I want you to watch as you make yourself feel good." He juts his chin, his eyes on something behind me. That something being the mirrored dresser.

My mouth pops open at the idea of watching us.

"Crawl over to me," he instructs.

I do as he says until I'm between his legs, where I twist my body and lay back against his chest.

"Keep your eyes on us. If I'm going to teach you how to be a good girl for me, then you need to pay attention."

Who is this man, with words that are sexier than anything I've read or heard before? Because every time he says something dirty, my entire body burns.

My eyes flit to the mirror, noting the stark contrast of my naked body against his fully clothed one. Somehow it makes this even hotter.

Theo moves my hair over one shoulder, peppering kisses along my neck that cause me to release tiny whimpers and moans. He grabs my left hand in his, and moves our hands up, over my stomach and up to my breast, squeezing it.

"So perfect," he murmurs to himself, but his words fade away when he twists my nipples with both of our fingers, making my back arch off his chest.

He cranes his head, his warm breath hitting my neck, sending a shiver down my spine. "Roll those pretty nipples for me."

His hand lets go of mine, and I mimic what he just did, rolling my nipple with my fingers.

"That's it. Make yourself feel good."

Warmth spreads throughout my body as a stream of pleasure follows in its wake.

His hand goes back on top of mine, stilling my movements. "I could watch you do this all day, but I'm guessing you need relief, and the fastest way is to touch your pussy. You ready for me to show you how to do that?"

"Please," I whimper, and I don't think I've ever sounded more needy in my life. As if the need to come is a matter of life or death.

With Theo in charge, he leads our hands back down my stomach, over my hip, and down to my pussy. He puts two of his fingers over two of mine, and then pushes them further down until they reach the slickness between my legs.

"Fuck, you're so nice and wet," he groans, gliding our fingers up and down my pussy, coating them in my arousal.

The motion feels good, but it's not enough.

"More," I demand, every nerve in my body on edge.

With his pointer finger over mine, we move in unison as we part my pussy and touch my clit, making me nearly scream.

"This might feel sensitive at first, but it's going to feel good. Trust me," he murmurs into my ear, biting down on my lobe as he draws circles on my clit with our fingers.

He shows me different ways to touch my clit in circles, moving up and down, side to side and even pressing down on it. Each one makes my thighs shake as I get closer and closer to the edge.

Theo then released his fingers from the top of mine, and says, "Play with your clit. I want to see if you were good and paid attention."

I gulp, not in fear but from determination. I want to do this, not just for myself, but I want to show him how good I can be.

I bring the tips of my two fingers to my clit, rubbing in a circular motion that makes my eyes flutter. I move my fingers up and down, increasing my speed as I climb higher and higher towards my peak. Not wanting our lesson to be over just yet, I switch tactics, rubbing my clit from side to side, seeing how good it feels to play with my body and see what it likes.

"God, this is so fucking hot. You're incredible," he praises, his eyes locked on me in the mirror, watching my every movement.

"More," I pant, needing to feel full.

Theo places his hand back on top of mine at my knuckles, and this time when he pushes further down, he manages to get my fingers inside of me. I gasp at the intrusion, as my body tingles with pleasure.

Theo uses his hand to guide my fingers further into me, and I clench around them.

"I'm gonna show you how to fuck your fingers." He tries his best to get the words out clearly, but I think he's as affected as I am right now.

This is hot, there's no denying it.

His hand wraps around my wrist, pulling my fingers back until the tips are at my center, and then he thrusts them back inside, over and over, faster and faster as my moans become louder and louder.

Watching it all happen in the mirror only adds to the erotic scene we're creating.

It's silent except for our heavy breathing and the sound of my fingers moving in and out of me, increasing the heat crawling over my body.

"Oh my God," my words are breathy as the pleasure pools down in my core, making me teeter over an edge I've never experienced before.

He lets go of my wrist. "Now, show me how good you can fuck your fingers, pretty girl."

Listen, Theo is already good looking, but with this filthy mouth of his? He's what every girl dreams of.

I do as he says, moving my fingers in and out of me as he was, my eyes locked on the reaction my body has. I watch in fascination that *I* can make myself feel like this. Theo reaches for my free hand and brings it down to my pussy, resting right above my clit that Hunter never seemed to have cared to pay attention to.

"Touch yourself here at the same time," he says roughly. Theo removes his hand and presses a kiss to my forehead. "Now be a good girl and make yourself come."

My breath hitches as my fingers move faster inside of me, and my finger on my clit moves just as quickly, side to side. I moan and mewl as my movements become more urgent, desperate for the need to come and finally burst this tight bundle of pleasure sitting in my core.

"That's it. You're doing such a good job," Theo encourages, brushing loose strands of my hair away from my face.

His words send me flying off the edge as I have an orgasm for the very first time. My entire body heats and sparks with pleasure as it flows over me in waves that never seem to want to end. My mind stills as euphoria fills my entire body, and my eyes close as I bask in the feeling I've never ever had before.

Once the high settles, and I regain awareness of where I am, my eyes settle back on the man behind me who looks … distraught.

"Theo, are you okay?" I ask, concerned as I crane my neck to look up at him.

He shakes his head. "No, I need to taste you. Desperately."

In the heat of the moment, I find myself wanting that too.

"Please," I plead, wanting to know how it feels.

His eyes are hooded as he stares at me. "Then get up here and sit on my face."

My mouth opens, closes, and—

"Stop thinking," he says as he scoots forward and lays his head back on my pillow. "And get that pussy on my tongue."

I'm about to shift my body so that I can hold onto my headboard when Theo moves his finger back and forth.

"Nope, I want you to watch. Face that way. You'll still be able to hold onto the board."

I do exactly as he says, propping myself up onto my knees on either side of his chest and then I scoot myself backwards until I'm hovering over his face.

The image in the mirror is unlike anything I thought I'd ever see, making me like it that much more.

Theo grips my hips and pulls my pussy flush to his face, his tongue going right for my already sensitive clit.

"Oh my God, Theo," I moan, gripping the headboard for dear life because not only is his tongue driving me insane, but so is the image in the mirror. Me straddling his face, his hands gripping my hips tightly as my breasts bounce with the roll of my hips as I begin to ride his tongue.

"You're easily the best thing I've ever tasted," he manages to say as he lifts me for a second, then pulls me back down onto his face.

His tongue dives back onto my pussy, licking up and down my slit. Theo eats me like I'm his last meal. It's passionate, and real. He's not doing it because it's a chore. He's eating me with pleasure for himself.

His tongue circles my entrance, then prods it rapidly. My thighs shake uncontrollably as I rock against his face while I whimper and moan. Theo moves his tongue back up my slit, his lips suctioning on my clit.

"Theo," I moan, not having any sense of where I am, as my body begins to heat up once more and that tight bundle of pressure returns.

He lifts me up slightly. "Yes, pretty girl?" His voice is hoarse with lust as he presses a kiss to my inner thigh.

"I think it's too much," I breathe.

"You can take it," he encourages.

"If you don't want to finish or—"

If Hunter was disgusted by it, there's no way Theo's actually enjoying it *this* much, right?

Theo squeezes my ass, then kneads it with his hands, unable to keep his hands off me.

"Oh, I'm finishing and so are you. Fuck, if you were my girl, I'd have my head between your thighs any chance I got."

Guilt momentarily punches my stomach when I'm reminded that this is all fake, but I ignore it because this feels too good, and Theo agreed to this. He's not doing it against his will.

"I think we can add that to our rules." I smile, biting my bottom lip.

"Yeah?" he grins, his voice low and sexy as it skates over my pussy. "You want my mouth on this pretty pussy of yours?"

"Please," I beg.

Theo reaches for my hand, intertwining it with his as he rests it on top of my thigh.

"Then stay like that and keep your eyes on us."

His tongue returns to my clit, flicking it rapidly up and down, making my eyes close as the pressure begins to build once again.

"I'm so close again," I tell him, breathless.

My body naturally begins to grind against his tongue, creating a delicious friction that has my entire body on fire. My core coils tightly and I'm sent off the edge once again as another orgasm washes over me.

I can't help it now. My body falls forward, my elbows on his thighs as he continues to devour me during my high. He sends my body into overdrive as I convulse and moan his name over and over again, until my body finally calms and he removes his mouth from my pussy.

My body rolls off him and to the side, and as I lay there catching my breath, I'm vaguely aware of the sound of running water in the distance. Moments later, Theo presses a warm washcloth between my legs, cleaning me up.

"Thank you," I murmur as anxiety begins to unfold. Does he feel differently now that we hooked up? Will he not be able to fake date me anymore? Will he want more? Will he be disgusted with me? Will this actually help me, or did I just ruin our friendship?

"Get out of your head," Theo says, reaching for my hand and helping me up.

"Sorry," I tuck my hair behind my ear, feeling shy with the heat of the moment gone.

"Don't be," he reassures me with his wide smile. "Everything's the same. Except now I get to taste you whenever I want. For book research purposes, of course, because every time can be a new experience to give you inspiration."

"Yes, exactly. For the book." I nod, trying to convince myself and him. "And maybe other stuff too? I can't only write about what we just did."

Theo's face scrunches. "Pfffft, why not?"

"Because there's more things."

"Alright, whatever you need." His hand wraps around my wrist, giving it a squeeze.

"Speaking of comfort, are you okay?" I gesture toward his erection trying to poke a hole through his sweatpants

"I'll be fine."

"Are you sure? Because I'd love for you to let me help with that. Hunter never did, because he said I sucked at it." My eyes trail downwards, unable to look at him.

His fingers grip my chin and gently force my gaze back up to his.

"Fuck. Him," he growls, jaw clenched. "If you want to suck my cock, you're more than welcome to."

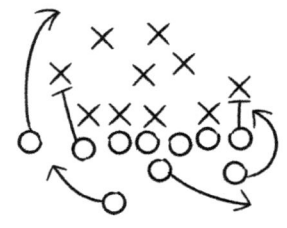

Chapter 21
Theo

Marcela lowers herself to her knees as I stand, and it's the prettiest sight I've ever seen.

"You're ready for lesson two so soon?" I drawl, caressing her cheek as I stare down at her.

"Yes," she tells me, her desire clear in the way her nipples pebble. "One thing though, can you lose the clothes too?"

"Ooh, you want me to strip for you, Celly?" I chuckle, and she shakes her head.

"Just do it," she urges me.

"With pleasure."

My hands find the bottom of my long-sleeve, and bring it up and over my head. I toss it on her floor, not at all minding her hungry eyes as they roam over every muscle on me. She starts at my chest, her tongue swiping out to lick her lips as she moves her gaze to my abs.

I cock my head to the side. "You okay down there?"

"Yes," she says with confidence, but her eyes tell me she's slightly nervous.

A smirk forms on my lips as I begin sliding my sweatpants and boxers down until they are both on the floor.

She stares at my cock in front of her face. A look of trepidation crosses her face for a moment, followed by pure desire as her hooded eyes meet mine.

"Celly?" I say, sounding amused.

"Hmm?"

"Are you going to just stare at my cock or put it in your mouth?"

Her lips pop open at my words as her hand wraps around the base of my cock, stroking me up and down.

I suck in a breath as my head falls back. Fuck. This feels way too good, and she hasn't even put her mouth around it yet. I need to rein in my control right now.

Just when I think I have it under control, her lips wrap around the tip of my dick.

"Fuckkk," I hiss through clenched teeth.

Marcela responds by moving slowly, bobbing her head up and down on my cock as she tries to take more of me into her mouth each time. Her hot mouth feels so good, and knowing it's her on her knees for me only intensifies the pleasure running rampant in my body.

"Goddammit," I grunt as my hand comes down to fist her hair.

A satisfied hum courses through her as she brings her lips back up to wrap around my tip, sucking right there.

A strangled groan leaves my lips, making her increase her efforts.

"You look so damn pretty with my cock in your mouth," I rasp as I tug on her hair. Her pretty eyes lock onto mine, batting her long lashes as she continues to drive me crazy.

"And you're being such a good girl for me, sucking my cock exactly how I like it," I add, wanting her to know she's doing an amazing fucking job.

She continues sucking and pumping me, licking along my length as she takes her time getting to know my cock. I honestly think she's having fun, and each time she draws out a different kind of sound from me, she moans around my cock, nearly making me explode.

I trail my hand in her hair down until it's caressing her cheek, making her look up at me.

"Fuck anything you've ever been told," my tone is icy, so unlike the usual me. "You're amazing at this. Pretty sure your lips were made to be wrapped around *my* cock, and that's why it never worked for him."

I think my words propel her because she grips my cock tighter at the base, bobbing up and down quicker than before. It puts me right on the edge, ready to come but I try to hold off.

She releases me for a second. "Come in my mouth."

"Are you—"

"Please," she nearly begs, my undoing.

"So goddamn perfect," I mutter, stroking her hair as I push myself back between her lips and into her mouth.

Using two hands this time, she pumps my cock while her mouth sucks the tip, and within seconds, my entire body stills as I come.

"Fuck, Marcela," I grunt, still spilling into her mouth. She waits until I'm finished, and then pulls off of me and swallows, making me shiver.

I lean against her dresser with my hands in my hair.

"That was …" I trail off, still trying to collect my bearings. "Fucking amazing. I don't think I've ever come that hard."

She laughs at that, looking proud of herself. When she stands and attempts to move, she ends up halting immediately. And it's then that I notice the wet spot on the floor.

Marcela looks up, fully embarrassed with her pink cheeks. I shake my head at her. "It's hot that you were that turned on during it. It doesn't bother me at all. I'll take care of it while you clean yourself up and get ready for bed."

She stares at me with a look of gratitude.

"You don't even know where my cleaning supplies are," she tries to deter me, crossing her arms over her chest.

"If you're like any other person I know, they're probably under your kitchen sink," I point out.

"They are," she admits. "Okay, fine, and thank you," she smiles, reaching behind me and into her dresser for an oversized shirt before tiptoeing into her bathroom.

Minutes later, after I clean up the carpet, I plop down onto her bed and pick up *Love Bites* from her bedside table. The spot she's currently at seems beyond what she's filled me in on in the story, but I read it anyway.

"You look comfy," she teases, leaning her hip against the doorway.

"I am, but I should get going. I have an early rehab session tomorrow," I say, upset at the idea of leaving.

"I hope it's healing well?" her words come out like a question, probably because she doesn't know what I want. For it to be healing and to play the rest of the season without my dad on my back about it, or to be out for the season and not have to play another game.

I laugh and shut the book, placing it on the table with the bookmark still in place. "You get me so well."

She walks me to the door, hugs me goodbye and we talk on the phone my entire walk home. Once I'm finally in bed, about to drift off, it hits me then that everything between us has changed.

Now that I've got a taste of what it's like to be with her intimately, it's all I'm going to want. The way our bodies were attuned to one another's, electric sparks going off in my body when she touched me. By her reaction, I'm assuming she felt the same way too.

I'm beginning to think Marcela is it for me. I'm not sure about a lot of things in my life, but I've got a really good feeling about this.

I hope.

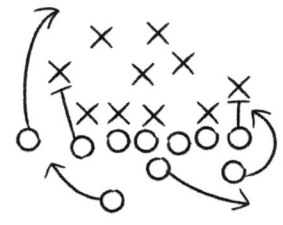

Chapter 22
Theo

*M*arcela asking me to give her sex lessons for research for her book has been the best thing to ever happen to me.

Knowing I'm the one that's going to make her feel good and get through her writing block is an honor I don't take lightly. She trusts me wholeheartedly.

Which is exactly why I'm doing this for her, because this will all be worth it to see Marcela happy and thriving.

My mood might change when all of this is over and I'm devastated, but for now, I'll just enjoy it.

We hadn't seen each other since that night, but we texted or talked on the phone whenever we got the chance. But today, our friends are in town for Thanksgiving and to celebrate Aurora's birthday, so I finally get to spend more time with Marcela.

The girls are all currently huddled around Aurora in the kitchen, gushing over the custom engagement ring Cameron had made for her. It's inspired by Iron Man's reactor, since they first bonded over their love for superhero comics. Nerds.

My eyes are drawn to Marcela, noting how wide her smile is and the way her eyes light up to match it. She's genuinely happy, a sight that makes me happy too.

Seeing her for the first time since then hasn't been weird at all. We're completely normal around each other, if you disregard that my thoughts are constantly about her. How I want to be with her for real. How I think she's the most precious thing in my world. How I want to be the one to make her feel good.

"How is the whole fake dating thing going with Marcela?" Ryker asks and I turn my attention to him as he sets his "*On the naughty list*" mug on a table.

Ryker, Cameron, Elio, and I are sitting around a fire pit outside of Jasmine's and Elio's new house.

My initial reaction must say it all, because everyone suddenly sits up and leans in closer to me.

"What happened?" Elio sighs, like he already knows what my answer will be.

"A gentleman never kisses and tells," I whisper, drawing them in closer.

"Fuck," Ryker groans, running a hand through his long hair.

"This is not going to end well," Elio adds before taking a sip from his mug.

"She asked me to help her, so I agreed," I say defensively.

"Hey," Cameron says softly. "I think we should trust that Theo knows what he can and can't handle. And if he's doing it to help her, we should be happy that they're able to work through whatever it is together."

"That sounds nice and all, but Theo is in love with that girl. Now you add in them hooking up? She's going to break his fucking heart when this is all over." Ryker scoffs.

"Pssh, who says I'm in love?" I chuckle.

They all glare at me. My heart starts to beat wildly in my chest and thoughts begin to swirl. Am I actually in love with her? I knew I was into her, that I like her. Whatever you want to call it. But ... *love*?

"Is she the first thing you think of when you wake up?" Elio asks.

"Do you constantly think of her? Worry and hope that she's okay?" Cameron adds.

"Does everything suddenly feel better when she's around? Like she shines a personal light on you since you've been together?" Ryker says, looking at me with an incredulous expression.

"Is there absolutely nothing you wouldn't do for her?" Elio looks at me pointedly, probably because I'm already showing my answer to this question with our fake dating arrangement.

I internally answer *yes* to all their questions as my mind begins to settle all at once, at peace with one clear thought.

I love *her*.

"Fuck," I mutter, leaning back into my chair. "I *am* in love with her. What am I going to do?"

Elio is the first to offer advice. "Not tell her, that's for sure."

"What if she likes him back? It *could* work out," Ryker counters, oddly optimistic.

A throbbing headache blooms at my temples at the potential disaster this could be. My hand reaches into the pocket of my candy cane pajama pants, fiddling with my fidget cube.

"What if you don't say anything?" Cameron suggests, his voice calm and confident. "Keep things as they are, with the new ... benefits. If she somehow manages not to fall for you by the time this is over, then you move on. It wasn't meant to be. But, if she does fall for you, then you have nothing to worry about."

"That does not sound like a plan," Ryker retorts, crossing his arms against his chest.

"No, it's perfect." Elio leans his forearms on his knees, speaking quietly. "At this point, you can't change the fact that you love her, nor the arrangement you're in. Whether you end it now or in the future, it'll break your heart."

"Gee, thanks."

Elio rolls his eyes at me. "What I'm saying is that Cameron is right. Keep things the way they are, and don't tell her how you feel. Let this whole thing play out, and hopefully she falls for you along the way."

I sit with his words for a moment. Marcela could either fall in love with me too, or she could break my heart. It's not like I hadn't thought about it when I suggested we fake a relationship.

Yet hearing it out loud makes it seem all the more real.

The mere thought of losing her after all of this sends my mind spinning, because I don't think my heart would ever heal if she doesn't end up feeling the same way I do.

"Elio is the oldest, so we should listen to him," Ryker concedes, making Cameron nearly choke on his hot chocolate.

"You mean my idea?" Cameron says with a raised brow.

"Yeah, yeah. Let's do that," Ryker says, making us chuckle.

"I guess Ryker is accepting decisions for my life on my behalf," I joke, trying to ease the seriousness of the conversation. Talking about my feelings with anyone is something I try to avoid.

"When you can't be trusted to make good life choices, then yes," Ryker retorts.

"Hey!" I say defensively. "When have I ever made a bad life choice?"

"How about when you opened your big mouth to Isaiah about Jasmine and me? Outed us to her father?" Elio asks pointedly.

"Blame Cameron for outing it to me in the first place!" I nearly shout.

"My future brother-in-law can do no wrong. Leave him out of this," Ryker says.

"Boys, boys, boys," Aurora yells over our voices as she and the girls decide to join us, each exiting the kitchen through the sliding doors. "What is going on out here?"

All four of us eye each other, obviously not wanting to share what we were just talking about.

I speak up quickly. "We were deciding who should give Cameron the '*hurt her and we'll kill you*' talk. Now naturally, Ryker wants to do it because that's his future brother-in-law, and he's the scariest out of us all. But Elio being the oldest gives him a competitive edge—"

"Does he have an off button?" Elio groans, running a hand over his face.

Jasmine slides onto his lap, and they look adorable in their matching flannel pajamas. "Be nice," she says, kissing him on the cheek.

Camille cuddles next to Ryker, draping her legs over his lap. They're wearing matching gingerbread pajamas and seeing Ryker in them makes me laugh, because I never thought I'd see the day.

Aurora loves the holidays and wanted to celebrate by having us all dress up in holiday pajamas while we drink hot chocolate, and play various board games. She nestles herself between Cam's thighs, and he wraps his arms around her. Their pajamas have holiday lights on them.

Marcela and I are the only two who aren't matching, a subtle reminder that our relationship isn't real.

But instead of the usual dread that follows that thought, I find myself fueling up on optimism. If I need to give it my all, in the hopes that she'll fall for me too, then I'm ready to take on the challenge. It's the first thing I've felt passionate about in a long time, honestly.

Marcela sits next to me, with a pink mug in her hand, leaving a small amount of space between us.

"You okay?" I ask, nudging her shoulder with mine.

"Honestly," she starts, and then a breathtaking smile takes over her face. "I've never been this happy before."

My face matches hers as my own smile pulls at my lips. "Good. I like seeing you happy."

"Me too," she says softly, and then to my surprise, she closes the distance between us, putting her thigh next to mine as she rests her head on my shoulder.

On the inside I'm doing my happy dance, but I play it cool as I shift my attention back to the group.

"When are you guys thinking of getting married?" Camille asks.

Aurora looks to Cam who gives her a small nod, "We want to get married next December, because, duh, I love the holidays."

"That's going to be so beautiful, I can see it in my mind already," Jasmine says excitedly.

"What about you two?" I ask Jasmine. She and Elio got engaged this summer, but haven't told us about any wedding plans yet.

"Next summer," Elio says. "We want to go back and have the wedding in Bora Bora. Of course, you all are invited."

Elio and Jasmine went to Bora Bora for a friend's destination wedding last year, and it's where they said they loved each other for the first time, making it a special place.

"Can you believe we're getting married next year, Minnie?" Aurora shrieks, making Jasmine smile as they bask in their pre-wedding bliss.

While I'm excited for them, all I can think about is how much I hope Marcela is by my side at those weddings.

"I'd better start saving money now," I joke, sipping my white hot chocolate.

"No one is paying to come to ours." Jasmine shakes her head. "Elio is taking care of it."

"Next year is going to be *so* much fun," Camille says with a grin.

"And don't forget the Olympics are next year too," Aurora chimes in.

"We'll all be watching and cheering you on," Jasmine says.

"Hell yeah, we will," I add, excited to see Aurora fulfill her dream. Her mom died a few months before she was supposed to represent Team USA for volleyball, and Aurora will get the chance to live out that dream for her.

I love seeing that my friends are doing what they love and are passionate about. I just wish I knew what that looked like for me—something that drives me as much as it does them.

"We've got it pretty damn good, don't we?" Aurora sighs contentedly, pulling me out of my thoughts as she looks around the group.

"We do," I say as my eyes meet Marcela's.

Her gaze drifts to my lips for the quickest second, before she looks away. Not wanting to overthink what it means, I wrap my hand in hers on my thigh and kiss her forehead.

Because for right now, I've got all I need. And it *is* pretty damn good.

Chapter 23
Marcela

We've been driving for just over an hour on the freeway, with a blur of pine trees passing as we go. Theo stopped to grab us drinks for the drive, getting my favorite chamomile tea. I don't even remember telling him it was my favorite, but he somehow knew.

I'm slightly nervous to meet Theo's family, especially since his dad looked intimidating the last time I saw him, and Theo seems to despise talking about him. Spending Thanksgiving with his father isn't exactly high on my list of things I'm excited to do.

But knowing Theo will be there eases most of my worries, because if there's something I know for certain, it's that I'll always be safe with Theo. It's why I found myself gravitating toward him at Aurora's birthday party yesterday.

And absolutely nothing to do with the fact that we've gone down on each other.

Theo takes the exit off the freeway, and within minutes we're going down a lone country road with a house every once in a while. There are bushes and trees everywhere, and we're surrounded by farmland. It's a stark contrast to the white picket fence suburban life I was raised in.

I like it a lot. Seeing kids and animals run around with freedom, and nothing but an open field makes my chest feel warm in a way I never expected.

I've never been to a farm before, but I'm beginning to think I might enjoy today more than I'd anticipated.

Theo turns into a long winding driveway where a white ranch-style home and a few large red barns come into view. It's a picturesque country home with a wraparound porch, a swing loveseat, and a dog that is eagerly waiting for us to get out of the truck.

Theo shuts the engine off, exits his door, and runs around to mine to open it for me. But before he can say anything, the fluffy black, white, and brown Australian shepherd is on his hind legs, jumping up at him.

"Sorry, Louie. I had to be a gentleman, but I see you, buddy." Theo crouches down as he scratches the dog's ears, who gives him a lick on the cheek.

As soon as my feet hit the ground, Louie loses his interest in Theo and turns his attention to me, his tail wagging excitedly back and forth as he sniffs my hand.

"Lou, this is Marcela," Theo introduces us.

"Hi, Louie," I greet him, my voice a higher pitch, as I crouch down to pet him.

"Uncle Teooooo!" a young voice squeals, drawing my attention to the porch where a small brunette boy is excitedly running down the wooden steps.

"Sunny boy," Theo shouts back, lifting his nephew Mason in his arms.

Mason looks at me with his big, brown eyes. "Wow, you're pretty."

I blush at that. "Thank you. I'm Marcela," I introduce myself.

"I'm Mason, and I'm three. My mom is Allison and my dad is David. My gramps lives here too," he overshares, with an excited smile on his face.

"Well, Gramps had to help our aunt in the city, so he's not here," A woman with shoulder-length, light-brown hair and brown eyes says as she bounds down the steps toward us.

Theo lets out an audible sigh of relief. "Really?"

Knowing his dad won't be here today causes the tension in my shoulders to melt away. Not only was I worried about dealing with him, but I was worried about Theo too. Now we get to both relax and enjoy the day with his family.

"Yup, it's just us four today," his sister explains. "I'm Allison by the way. It's nice to finally meet you." She smiles before wrapping me in a hug. Clearly, the Millers are huggers. I kind of love it.

I wrap my arms around her and hug her back. Once we separate, I say, "It's nice to meet you too."

"Where's David?" Theo asks as Louie and Mason begin chasing each other around us.

I remember Theo telling me about how his sister and her husband met. David, who's sixteen years older, used to be one of her professors at RLU. Being a reader, I'll never judge a love story. If anything, it makes me intrigued to hear more about how they fell in love.

"He had to fly back home this weekend to see his dad. Robert's not doing great—stage four lung cancer," her voice lowers to a whisper, a knowing look across her features. Their own mom passed away from cancer, so I can only imagine what feelings that brings up.

"Shit," Theo murmurs. "I'm sorry."

Allison nods, and her lip quivers. "Yeah, it's just a lot. It's a holiday and Dad's gone, and now David too. I love Mason more than anything, but he's driving me up the wall today and I need to get some work done this weekend. Our busiest time of year starts next week, and I need to get things ready."

From what Theo has told me, Allison oversees the business side of things at the farm. She plans events and activities with local businesses, and deals with logistics. Basically, she's the brains of this place, while their dad does the physical work.

"I can hang out with him while you guys get some work done," I offer, knowing I'll most likely be useless at whatever manual labor needs to be done in the barns.

"No, you guys came to visit, not to work," Allison says, shaking her head.

Theo rests his hand on her shoulder. "You already know I love working on the farm, it's no problem. Just tell me where to start," he tells her softly, letting her know he's not budging on this.

"Okay," she concedes as her shoulders sag in what must be relief. "Dad already did all of the barn work before he left. All that's left to do is some inventory stuff, and I'm going to get a head start on pricing the Christmas trees. You can't help me with that, but you could take the horses out for a walk. They need it."

"You're sure nothing else needs to be done?" Theo double checks.

"Yes," Allison groans, shoving his hand away. "Now get out of here and watch your nephew for a few hours. I'll be done in time for dinner."

"Whatever you say, Ally!" He gives her a salute, before walking toward Mason.

She rolls her eyes at his antics, chuckling. "I can't believe you're signing up for this," she says, meeting my gaze.

"He makes life fun."

Theo's not afraid to be loud and excited, or do the silliest things to make people laugh. It's genuine and real, something a lot of people are afraid to be.

"That he does." Her eyes warm as she watches her brother putting Mason on his shoulders. "Drop my son and you're dead!" she chastises him as Theo and Mason head for the barn.

"Uncle Theo never hurt me," Mason yells, hanging upside down across Theo's shoulders.

Theo turns and motions for me to join them. "Celly, follow us."

"I'm coming," I shout after them, and turn to Allison. "I'll see you later."

"Have fun," she winks, then spins on her heel and heads towards the house.

I jog the few steps to catch up to them, thankful I wore my pink cowboy boots just like Theo suggested. I bought the pair with Jade on our family vacation to Nashville years ago. I never really got an occasion where I could wear them, but they're perfect for today.

Once inside the barn, my nose crinkles at the smell, not used to it. There's stall after stall of horses, and they all begin to neigh happily as Theo walks by.

He mentioned how much he loves being on the farm, and now I'm beginning to see it. Theo Miller seems like a country boy at heart.

And I must say, he fills out a pair of jeans pretty well. Who am I kidding? More than pretty well—especially with his cowboy boots. He looks hot. Really, really hot.

Theo sets Mason down on the hay-scattered ground, reaching for the cowboy hat hung up on the wall. He places it on top of his nephew's head. "Mason, stand with Marcela while I get the horses ready, okay?" Mason nods before coming to stand by my side.

We watch as Theo rolls up the sleeves of his button-up, and my mouth suddenly starts watering at the sight. Why is this so attractive? There has to be something in the country air that they don't tell people about.

Theo unlatches the stall closest to him, taking out a midnight-black horse. He gives it scratches and the horse nestles its nose against him, clearly familiar with Theo.

"How's my Stormy girl doing?" he coos. "I missed you too."

He walks her over to the open fenced-in area outside the barn, tying her to the post as he begins to saddle her up. His arms flex with each movement, and the image of his arms doing the same thing while driving inside me blooms in my mind, sending warmth to pool low in my core.

Once Stormy is ready, he returns to retrieve a sandy-colored horse named Maple, and Mason and I watch as he repeats the same process. With Maple and Stormy both ready to be ridden, Theo claps his hands together coming to stand in front of us.

"Who's ready to go for a ride?"

Me, my brain responds almost instantly.

"Meeee!" Mason exclaims, pulling me out of my very inappropriate thoughts.

"You have to ride with me, Sunny. Okay?" Theo tells him, giving his head a ruffle.

"Okay. But one day I be big enough to ride myself," Mason points to his chest as he looks to me.

"You sure will, buddy," I agree, giving him a big smile.

"Celly, will you be okay to ride by yourself? Maple is our best-trained horse, she's perfect for beginners. I'd trust her to take Mason by himself if I didn't think my sister would kill me."

Nerves churn in my gut, but I do my best to ignore them. If Theo says it will be safe, then I know nothing bad will happen to me.

"Sure, sounds good. I might need help getting up there though," I say, gesturing to my five-foot-five frame.

"I've got you." He eyes me intently, and without breaking eye contact, he says, "Mason, wait here while I get her up on the horse."

"'Kay," Mason gives us a double thumbs up, making me laugh. This kid is so sweet and silly, it's adorable.

Theo takes my hand in his, leading me out towards the area where the horses are waiting. "This here is Maple." he pats the sandy horse on the back.

"Hi, Maple," I say sweetly, walking around to face her and let her sniff me. She does exactly that, and before I know it, she nibbles on my hand.

I giggle and back away. "It's nice to meet you too, girl."

"Huh," Theo tongues his cheek.

"What?" I ask, giving Maple a scratch on the nose.

"She likes people, don't get me wrong, but I've never seen her do that," he remarks, then holds his hand out to me. "C'mere, let's get you up on her."

I take his hand and let him guide me to Maple's side, where a step stool rests.

"Step up on that and then I'll help you swing your leg over," he instructs and I do as he says.

Theo steps up behind me, his body crowding mine, and it makes a shiver roll down my spine. His hands land on my hips, and that rough, sultry voice of his hits my ears. "Lift your leg up."

My mind instantly transports me to when he told me to spread my legs for him, and it takes everything in me to not react. Instead, I lift my right leg and suddenly he's lifting my entire body up and onto Maple.

She sways slightly underneath me, and I grab onto the thing sticking out in front of me.

"Good girl," I hear Theo whisper as his hand squeezes my thigh. My hips buck forward on their own accord, his words a shot of warmth to my core.

His hand lingers, slowly trailing from my thigh down to my calf. My eyes don't leave his, watching as they darken with desire.

I swallow as our eyes lock while his hand switches from a light caress to a tight grip around my leg that has my core tightening. His bottom lip lowers as the tip of his tongue glides along the top of his lip, with his eyes not once leaving mine.

Stormy neighs, interrupting the moment as we both snap out of it. Theo releases his grip on me and takes a step back.

"That's called the horn. Hold onto it to keep your balance and use your legs to keep you grounded," he explains as he hands me the reins. "Use these to guide her. If you pull really hard, she'll come to a stop, and if you pull slightly one way, she'll follow. But you shouldn't have to do either, she'll follow us with ease. Okay?"

I nod as I take in all the information while trying to decipher why I wanted to kiss him just now. "Yes, I think so."

"I'm going to untie her and then get Mason and myself up on Stormy. I wouldn't put you up here if I thought you'd get hurt, you know that right?" his light-blue eyes bore into me, intent and serious.

"I do."

"Good," he tips his cowboy hat at me, giving me a wink before he turns to untie Maple. He's completely unaware of how attractive he looks right now. I'm thankful we're not in this setting everyday, because I think we'd be getting through our lessons *very* quickly.

A few minutes later, we're slowly moving through the property and out onto a wide expanse of green grass that never seems to end. There are mountains in the distance, and a clear blue sky above, making it absolutely breathtaking.

Theo leads with Mason on Stormy, while Maple and I trot slowly to the side and behind them. It gives me the perfect view of Theo smiling widely, and this look of content on his face that I've never ever seen before.

It's even better than the view.

He makes Mason laugh as we move along, and he constantly looks back to check that I'm okay. Each time, it makes my belly swirl with butterflies at the thoughtfulness. But I try to remind myself every time that he's just being a good friend. Although, my previously trusted reasoning is beginning to weaken every time that I'm with him.

The day goes by better than I could have imagined. Our horse ride was relaxing but fun, and I got to see so many beautiful sights along the way, Theo's unbidden joy being my ultimate favorite one.

It gets me thinking that this place is where Theo is truly meant to be. Surrounded by nature and animals. With his family.

We're sitting around the dining room table, and it's the first time I've sat at dinner and wasn't afraid of someone yelling at me.

Every time I have dinner with my parents, there's always an underlying fear of not knowing when things will get worse.

"So, Marcela," Allison says, snapping me out of my thoughts. "Tell me about yourself."

My stomach sinks. That is quite literally the worst question you can ask me.

"Ally, I talk about her all the time." Theo eyes her over a forkful of his roasted veggies.

"Zip it. I want to hear from her." Allison shoos him with her hand.

Theo mocks her under his breath and I stifle a giggle.

With a deep breath, I answer her the best I can. "I was born in Costa Rica, but my mom and I moved here when I was two after she got remarried. I'm studying English literature, and love books, tea, anything pink, and my mom's cooking."

"Do you ever go back home and visit?" she asks.

"We try to go every year, yes."

Wanting to shift the focus off me, I quickly add. "Tell me about you and David. I love romantic stories."

"Yes, Allison. Tell us all about your forbidden relationship," Theo grins, placing his hands under his chin.

After horseback riding, Mason was exhausted and Allison tucked him in for a nap, so I'm hoping she'll give me the full story since he's not around to hear it.

She takes a small sip of her wine. "I was twenty when we met in my fourth-year business ethics course. He was my professor, and obviously I had a crush on him, like the other girls in my class. He's gorgeous, how couldn't I?"

"Gross," Theo mutters.

I shush him, wanting to hear this.

"So, I set my mind and pursued him. I wore my best outfits to class, and showed up to his office hours to ask about assignments I absolutely didn't need help on." Allison chuckles, making me laugh with her.

"We formed this unexpected bond and ended up talking about everything. I would catch him staring at me, and honestly, I couldn't take my eyes off of him either. I know it probably sounds strange, but we were drawn to each other. One thing led to another, and here we are. I never expected to fall for him, let alone have him feel the same way."

I open my mouth to ask Allison more about her relationship, when suddenly we hear a cry on the baby monitor.

Theo stands from his seat. "Don't worry. I've got him," he says, before exiting the dining room. We hear the thump of his feet on the steps as he goes to get Mason.

"How did your dad take the news of your relationship?" I ask.

"I thought my dad was going to kill me. But now, he and David are besties." She shrugs just as Theo and Mason enter the dining room.

"Mommy!" Mason yells, squirming out of Theo's arms.

He jumps right onto her lap and they snuggle into each other. The sight makes me smile and think about how I can't wait to have kids of my own someday. Not everyone dreams of being a mom, but it's something I've always wanted.

After finishing dinner with Allison's homemade pumpkin pie—which was absolute perfection—Theo and I offered to clean up, since she cooked.

We're side by side, him washing and me drying the dishes, the atmosphere feeling peaceful while we work together. I immensely appreciate it after a day spent socializing in a new environment.

Once we're finished, Theo puts a hand on the small of my back as he guides me to their living room, where Allison and a sleeping Mason are curled up on the couch watching a movie.

"We're going to head out," he tells his sister. "Thanks for everything, Ally," She moves to stand, but he gestures for her to stay put. "Don't get up. We'll walk ourselves out."

"Thank you for coming and hanging out with Mason while I got some work done," she whispers back, not wanting to wake her son up.

"It was so nice to meet you, and thank you for dinner. It was amazing," I say.

"Come back soon," she says, waving to us as we exit the front door.

Theo and I make our way to his truck when he stops me.

"How comfortable would you feel driving my truck?" His voice is curious with a hint of playfulness.

"I've driven my stepdad's truck before, so I'd be okay. Why?" I ask, intrigued.

He takes a step forward forcing my back against the hood of the truck. Theo dips his head lower, his lips brushing against the shell of my ear. "You've been driving me crazy all damn day with your pink cowboy boots and tight jeans. It's time for a lesson."

I inhale a sharp breath.

"I saw the way you were staring at me all day, pretty girl. Have a thing for cowboys, do you?" he drawls.

"I might now," I say breathily.

Theo's lips press against my neck, and I gasp. He continues pressing kisses up my neck as his hands grip onto my hips, keeping me in place. My hands latch onto his thick biceps, squeezing as he drives me wild with kisses.

I feel him harden against me, and I instinctively grind against him. Just as his lips are about to press against mine, he pulls back, leaving me breathless and panting for more.

His hand travels from my hip to my ass, giving it a squeeze.

"Get your perfect ass in the truck. Class is about to be in session."

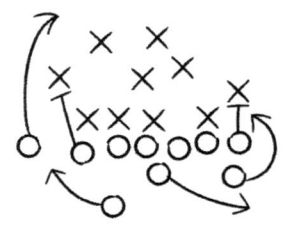

Chapter 24
Theo

Marcela has been driving me insane all goddamn day. Those tight jeans she has on are molding her curves perfectly, paired with the pink cowboy boots that are making my cowgirl fantasies come to life.

But seeing how easily she fit in with my family and how much they liked her, made me like her even more.

I know I'm playing with fire, but we're too far in to stop now.

Marcela turns the key in the ignition, roaring the truck to life. "What now?" Her voice is thick with desire. Knowing it's all for me turns me on even more.

"Make a left out of the driveway." I scoot over to the middle seat to sit next to her. We should be taking a right to make our way back to the freeway, but I want to have a little fun first.

Marcela makes the turn and begins heading down the empty road with her hands tightly gripping the steering wheel. She's just as on edge as I am.

"Drive slow and focus, okay?" I say as my hand grips her thigh and slowly trails upward. My lips move across her neck, making her moan softly as my hand reaches the button on her jeans.

"What are you doing?" she asks breathily, her eyes focused on the road.

"Teaching you what it feels like when I can't stand not touching you for another second." My jaw clenches as my dick hardens in my jeans, painfully aware of how much I want her. "That okay?"

"Yes," her voice is thick with lust.

"Then keep your eyes on the road like a good girl while I make you feel good," I order, grazing the skin below her ear with my teeth, before peppering her neck with kisses.

She squirms, and I take that as my signal to undo the button on her jeans and pull her zipper down.

Fuck. Me.

I look down to see that her satin pink panties are soaked. It makes me want to put my tongue all over her pussy, but we can't quite do that right now.

My hand makes its way to her pussy, cupping it over her panties as I rub my fingers up and down her slit.

"God, Celly," I whistle lowly. "You're soaking me through your panties."

She doesn't say anything, only moans as my thumb begins to press circles against the fabric right where her clit is.

"Theo, I can't—"

"What's that?" I hum, pressing a kiss to her jaw as I move her panties to the side. My thumb continues to work her clit and my two fingers move up and down her slit.

"How am I supposed to drive?" She stumbles her way through the words as I continue my ministrations.

"You can do it. And you're doing such a good job soaking my hand, but I need you to come all over it now," I order her, my voice almost unrecognizable.

My thumb circles her clit and my fingers on her slit rub her harder as I suck on her neck.

"This pussy has been driving me wild since I tasted it, you know that? Can't get it or you off my mind," I grunt as I palm my cock over my jeans, feeling myself on the verge of coming too.

"Theo," she moans my name, and it's music to my fucking ears as she finally comes, her thighs squeezing my hand as she pants wildly. It sets off my own orgasm, my moans ragged as I rub out each ounce of her pleasure I can.

I plant soft kisses all over her face as she comes down from the high. Once she releases me, I remove my fingers from her pussy and put them right to my mouth as I suck her arousal off.

"I—I—" she pants. "Have no words."

I grin cockily. "I made the author speechless. Go me."

She chuckles and it makes my entire body light up. It's easily the second-best sound—the first being hearing my name out of her lips when she comes.

"That was quite the lesson," her voice is airy and light. "Do we have time for a repeat?"

She wants more?

Although surprised by her request, I say, "If I ever say no to that question, call for help, because there's something seriously wrong with me."

Her laugh is quickly transformed into a low whimper when my thumb returns to her clit. By the time we make it back to her apartment, she's had four orgasms, each one better than the last.

Marcela moves to zip up her jeans, when I put my hand over hers to stop her. "Do you remember agreeing to me putting my tongue on your pretty pussy whenever I wanted?" I lick my lips, eager to taste her.

"Yes," her lips part. "You want to do it here? What if we get caught?"

"There's no one around. It's late and cold outside. Plus, we're facing the trees, so no one will be coming this way. But if you're not comfortable, I get it."

Her eyes dart between mine and then my lips. "Lesson three could be doing things in public?"

Fuck. Yeah.

I answer her with a kiss and she opens for me instantly. Her lips are soft yet fierce against mine, kissing me with the same fervor.

I push her down on the seat and we make out for what feels like forever. My body is on top of hers as we grind against one another. I pull back, my lips brushing hers, and my hips give a shallow thrust upward.

"I can't wait to feel you come around my cock one day," I groan.

Her eyes widen for a fraction of a second, and then she's biting her lip. "Me too."

I know she asked for help to feel more comfortable being intimate, but I honestly wasn't sure what it included. I'll be sure to have a conversation with her when we're both not pent-up with lust.

My lips dive back onto hers, kissing her for a beat before making my way down her jaw, to her neck and her cleavage.

I'd love to play with her nipples with my tongue, but I'm starving. I help her out of her jeans and make my way between her thighs, feeling cramped in this position, but I'd do just about anything to get a taste of her right now.

My nose notches against her pussy, inhaling deeply. "I love the way you smell."

Her fingers dive into my hair, tugging and I press a kiss to her inner thigh.

"I've got you, Celly," I tell her as I drag her panties off. And then I dive into her pussy, not wasting any more time. I lay my tongue flat against her and her body twitches at the contact. Her hands tighten in my hair, urging me on.

I lap at her clit, alternating from a light amount of pressure to hard, then I circle it with my tongue. Marcela moans, making me grip her thighs tightly as I devour her. There's nothing better than this. She's feeling good and moaning because of me, my tongue on her pussy, lapping up her sweet taste.

"Mmm," I hum, catching my breath for a second. "Such a good pussy," I mumble against her.

"Oh my gosh, Theo," she whimpers, her hips driving up and seeking my tongue.

I lay my tongue flat again, licking her up and down, then return to her clit where I give her hard flicks.

I feel Marcela tense underneath me, and I know she's close and it pushes me to go harder. I suction my lips around her clit, sucking hard as she screams my name and her hands yank on my hair.

"That's it, Celly. Let everyone know who's making you feel good," I say, my voice husky and low.

Her thighs begin to shake around me as I continue to flick her clit rapidly with my tongue, her moans getting louder and louder. Knowing my quiet girl is losing it for me—and quite loudly—is a huge fucking turn on.

That's why when she comes on my tongue, her moans unrestrained as her thighs clamp around my head, I find myself unable to stop from coming in my pants for the second time tonight.

I continue lapping at her through both of our orgasms, making her shiver and twitch beneath me, until she's finally calmed down.

"Five orgasms in one night," she pants heavily. "I never thought it was possible."

"Always expect the unexpected with me," I wink, wiping her arousal from my face.

"You really do enjoy doing that, don't you?" She looks at me as if I've grown five heads.

"Why wouldn't I? I like your pussy," I say nonchalantly.

Marcela covers her face with her hands. "God, where do you come up with that stuff?"

I laugh at that as I hand her panties back to her. "I just say the truth and what I'm thinking out loud."

Marcela plops back down on the seat, rolling her jeans up her legs as she contemplates what to say. A small, shy smile plays on her lips as she tilts her head to the side. "You're something, Theo Miller."

"Just when it comes to you."

"On a serious note," I clear my throat, drawing her eyes back to me. "Thank you for coming with me today."

"Theo, you don't need to thank me. I was more than happy to be there. Your family is great," she says wistfully as her eyes take on a faraway look.

"That's because my dad wasn't there," I mutter quietly. Not wanting to talk about it further, I open my door. "Alright, time for bed. I have an early workout tomorrow."

Marcela's brows pinch in a puzzled look. "It's Thanksgiving weekend."

I sigh. "My personal trainer, Rob, doesn't take holidays off when my dad is paying him an insane amount of money."

"Okay, but you deserve a break."

"Oh, believe me. I know I do, but it's not worth the argument."

Her face falls as pity takes over.

"No, don't do that." I shake my head.

"I know you don't like talking about it, but maybe you should. Maybe it'll help you figure out what to do," she suggests, her voice gentle.

"There's nothing to do," I glance away from her, staring into the darkness of the sky.

"Everyone has a choice."

"I get that. I really do. But do you know how hard it is to make that choice? How upset my dad would be if I walked away from this? How hard he's worked his entire life to get me here? I can't do that to him."

"So instead, you work yourself to the bone?" she counters, sounding rather protective. Part of me wants to dive more into defensive mode. On the other hand, she's right even though I don't want to admit it.

"It's comfortable, being the guy who doesn't upset anyone. I know my role," I pause, pressing my lips together. "I don't know who I am or what I'd even do if I wasn't that person."

Marcela inhales sharply, drawing my gaze back to her. "Theo," her voice cracks.

"Celly, it's okay. I'll go to the NFL for a few years, make my dad happy, and then retire once I get injured or something."

Before I know it, Marcela shifts so she's straddling me. She places her hand on my cheek as she rubs a soothing circle there. "I know exactly who you are, Theo."

"Yeah, who's that?" I ask, desperate to know how she sees me.

"You're the guy who makes everyone's life brighter. You make sure everyone is included and having fun. You're a great friend, and even though you're the life of the party, you have a serious and deep side that you don't show everyone. And it's okay. No one has to be the fun one all the time," she says softly, her eyes never once leaving mine.

"You love your family fiercely. You're a great uncle, brother, and son. And I think where you're meant to be might just be where you started. I saw you come alive in a way I've never seen before at the farm. I've never seen you so happy."

I swallow harshly, trying to push down the emotions that want to break free. My hands find her hips and I pull her closer to me. Marcela lays her head on my chest, right over my heart as I hug her tightly.

For once, I am at a loss for words as I try to process what she just said. I know my friends and family love me, but damn. I've never had someone say things with such honesty and sincerity.

It only makes me love her more, despite knowing better.

Saying it in my mind sends a chill down my spine, because I know there's no way to undo how she makes me feel, and that's eventually going to change things between us.

Either for better or for worse.

Switching my thoughts, I reflect on what she said about the farm. Everything has always felt lighter when I'm there. The anxious pit in my stomach is absent and my mind always seems clear and free there.

It's the only place I feel like I'm at peace, other than when I'm with Marcela.

It's easy and makes me feel carefree.

The complete opposite of football.

If I were to quit football just to end up exactly where my dad did, he'd probably lose his mind.

But the difference between us? He didn't have a choice back then, but I do.

And I want that life. Simplicity and slower days. Not grueling workouts nor flying across the country multiple times in a month.

I want to take care of the place my mother loved the most.

I want to do all of that and spend my days with the love of my life by my side.

Chapter 25
Marcela

Locking myself up in my room to write during a visit home to see my mom sounds like a typical night for me when I'm home. Especially because my stepdad is here, and I'd prefer to limit my interactions with him. I told them I had a headache from the school day and needed to lay down for a bit.

Meanwhile, I've been in my room finishing the spicy scene between Marissa and Dom.

My writing has been seamless lately as the creative flow is hitting me like it never has before. I'm almost done with my novel—seventy-five percent finished, which is something I never thought I'd say. I've always wanted to write a book, but I never thought I'd actually finish one.

I'm about to start a new chapter when I hear footsteps coming up the staircase, just outside my room.

Seconds later, I hear, "Ohhh, Mar!" as Jade sing-songs while she knocks on my door.

"Come in," I call out to her as I set my phone down.

Jade comes in and closes the door behind her, then plops down onto my bed.

"Why are you hiding in here?" she asks, flipping her blonde-highlighted hair over her sun-kissed shoulder.

"Why do you think?"

Her shoulders deflate, a knowing look in her brown eyes. "Sometimes when I'm away for so long, I forget what it's like to be here day in and day out."

When there were really bad fights, Jade and I would hide in my room together, our ears firmly pressed against the door. I'll never forget the way my legs would shake from fear as my stepdad's voice would rise in anger. But despite how afraid we were, we wanted to make sure my mom was safe.

My mother has always considered Jade one of her own, especially since Jade's mother disappeared after she was born, claiming she never wanted to be a mom. In a way, it's like it's been the three of us against him for our whole lives.

We always promised to stick together.

"He's been fine so far, but I still don't like to be around him, you know?"

She nods along. "I get it," she blows out a breath. "It sucks, because he's not an awful person when he's sober. But when he's drunk … he becomes someone else entirely."

I play with the ends of my hair, my eyes fixated on the pink florals on my comforter. "I don't know how Mom has put up with it this long."

"Do you ever think maybe it's because she knows how messy leaving would be? Sometimes it's easier to stay," she says, her voice going quiet.

"How is it easier to stay with someone who treats you and your kids that way?" I counter, feeling myself getting upset.

"It's easier said when you're not so deeply involved. Love changes your perception. Trust me, I've watched and studied movies my entire life. You learn a thing or two about how love controls everything, including people. It makes what seems like easy solutions not so easy."

"You really think she still loves him?"

Jade's quiet for a moment before she speaks up. "I'm not sure, honestly. Part of me thinks yes, because she's still here. But then there's a part of me ... I don't know."

"No, say it." That usually means she knows *something*.

Jade eyes me with caution, and that has me sitting up straight. "Jade," I say, urging her on.

"It's only a hunch," she warns, holding up a hand to me. "But last year, Dad was at work and I was alone with Mom all day. She took a phone call from your aunt, and I may have eavesdropped. While my Spanish isn't great, I could understand some of what she was saying. It sounded like Tía Isabella was asking her why she's still with him. I don't know if I'm right, because like I said, my translation isn't great, but she said something about waiting until we had our careers established. She didn't want him interfering with us in any way."

My stomach drops. My mom has been sacrificing her own happiness for us over the fear of what my stepdad might do if she tried to leave him.

"So it's our fault," I mumble, feeling frozen to the bone.

"No," Jade says firmly, grabbing my hand in hers. "This is why I didn't want to tell you."

"How is it not our fault if she's literally waiting for us to be independent?"

"Because what if I misheard or misinterpreted what she said?"

"So then why say anything to me now?" I ask, feeling confused and sad. My mom should have left him years ago if that's what she wanted. It's what we've all wanted.

"You're almost done with school, and I wanted you to be aware of what might happen after."

"What do you mean?" I ask cautiously.

Jade sighs. "You know what my dad is like. If she tries to leave him ... he's going to destroy her ... and you. Because he knows that's what will hurt her the most. He'll freeze her out of the bank accounts and ensure she doesn't get a cent of his money in the divorce. He'll ruin your reputation and you'll never be able to outrun his influence. He'll take everything you love and drain it dry."

I swallow as the reality of what could happen sets in. I know Chris Bass is a powerful man, yet I'd let him ruin me if it meant my mom could live a life where she doesn't have to fear her husband. Especially when he's had one too many drinks. A life where she isn't free to be herself.

I don't care what happens to me, so long as my mom is happy.

It's all worth it to me. No matter how terrifying that all seems.

"I hear what you're saying, Jade. But if she is willing to leave him, I'm going to support her and encourage it. I don't care if he tries to ruin my future."

"Let's not get ahead of ourselves. We don't even know if what I heard was correct. But if it was, who's to say she'll actually go through with it?" Jade points out.

"True," I sigh in agreement.

"At least you know we will have options if he does anything. It's a good thing I just got a job and can afford a good lawyer," she teases, trying to lighten the mood.

"We?"

Jade looks at me as if I've grown a second head. "Well, duh. You two are my family, I don't care what biology has to say about it."

"I couldn't agree more," I say back, my voice growing thick with emotion.

"Nope, no getting sappy with me," she flails her arms, searching for a pillow which she tosses at my head.

That earns a genuine giggle from me as I take it and throw it back at her.

Her mouth gapes, followed by a boisterous laugh. It reminds me of when we were kids and we do this in the forts we used to make.

"I've missed you," I tell her once we stop laughing.

"Me too. Tell me what's new with you? I heard you have a new man?" She wiggles her brows at me.

I faceplant into a pillow and groan. The last thing I want to do is to talk about how much I like Theo, when I need to keep the lines clear between what's fake and what's real. Especially with everything that's been happening between us recently.

Because at least for that part, I know it's very real. The way my body burns for his touch, the way my stomach leaps whenever I'm with him. That can't be faked.

At least, I couldn't fake it *that* well.

Jade pulls the pillow out from under me, forcing me to snap back up.

"You like this one, don't you?" she drawls, rubbing her palms together like she's uncovered a secret.

I push whatever I really feel for him to the side and slip back into the role of the perfect girlfriend.

"I do. He's my best friend too, and it just feels so natural. I even enjoy talking to him, which isn't common for me," I say, putting some of my hair behind my ear. "It's different than it was with Hunter. Theo is calm, understanding, and thoughtful. Hunter was never any of those things. I don't think I realized all of the things he wasn't, until Theo came and gave me all the things I should've had."

"Hunter is a piece of shit." Jade crosses her arms against her chest. "As much as what happened sucked, I was relieved that he was finally gone."

"Why didn't you tell me you didn't like him?"

"Because you were young and thought you were in love. You had the rose-colored glasses on, and I didn't want to be the one that took them off for you. But looking back, maybe I should've said something so things didn't end the way they did. I'm sorry," she apologizes.

I reach for her hand, giving it a squeeze. "Don't feel bad. Oddly enough, everything worked out the way it was supposed to. I'm much happier now."

Jade grins at me. "I know you are, I can see it. I'm proud of you."

Tears prick my eyes, because hearing those words never fail to stir emotions within me. I've been through a lot this year—hell, my entire life—and I'm pretty proud of the life I'm making for myself too.

"Thank you," I sniffle. "I'm proud of you too. My sister is about to be famous soon."

She rolls her eyes, but I don't miss the excited smile she wears. "Yeah, yeah."

Suddenly, my mom's voice is booming up the stairs, "Girls, dinner!"

Jade and I stare at one another as we inhale and exhale, ready to take on whatever happens at dinner.

Things have been fine … so far.

Chris hasn't lashed out and or said anything hurtful, since he doesn't appear to be drunk. *Yet*, my mind adds, as I watch him signal the staff for another drink.

"It is so nice to have you both home with us," my mom gushes as she takes a bite of rice and black beans.

"I agree," Chris clears his throat. "The Bass family needs to get together more often. Especially now that Jade is in the public eye, we can use it to further promote the business."

As if our five-star hotels needed any more promotion. They're already well-known across the globe and are sometimes booked out years in advance.

"I can't wait to watch you on TV and brag to all my girlfriends that my daughter is a movie star," my mom gushes.

"Oh, stop," Jade blushes as she downs a mouthful of steak.

"Then my Marcie's graduating so soon. I couldn't be more excited," my mother continues.

"And what exactly do you plan on doing with a degree in literature?" Chris eyes me over the rim of his glass.

"Just like we talked about, Dad," my words are slow and practiced, careful not to upset him.

"Good, I'm glad you're sticking to that plan. Darla, our marketing coordinator will be more than happy to sit down with you after graduation and talk about how your ... way with words can be used in our company."

"Of course," I agree, nerves pricking my stomach. I don't want any part of this plan.

I twirl my fork around my plate, mixing the beans, rice, and veggies together as I hope the attention shifts away from me. Jade and my mom talk while my dad continues to drink, throwing back two more glasses of whiskey. Each one makes me more on edge.

Dessert is brought out, making me nearly sigh in relief that this dinner is almost over. My mom made *arroz con leche*, and Jade and I always liked to add our own twist to the dessert, drizzling Nutella on top of it, so I'm not surprised when a squeeze bottle of it is placed between us.

Excitement bubbles to the surface as I reach for the bottle, only to knock over the pitcher of water, spilling it right onto my dad and soaking his shirt.

"Are you fucking kidding me!?" he shouts, and I flinch from the force of it.

"I—I'm sorry," I stutter as my nerves turn into full-fledged nausea.

"It's okay. It was just an accident," my mom tries to calm the chaos.

"All because your daughter needed some extra calories on her dessert. Neither she nor Jade needs to gain any more weight. In fact, take it off the table," he scoffs as he tosses it.

The bottle clatters against the wooden floor. I wrap my arms around my waist, suddenly feeling self-conscious.

"Dad, stop," Jade cries out.

"Put your fucking tears away, you little shit. It's the truth. You think the network will keep you on if you gain weight? I'm trying to help," he shouts even louder as the waitstaff dabs at his shirt.

My entire body tenses as my breathing becomes erratic.

"Chris, it's okay. Let it go. This is silly," my mom says as she tries to talk him down.

"Fuck this," he stands and whips his empty glass at the wall, making the entire room go still. "I'll be in my study."

We sit in silence as he exits the room. Once we hear the slam of the door upstairs, we collectively sigh and sag back in our chairs.

My mom waves his tantrum off. "Ignore him. Now we can have girl time."

My eye meets Jade. How can she not say anything after that? How can she be this calm?

"Mom," my voice is tight with emotion.

"What's wrong, Marcie?"

"What's wrong?" I repeat her words, baffled that she even has to ask.

"Marcela …" Jade warns me, but I don't think I care much anymore.

"Mom, how can you not see what's wrong?" I crack, not able to hold it back.

Her face softens, her eyes closing briefly, and when they reopen, I see sadness in them. "Marcela … It's complicated."

"What is so complicated? Chris is an alcoholic who treats all of us like shit. He's abusive, Mom. We all deserve better," I plead, feeling a tear roll down my cheek.

"She's right, Mom. Hell, he's my own dad and I agree with her. I don't know why you haven't left him yet," Jade chimes in.

My mom lets out a shaky breath.

"I know that, girls. I do, but it's complicated."

My fork clatters to my plate at her admission. So she *is* aware of the abuse that we've all tolerated for years, yet has never talked to us about it? Why?

Sadness and anger consume me, not just because of what we've been through, but because of how hard this must have been on my mom to stay silent all these years.

But there's also an overwhelming amount of shock I'm feeling, because I have no idea how she put up with this and it seems like nothing is wrong.

"What's so complicated? Would you want me or Jade to be with someone like that?" I ask quietly.

My mom's eyes well with tears as she shakes her head.

"Then why?"

"Because I wanted to make sure the two of you were off living your own lives before I made any changes to mine," she says, confirming what Jade said.

The room is quiet for a moment before my mother speaks up again.

"It wasn't until you were ten years old, Marcela, that I noticed his drinking problem. But by then, I was so in love with him, I thought that it was something I could look past. When it became worse and he started to be verbally abusive, that's when I started to question if I wanted to stay. I made a plan to start my own private catering business, which he has no idea about. That way I'd have my own money in case I ever did leave."

Shock ricochets through me at the news.

I was wrong.

This whole time I thought my mom needed saving, and that I needed to be the one to do it. It's why I played by the rules and agreed to anything my stepdad ever asked of me. So I could be successful and eventually help her leave.

But it turns out, she's saving herself.

A sense of pride washes over me because my mom is the strongest person I know. She's been through so much and I wish I'd talked to her sooner. I wish I'd been able to be there for her more.

"Once I realized how powerful he was … I will admit I was afraid to leave. I didn't want him ruining your lives before they even started. So I made a promise to myself that once the both of you graduated and settled into your adult lives, I would leave him, and that way he couldn't hurt either of you, because you would be independent from him."

My heart aches for my mom at what she's gone through to protect my sister and me.

"Mom, you didn't have to do that for us." I sniffle, wiping away another tear.

"You girls are my life. I needed to make sure you were both okay before I did anything," she takes a drink of her water, her hand slightly shaking the glass as she sets it down. "Marcela, do not take that job at Bass Hotels unless you really want it. If you do, I will support you and stay with him."

I fumble over my words. "I … I don't want to take it, I never have. My plan was to get my master's in English literature and work at a publishing house while I worked for him. And then maybe one day …"

"What?" my mom and Jade both ask at the same time.

My stomach sinks at the fact that I'm about to share this part of myself with them, but if we're all being honest here, I might as well join in.

"One day, I'd like to publish a book. I love writing," I say, my voice growing more confident as I think of how awestruck Theo was when I told him. "I'm really good at it—at least, that's what over fifty thousand people on the internet think."

My mom's hand flies to her mouth. "Oh my, Marcie, that is wonderful. I'm so proud of my little girl."

"That's amazing, sis. Proud of you." Jade smiles, her eyes watery.

"Sí, I'm so proud of you both," My mom says, her voice fading at the end as she begins to cry.

It instantly breaks my heart, making my own eyes well up with tears.

She begins to sob into her hands, her body shaking as her emotions take over. Jade and I get out of our seats, rushing to her as we envelop her in a hug between us.

"You're so strong, Mami," I tell her as I breathe in her comforting scent of apples.

"I can finally leave," she says between her cries. "I never thought I'd see the day."

"We will be here for you," Jade tells her. "And support you in any way you need. I'll have my own money soon from this job. You can stay with me."

"Thank you, Jade," she says. "I don't know how or when, but I will do it. Even if it will break my heart, because for whatever reason, a part of me still loves your father."

"I get it. Love isn't always easy. But you can't live like this forever," I tell her.

With what I learned today, I know it's not an easy thing to do. But it's time for her to have her happiness back.

"I know," my mom affirms.

"There's no rush or pressure. We just want you to be happy," Jade says.

"You deserve it," I add.

"I love you both very much. Thank you for understanding," my mom says, wiping her eyes.

"We love you, Mom," Jade and I say in unison, squeezing her tightly between us.

Seeing that my mom has a plan and is going to go after her own happiness inspires me. It makes me wonder if I could do the same. Maybe, just maybe, I could actually publish this book I'm writing. Just like I've always dreamed.

Why wait years to try? Life is unpredictable, and anything can happen. And I know that at the end of my life, I want to be certain I've done everything I could possibly want to do.

No matter how it turns out, I want to say I did it. All by myself, for myself.

I think it's time I start creating the life I want to live.

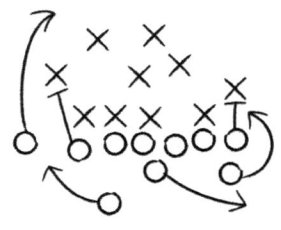

Chapter 26

Theo

"It's the most wonderful time of the yearrrr!" Dale sings loudly enough that I can hear him from within his room as I pad down the hallway from the bathroom.

Chuckling to myself, I make a stop at his room. "There will be parties for hosting, marshmallows for toasting and caroling out in the snowww," I sing, finishing it for him.

Dale turns away from his dresser where he seems to be packing his bag for the holiday break. "Shit, could you hear me singing?"

"I'm pretty sure the neighbors could hear you," I laugh, and he joins in, not taking himself too seriously. "What has you in such a good mood? Weren't you nervous to go to Robin's parents' for the holidays because you still haven't told them about the baby yet? Otherwise known as our assistant coach's house?"

"Oh, dude, don't get me wrong, I *am* nervous as fuck about that. My stomach has been upset all day thinking about it. Her parents will be supportive, I think. but I know they won't be too happy initially. Especially Coach Sanders."

"Well, rip the Band-Aid off and give them time to process it. If you know in the end they will be supportive, try to let go of whatever reaction they give you at first. Coach Sanders might yell at you, but I don't think he can bench you or anything." I've never been in a situation like this, and my advice might not be the best, but it's all I can think of.

"That's what I've been telling myself. I'm sure I'll keep repeating it until we get to their vacation home in Arizona," he says, throwing a toiletry bag in his duffel bag.

"You've got this. And if you need anything, you know I'm here," I remind him, and he gives me a nod in appreciation. "Now, what's the cause of this good mood?"

Dale looks almost shy and I watch as his eyes go glassy. "We're having a boy. We found out yesterday."

I immediately take the few steps into his room and wrap him into a hug, squeezing him hard. "Dale, that's amazing. Congrats, man."

"Thanks, Theo," Dale says, patting me on the shoulder as we part. "I can't believe it's happening."

"I'm so excited for you two. Do you have a name picked out already?".

"Hudson. It was my grandpa's name."

"Wow," I breathe, finding myself getting emotional. "That's sweet. I'm sure your parents will love that."

"Me too. We're telling them after we tell Robin's parents."

I check my watch, seeing that it's nearing five o'clock, which means Marcela's shift at the bar is almost over. I wanted to surprise her at work today, so I need to get out of here.

"I've gotta get going, but congrats again and good luck with everything. Let me know how it goes," I say as we slap our hands together.

"Thanks. Theo. Have a great holiday. Try to enjoy yourself," Dale says, knowing how much I'm not looking forward to seeing my dad.

Which is why I'm only going for Christmas Eve and Day.

It'll give me plenty of time during our break from school to spend time with Marcela.

We can kick our feet up and relax for once. Maybe she can read me her book, or we can watch a movie. I don't really care what we do, so long as we're together and she's happy.

All I want to do lately is be with her.

The line of what's real or fake is becoming blurry. We text all the time. We're intimate. We've gone to each other's houses for family dinners.

And if she agrees to go on a date with me, knowing Hunter and Ruby won't be there. What does that say about everything we thought we knew?

I won't know until I ask.

I push through the doors of Beers 'n' Cheers, stomping my snow-laden boots on the mat to clear the snow as I search around the room for my girl.

My heart skips a beat when I see her at the bar, wiping it down, but my mood quickly changes when I see a guy sitting in front of her, his eyes glued to her breasts.

I can't make out what he's saying, but I can tell Marcela is uncomfortable, because she's not saying anything back.

He looks old enough to be a senior, but I've never seen him on campus before. All I know is that I've never wanted to punch a stranger more in my life. I'm not a confrontational person, but where Marcela is concerned?

Yeah, I'd do just about anything to protect her.

My anger propels me towards the bar. I try to keep my cool on the outside, but on the inside, I'm boiling.

I make my way behind the bar, not caring if I get in trouble. Marcela looks up and relief washes over her pretty face when she notices it's me.

As soon as I'm close enough, I hear him say, "Do you want to go out sometime?"

A green wave of jealousy clouds my vision, and I have every intention to let him know who she belongs to. "There's my girl," I hum right before I grab her face in my hands and plant a chaste kiss on her lips.

I know I'm breaking our no kissing rule, but I find myself unable to care right now.

When I pull away, I turn to face him with a cocky smile on my face. "Hey, I'm Marcela's boyfriend. And you are?" I ask, putting my hand out to shake.

The asshole must get the hint, because he ignores my hand, throws some cash down the bar and walks away without a single word.

"Jealous?" Marcela says with a laugh as she pulls out of my embrace.

"Pfffft," I sputter. "I know you're mine, and I have no problem reminding people."

"I hoped he would stop if I didn't reply. I mean, he didn't say anything awful," she adds in quickly, having noticed the look on my face. "I would turn him down anyway. I'm yours… for now."

Although she whispers the last part, it doesn't stop the ache in my heart at hearing her confirm that she's only mine temporarily. *Stop*, I tell myself before my brain spirals over those two words.

"Since your shift is over," I say, changing the subject as I point to the clock behind us. "I have something fun planned. You free?"

"Bold of you to plan a date without asking me first," she teases, which is becoming more and more natural for her. I love it.

"Does that mean you're turning me down?" I ask, eyeing her up and down. God, she's sexy in her tight black T-shirt and leggings.

It's so different from her usual style, and there's something about seeing her in all black that drives me wild.

"No, I'm not. What did you have in mind?" she says with ease, not thinking twice about the fact that this date is just for us.

Maybe it means we're moving past all the fake dating. Maybe she's developing *real* feelings for me.

"It's a surprise. Get your jacket and let's go. I'll drop you off here later to get your car," I tell her, and she does exactly that as she heads to the staff room to get her things.

Marcela and I are going on a date, a real one. I'm not sure if that's clicked for her yet, but it doesn't matter.

It's just me and her.

What could go wrong?

Chapter 27
Marcela

I've been dying to know where Theo is taking us this entire ride. I've tried to goad him into telling me, but he's locked up like a vault.

We exit the freeway, and I can't say I'm familiar with the area. We drive for a few more minutes, and eventually Theo makes a left turn into a parking lot with a building with a sign that says "Fun Zone."

"What is this place?" I ask, noting the bright neon colors the building is painted with.

Theo parks and turns to me with a wide grin. "It's exactly that, a fun zone. There are arcade games, laser tag, mini golf, and even fowling."

My brows pinch together. "What is fowling?"

"It's a mixture of football and bowling. You use a football to throw at large bowling pins."

"You'd be okay to play that?" I ask, knowing his distaste for football.

He shrugs as he unbuckles his seatbelt. "Of course. This is for fun, and it's with you. I'll love it."

My stomach flutters at his words, unable to ignore the way they make me feel. Knowing he enjoys spending time with me makes me question if the line between real and fake is beginning to blur. Not just for him, but for me too.

Because I enjoy spending time with him, so much so that I agreed to this date without the guarantee that we'd run into Hunter or Ruby.

I push those scary thoughts about the reality of our relationship away, when Theo opens my door and we walk hand in hand inside the building.

"Where do we even start?" I ask, overwhelmed by everything around us. It's loud with kids, teenagers, people our age, and adults moving around the place.

The center is filled with arcade games, from the classic Skee-Ball to newer machines like Flappy Bird. I think fowling is near the back wall, and the sound of pins being knocked over confirms that.

"Let me take care of you. I've got this," Theo gives my hand a squeeze as he leads us to the front desk where he pays for two passes that give us access to both fowling, laser tag, and tokens for the arcade games.

"Thank you," I say as we move out of the way for the next people in line.

"What do you want to do first?" he asks, giving me a choice.

I look around the bustling building, overwhelmed by how much there is to do. I decide on the first thing I can think of.

"Wanna fowl?"

"Sure," He smiles, taking my hand in his once again as he leads us to the fowling area near the back of the building.

There are four lanes with ten pins at each end. Players stand on opposite sides, throwing footballs at the pins. Some people seem to be in teams, while a couple is playing against one another next to the empty one we walk up to.

Once the attendant stamps our passes and explains the rules of the game, we're ready to play.

Theo's about to walk to his side of the lane when I stop him. "Wait," I rush out.

"What is it?" he asks, looking concerned.

"I've never thrown a football in my entire life. Can you teach me how?"

"Another lesson," Theo winks. "I've got you, Celly."

I shake my head and laugh as he picks up the football and holds it out to me.

"Do you see these white lines here?" I nod and he continues. "Your fingertips should rest in between each line."

My hand wraps around the football, my fingers resting exactly where he told me. Theo then steps behind my body and lifts my arm that's holding the football up and back above my shoulder.

"Before you throw, bring it back up here to your shoulder. Then you're going to twist here with your hips," he says as his hand grips my hip and twists it for me. My heart skips a beat as my entire body heats just from his touch.

Wait ... why is this happening? We've been intimate before, and we're not actually dating. Yet, when he put his hands on me just now, it felt ... right, exciting, and good.

Theo stops my spiraling thoughts when his hand that's on my arm pulls it back, then extends it forward. "You're going to pull this arm back, then twist your hips like I just showed you as you extend your arm and throw the ball. You aim with your shoulders, wherever they're facing is where your ball will go."

I hear what he says, but it doesn't process because all I can focus on is how close his body is to mine. It makes me want to leave here and roll around in my sheets together. Naked.

The way I want Theo is unlike anything I've ever experienced before. I crave it daily, though I'd never admit that to him.

"Celly, you with me?" he chuckles as his free hand wraps around my stomach, and he rests his chin on my shoulder.

"Yeah," I say, my tone an octave higher than normal. "You ready to lose?"

Theo unwraps himself from my body, and comes to stand in front of me with a small smile on his face. "This is the most excited I've been to toss around a football in my life. Let's do it."

My heart clenches at his words. The relationship he has with football and his dad is complicated, so instead, I focus on the fact that this is going to be fun for the first time in a long while.

And that's exactly what we do—we have fun. We laugh the entire time, especially after one of my throws hit the lane next to ours. The couple was sweet and thankfully laughed it off with us.

I already knew that Theo is amazing at football, but watching him throw the ball with precision each and every time today was amazing. It proved that he has worked so hard to get where he is—time that he would've rather spent doing anything else.

After Theo beats me a few times with ease, we head over to laser tag where we face off against each other. Our laughter echoed off the walls as we chased one another around the arena, and we were out of breath by the time it was over.

To my surprise, I beat him. He took the loss with a shrug of his shoulders, not caring in the slightest.

Hunter would've cared a lot.

I wish I didn't compare the two so often, but when you've never received the bare minimum and then start to receive it, you quickly realize how much you were missing before.

We spend the rest of the night at the arcade playing the games and taking photos in the photo booth. The night ends with enough tickets to get a small stuffed penguin, which Theo lets me have.

It's truly one of the best dates I've ever been on. It's scary, considering I don't know if this is fake anymore. We didn't do this to show off to Ruby and Hunter.

We did this because we enjoy spending time together.

"Shit," Theo mutters under his breath as we exit off the freeway, heading toward my apartment complex.

It had begun snowing on the side of town we were just in, but here it's a complete blizzard. The roads are covered in snow, and it's coming down so hard he has the wipers on full blast just to see out the windshield.

"Just drive slow. It'll be okay," I say softly, trying to reassure him and myself.

And that's exactly what he does. He drives as slow as he can, allowing us to make it to my apartment safe and sound.

"I don't want you driving home in this. Will you please come in until it passes?" I plead, my stomach twisting at the idea of him driving a centimeter further in this weather than he has to.

"As long as you promise to read *Love Bites* to me," he says, making me roll my eyes as I smile.

"I'm going to buy you an audiobook membership," I chuckle as I reach for the door handle.

"Ah, ah, wait for me," Theo instructs before he hops out and runs around to my door. He opens it and lifts me out.

"Wrap your legs around my waist," he says hurriedly as the snow falls hard and fast around us.

I do as he says, clinging to him as he carries me into my building and onto the elevator.

"You didn't need to carry me," I say, lifting my head from his shoulder so we're now eye to eye.

"And risk you slipping and hurting yourself?" he says gently as he tucks my hair behind my ear. "Not a chance."

Words fail me as I try to make sense of what's happening between us. I know without a doubt that Theo cares for me in a way no one ever has. The things he's done for me with no one looking speak to that.

I get lost in the light blue of his eyes, and he stares right back at me. My nails scrape along the back of his neck as my eyes dart to his lips.

Theo notices, his lips parting slightly before he leans in slightly.

Do I want to kiss him? Even with no one around?

My breathing turns rapid as I shut my eyes and—

Ding.

The elevator doors open, ruining the moment. Theo pulls back as I release my legs from around his body, neither of us saying a word as we make our way to my apartment door.

I'm worried I've made it awkward by not kissing him right away, but Theo pulls me into a hug once we're inside my apartment.

I melt into his embrace, that feeling of pure serenity that I get with him coming back. "Why don't you take a shower and warm up?" he says. "You're freezing."

"Is that weird though? What will you do while I shower?"

Theo pulls back so he can look me in the eyes, giving me an easy smile. "It's not weird at all. I want you to be comfortable, okay? And I'll read the book while I wait. Then you can take over and read to me after you're done."

"Maybe I want you to read it to me," I quip, tilting my head up at him.

"Anything you want," he says softly, making my heart do abnormal things inside my chest.

Ignoring it, I run straight to the bathroom to shower.

Because the last thing I need to do is complicate things, especially when we're most likely going to be snowed in together all night.

This should be fine.

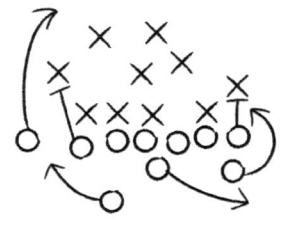

Chapter 28
Theo

I plop down into the desk chair in Marcela's room, spinning slowly in a circle as my mind runs through tonight's events.

Marcela going out with me, without the pretense of faking it for someone else, was huge. At least in my mind it is. Because it has to mean something, right?

What other reason would she go on a date with me if she didn't like me back?

And then the almost-kiss in the elevator? I'm not going to lie, it stung a bit when she didn't immediately lean in and kiss me, but I also know my girl better than anyone. I know that she needs time to process things, and think before she acts. It's not like her to be impulsive. If she wants to kiss me without an audience, it'll be on her own accord.

The chair stops spinning, placing me right in front of her laptop screen which is open to a word document.

She must not have a sleep mode activated, and forgot to close it before her shift today.

I know I shouldn't read her work without asking, but I can't help myself. Plus if I'm helping her with inspiration, I should be okay to read it, right?

The scene isn't finished, so I scroll up to the beginning of the chapter and my eyes widen when I read the first line.

"Can I put my tongue on this pretty pussy?" Dom rasps from between my legs.

Holy shit. I continue to read on about Dom going down on Marissa, and right away I notice how much it sounds like what happened between us.

My chest puffs with pride knowing I was able to help her write about sex in a way that she feels good about. She seems to have gotten through her writer's block, and she's a damn good writer from what I can see.

I read up until Dom's hovering above her, nearly about to insert himself, when the scene stops.

Huh.

I wonder if that's because she had to go, or … does she need more inspiration, since we haven't had sex yet?

"Sorry, I forgot to grab clothes. I ran right into the bathroom to shower," Marcela says, sounding flustered as she enters the room.

My eyes instantly dart to her, wearing nothing but a towel that's barely covering her.

I was already starting to get hard from reading that scene, and now this? I'm fucking rock hard looking at Marcela with her wet hair, and skin covered in water droplets that I want to lick off.

I try and fail to form words as my eyes don't move from her. Her cheeks redden as she leans against the wall.

"What are you doing at my desk?" she asks cautiously.

"I saw your book and I couldn't help myself from reading. It's really fucking good, Celly," I say. "I notice that you didn't finish it though."

The room goes silent as her eyes widen, lips parted. I watch as she swallows, then says, "I couldn't. My mind went blank whenever I tried, probably because of my past experiences."

I don't think I'll ever say it enough, but I hate that fucking guy.

Instead of focusing on that, I want to give her the chance to finish her scene and change her experience with sex.

It's what she always deserved.

"Why don't we write the future?" I propose.

"What do you mean …" she trails off.

"I mean that if you want, I'll give you a lesson to help finish the scene. And then in the future, you can successfully write a sex scene without getting a mental block."

I watch as she swallows, her eyes turning hazy with want as her fingers grip the towel she's holding tightly to her body.

Then to my surprise, Marcela lets go of her tight hold and the towel drops to the floor, displaying her gorgeous body.

"Yes," her voice is firm and confident, letting me know she wants this.

My brain nearly explodes at the realization that we're about to have sex for the first time. The girl I'm madly in love with wants me to make her have a better experience with sex, and honestly, I couldn't be more honored to fulfill that.

I swivel in her chair and stand. I stride towards her, not stopping until she's backed up against the wall. I don't miss how her chest heaves with each breath or the way her eyes are roaming over me with a want so powerful, it feels as if she's stripping me down completely.

I lean one forearm against the wall above her head while my other hand cups her cheek. "You want me to put my cock inside you?"

Her breath catches in her throat. "Please."

That's all I need to hear. My lips crash into hers as I press my hips into her bare pussy, letting her know how hard she makes me.

She moans into my mouth when I grind against her, and I instantly can feel through my pants that she's wet already.

Not breaking our kiss, I grip her thighs and lift her up. She wraps her legs around my waist, just like she did when I carried her in. Except this time around, she kisses me.

In fact, I would say she's in control of the kiss right now. Her lips are setting the pace as her hand grips the back of my neck.

I continue to grind, letting that friction build between us as I kiss her neck, allowing me to hear the soft sighs from her lips.

"I need to taste you. Right now," I say, my voice husky as I carry her over to the bed and gently lay her down on it.

"I want you naked first," Marcela says, shocking me at her bluntness.

"Whatever you want," I assure her before placing a kiss on her lips. Pulling back, I stand and begin to quickly strip off my clothes. Marcela watches intently, her eyes tracing each and every part of me.

And fuck, I am turned on, knowing she likes what she sees.

Not wasting any more time, I fall to my knees and grip her legs to spread her open for me.

Leaning forward, I run my nose up and down her pussy, inhaling her scent. "Fuck," I groan.

"What's wrong?" she asks just before letting out the sweetest moan as my tongue flicks over her clit.

"I could come just from sitting between your thighs and staring at your pretty pussy, but today, I'd like to fuck you first."

"Please."

"We're going to do this exactly how you wrote it in your book. I'm going to make you come on my tongue first, and then I'll slide my cock inside of you, nice and slow until you've adjusted, and only then will I fuck you. H*ard*."

"Fuck," she whimpers, and the sound turns me because Marcela never swears. Ever. Hearing her let go of her inhibitions might just be my undoing.

I nip at her thigh, causing her hips to buck before I dive back into her pussy, my tongue lapping at her like I haven't eaten in days.

My fingers slip inside her, curling at her inner wall as my tongue continues to flick her clit quickly. She's dripping down my chin, and I do my best to not waste anything, savoring every drop of her sweet taste.

Marcela's fingers tighten in my hair and I increase the pace at which my fingers fuck her.

"You're doing such a good job for me," I praise, taking a moment to look at what I am doing to her. Her nipples are taut, pussy soaking, chest heaving up and down with her eyes wild and full of lust. "Is my girl gonna come all over my face?"

"Yes," she moans her answer, making me smirk. She's always so quiet, and for once, I want to hear her scream.

I return my mouth to her pussy, but this time, my lips suction around her clit as I suck on it hard, and fuck her even faster with my fingers.

"Theo," she sighs, getting louder and louder as her thighs clamp around my head. I let her, holding her down with my free arm as I continue to push her over the edge.

Marcela screams my name as her hips lift and her legs shake, but I don't stop. If anything, I grip her thigh harder and continue to lap at her. Her orgasm seems to go on forever and I don't stop until she's completely sated, her body relaxing under me.

I stand and climb atop her, staring at her in awe. God, she's fucking beautiful.

I see her gaze focused on my lips so I ask, "Wanna find out what you taste like?"

Her lips open then close as she thinks for a moment. "Is it weird that I do? You seem to like it … very much, so I'm curious."

"It's not weird at all," I reassure her, leaning down so that our lips are a mere inch apart. "Never be ashamed of what you want. Okay?"

She nods, and lifts her head up to press her lips to mine. She kisses me tentatively, taking her time as our lips brush over and over again.

I pull back in time to see her licking her lips, a slight blush to her cheeks.

"Thoughts?"

"I like that you taste like both of us," she admits, her eyes blazing with desire as they bore into mine.

My body instinctively responds by grinding my painfully hard cock against her wet slit. We both moan at the contact while my lips dot kisses down her neck. It's the first time I've felt her without anything between us and it's like nothing I've ever experienced before.

"Theo, I need you," Marcela's words are filled with urgency as her nails dig into my arms. God, I hope she leaves marks. All I want is a reminder that I was the one making her lose control like that.

I sit back on my haunches. "How do you want me?"

"Like this, with you on top."

My head bobs in a nod as I take a deep breath, giving myself a quick moment to prepare myself to have sex with the girl I'm in love with. I push the thought away and focus my attention back to the present.

"Open up for me, Celly," I demand, my voice turning husky.

She does as she's told, giving me the perfect view of her perfect pussy. I've never been this addicted and this is all fucking mine.

At least for tonight.

I crawl back over her, resting on one forearm. I use my other hand to run down her slit to collect her arousal on my hand before running her over my cock, coating myself with her.

"Go slow," she whimpers, "It's been a while."

I smile and I lean down to kiss her forehead. "Of course. Anything you like or don't like, just tell me, okay?"

"Okay," she says softly, staring into my eyes with something I can't name.

I don't get time to be delusional about her feelings because the need to be inside her is making my cock ache painfully. I run the head of my cock up and down her slit, making her moan and arch her back. I swear I could come right now, seeing how much she wants this. I need to get it the fuck together.

"I need to be inside you" I grunt.

"Do it," she pants underneath me.

With her confirmation, I slide just the head of my cock inside of her, and my head falls back as I groan. "Fuuck."

"Oh my god," she moans. "Theo, more."

I oblige her, sliding in slowly as I fill her inch by inch until I bottom out inside her. My forehead drops to hers, our breaths mingling as we pant and attempt to catch our breath.

It's been a long time for me, but I've never been inside of a girl I'm in love with. It's making it ten times harder to control myself.

"Are you okay?"

"No, I need you to move. I'm aching."

I buck my hips, rutting in and out of her at a steady pace. Not too fast or slow as we find our rhythm together.

Our bodies move together perfectly, creating a sweet friction. Her hands are on my back, with her nails digging into it every time I slide back into her. And we're kissing the entire time, my tongue slowly exploring her mouth as she does the same to mine.

It feels like more than just sex to help her with her writer's block.

It feels like we're making love.

I pull away from her mouth as I stare into her eyes. My chest grows tight with the sight of her like this. Fuck, I love this girl.

"Harder," she pants, breaking me away from my thoughts of love.

My hands move down her body to grip her hips. "Be careful what you ask for."

Using the leverage gripping on her hips provide, I begin to fuck her hard. Our bodies slap against one another, the sound of wet skin echoing off the walls.

"So—" she breaks off into a whimper. "So good."

"What's that?"

"You feel so good, Theo," Marcela says, staring into my eyes as I fuck her.

"Celly, your pussy is unbelievable. You're so wet and taking me so well."

I pull out of her and move her body so that she's laying on her side, not missing the look of shock in her eyes as I take control. I lift her right leg up, giving me room to slide back into her.

"Theo," she whimpers at the new position. And fuck, I know exactly what she means. She feels amazing this way, so tight.

I grip her chin and press a kiss to her lips as I rock in and out of her.

Marcela kisses me back, our lips moving sensually, just like our bodies are. It's slow, sweet and makes my heart want to explode with the love I'm feeling for this girl.

My fingers make their way to her nipple, pinching it as my tongue enters her mouth. She moans around it, sending a vibration throughout my entire body.

"Play with your clit," I break away from her lips, kissing and sucking on the sensitive spot on her neck.

I know the moment her fingers meet her clit because she clenches around me, and her moans turn into desperate whimpers.

"You can come now, Celly. Let me have it," I grunt, biting down on her shoulder and following it with my tongue to soothe it.

It only takes a few more seconds of my lips on her neck, my fingers on her nipple and her own on her clit for her to explode.

Her pussy squeezes me, as I feel a rush of wetness hit my cock. Everything in my body tightens as the need to come becomes imminent, with each thrust more powerful than the last.

"I'm about to come. Where do you want it?"

"Wherever you want. I'm on the pill."

I can't help it at that, losing myself to my own orgasm as I groan into her neck as we ride out our mutual highs together.

I lay on my back, sliding out of her as I attempt to catch my breath. We're both sweaty messes.

It hits me then that I should've asked beforehand about protection and all that, but we were both so caught up in the moment that we couldn't stop.

I huff a laugh and ask, "Will that help you finish your chapter?"

Marcela giggles beside me as we stare at her white ceiling. "Yes, one hundred percent yes."

"That good, huh?" I say cockily.

She doesn't even give me shit, which normally she would when I'm like this. "It really was. I … I don't even know how I ever thought what I had before was special. It's never ever felt like this before."

I swallow roughly, trying to tamp down the hope I feel at her words and their possible implications.

"I'm glad I could help."

I feel her turn on her side, and I do the same, so that we're now face to face.

"And … you had fun too, right?" she asks cautiously.

My eyes nearly bug out of my head. "That was the best sex I've ever had. It's all I'm going to want to do now."

As soon as the words are out of my mouth, I want to take them back. I sound like a stage-five clinger, when all she wanted was experience for her book.

We're silent as we look at one another, and I'm sure my eyes are filled with the hope that she'll want to do this again. Meanwhile, I can't get a read on what she's feeling at all.

Her lips tilt up into a shy smile, and relief begins to flood my body before she even speaks. "Possibly, I might need to see what it's like in other positions. You know ... for the book."

"Of course." I say, although I don't fully believe her. Maybe I'm being delusional right now, but I swear I see it in the flicker of her eyes.

Fear.

She's scared of wanting this, *us*, for real. It's making her hide her real feelings by claiming this is all for her book or that this between us is still just to prove something to Hunter and Ruby. My mind sifts through all of our time pretending to date to see if there's ever been any indication that she liked me as more than just a friend.

Fuck, it's hard to determine what's been real or fake when everything has felt so natural between us. The way Marcela has begun to reach for me on her own, and melt into me when she's in my arms. There's no way that can be fake. I refuse to believe that.

"Marcela ..." I begin, but she suddenly cuts me off.

"Shhh, don't ruin the peace," she says quietly.

We lay there silent for a few moments as we cuddle. I never want to let go, but I don't want to overstep and assume I can sleep over. Besides, I have another grueling personal training session tomorrow morning before I have to head home for my family's Christmas dinner.

I sigh dramatically, making her giggle against my chest. "I sadly need to go. I have training in the morning."

She pouts at me, which makes me wonder if she wants me to stay but she follows it up with, "Of course. Let's get dressed."

We quickly get dressed, and once I'm done, I turn to find her in pink bow pajamas.

"I'll walk you out," she says.

Moments later, I'm standing outside her locked door, and I can't help but think about how what we did has changed me forever.

And I don't know what I'll do if it didn't change anything for her.

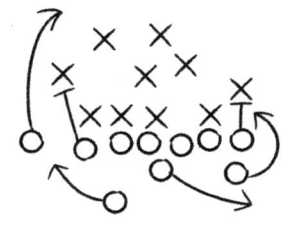

Chapter 29
Theo

A sense of dread fills my entire body as I park my truck in front of my childhood home, knowing I'm going to spend the entirety of Christmas Eve and Christmas Day with my dad. Usually, the athletic department banquet happens every Christmas Eve, but due to construction on campus, they moved it to the end of January.

I'm happy about being able to see my sister, her husband, and my nephew. But I could go without my dad talking my ear off about the upcoming draft and how I could do something better, how it's never enough.

As soon as my feet hit the dirt path, Louie comes running up to me and I take the time to pet him.

"Hey, Lou. I missed you, big guy," I tell him as I scratch behind his ears and take in the scenery.

Ever since my sister started helping out at the farm, it's looked better and better every year, especially since Christmastime is our busiest season. They had an entire barn built for a market, where local vendors can come and sell their products to holiday shoppers.

There are decorations and lights all around the property, and the large spruce tree in the front yard is the star of the show. It is wrapped with colorful lights and ornaments that kids make when they're here to visit the animals or craft events with their families.

A pang of longing hits me that Marcela isn't here, since she's also busy with family. I assumed we'd try to go to one another's holiday festivities, but Marcela said we should both enjoy the time with our families and not worry about it.

I tried not to overthink it and remind myself that we are supposed to be *just* friends, but I can't find it in myself to want to pretend anymore. Not when my heart races the way it does every time she smiles at me. Or the way my skin heats when she touches me. Don't even get me started on the feeling of being inside of her.

God, last night was … fucking phenomenal. She was. *We* were. The way our bodies fit so perfectly together isn't just a coincidence, Marcela is meant to be mine.

A door closing snaps my attention to the front porch, where Mason is running down the steps towards me. "Uncle Theoooo!"

His wide smile makes my entire body light up with joy, and I pick him up and snuggle him into my arms. "Sunny boy, I missed you," I tell him before putting him back down.

As soon his feet hit the ground, he grabs my hand and pulls me towards the house.

"We got so many plans. Santa is coming tomorrow, did you know that?" he exclaims, making me miss the excitement of being a kid on Christmas Eve.

"I hope I made the nice list," I tell him as we kick our boots off on the doormat.

His large brown eyes are serious as he looks up at me, finger pointed at my chest. "You better hope so. Or you'll have no gifts to open tomorrow."

I chuckle as we walk into the house together. "That's okay. I don't need gifts."

"That's okay, 'cause I got you—"

"Mason," Ally cuts him off with a warning. "Remember what we talked about? We don't tell people what we got for their presents."

"Sorry, Mommy," he apologizes, then runs off to the living room.

She shakes her head and hugs me. "He already told David what we got him. Little bugger."

"Hey, my nephew is perfect," I scold her mockingly.

David's six-foot-five frame makes its way down the steps, wearing Christmas pajamas. "If he's so perfect, you should take him for a full weekend and then get back to us on that," he jokes, bumping my fist.

"I'd love to," I tell him, because kids have never bothered me. Sure, they can be a lot, but I've always loved spending time with them.

The three of us make our way to the living room where Mason is on the floor playing with cars, and my dad is sitting in his recliner watching sports highlights on the large flat screen TV.

"Hey, Dad," I call out.

"Hey, son, how's it going?" he asks, looking me up and down. Probably to ensure I've been sticking to my diet and training.

"Happy to get a break from school for a bit, and you?" I say as I sit on the tan-colored couch, settling into the spot I sat in for years growing up.

It reminds me of early mornings with my sister, watching cartoons before school. Or that one time I was sick and slept on the couch while my dad slept on the recliner to keep an eye on me. The memory makes me determined to try to have a good visit, because things weren't always this way.

There were times growing up where every conversation was not related to football, when my dad and I had an actual relationship.

"I'm good. Ready to spend the day with my family and watch some football tomorrow," he replies, taking a sip of his beer.

It was a tradition in the Miller household. We start our Christmas morning by opening gifts, followed by a big breakfast. Then we spend the day watching football and preparing a big dinner. More often than not, I find myself in the kitchen with Ally, wanting to spend the least amount of time watching the game.

When you're forced to play football and it's all your dad talks about with you, it makes you hate even watching it. Which sucks, because as a kid, there was a time I did enjoy it. That was until it became a part of each second of every day.

"Where's Marcela?" Ally adds when I don't say anything.

"She has a lot of family things going on, so we couldn't make it work," I explain, my fingers twitching to text her. We've already spoken earlier today, but I find myself wanting to talk to her again.

"That makes sense. She's a lovely girl. I really hope you don't lose her," she says, giving me a warning look.

"Me either," I whisper to myself.

If only she knew.

After dinner, I head for the stables, craving some alone time. Dinner wasn't bad, but I found myself thinking about my mom a lot in what used to be her favorite place. I brush Stormy's coat as my thoughts drift.

Sometimes I think it's a blessing to not have distinct memories of her to haunt me. Sometimes it bothers me more that I don't have anything to remember her by, besides what pictures and stories Allison has shared with me. That breaks my heart.

A tear slides down my face as grief begins to pull me under. Feeling this pain while standing in the barn my mother's family built, the one she loved with all her heart, is making it hurt even more.

I wish she were here. I wish I could talk to her about Marcela, ask her what's the right thing to do. Ask her how I can move forward with my life without disappointing Dad or myself. My sister always told me how Dad was different when our mother was still alive, and I wish I could've seen that version of him.

Part of me doesn't blame him for being the way he is now, because if I lost Marcela the way my dad lost our mom? I'd be a fucking mess too. I'd just hope I wouldn't become a shell of a person I once was, channeling all my energy into pushing my son into something he doesn't love just to fulfill a dream I never got to accomplish.

Stormy nuzzles her nose against me, making me smile faintly as the tears continue to slide down my cheeks.

"Thanks, Stormy." I sniffle.

"Theo, are you okay?" Allison's voice startles me, making me jump back from the horse as I begin wiping at my cheeks.

"Oh yeah, why?"

She narrows her brows at me as she crosses her arms over her body. "Because you're crying and talking to a horse."

"I …" I begin trying to make some sort of joke, and fail as a heavy pressure sits on my chest. It's hard to breathe when my mind races.

My lip trembles as more tears threaten to break free, and all it takes is the look on my sister's face to send me over the edge.

I'm barely aware of what's going on when Allison wraps her arms around me while I cry into her shoulder.

"Hey," she says gently. "It's okay. I know the holidays are hard sometimes, but we have each other. Always remember that."

I nod, but can't form any words as I continue to let out what feels like years of pent-up feelings.

Allison strokes my back until I eventually calm down.

We take a seat on a bale of hay outside the stalls, and she looks at me with concern. "Theo, what's going on?"

I never told Allison any of this before, because I know she wouldn't have rested until I talked to Dad and figured it out. Back then, I was too afraid of facing him, but now that my life is about to change next year with the draft, I find myself wanting to tell her.

I can't keep this in anymore, and talking to Allison about it might help me come up with a plan to tell my dad. She knows him better than I do.

"I hate football," I whisper, my words barely audible. The entire barn seems to stand still in the aftermath of my revelation.

"Oh, Theo," her voice breaks. "Why haven't you ever said anything?"

"You know how Dad is with me. Everything's about football. My whole life has been about making me into the perfect athlete. It's all he wants for me. How can I take that away from him after so much already has been? His career? Mom?" My words come out almost frantic, feeling despair wash over me because I have no idea how to stop feeling like this.

"Theo ..." she says, her voice filled with sorrow. "Yes, Dad has been through a lot, but you need to think about yourself. What about your feelings? What about your life? Not to be morbid, but Dad will be gone one day, and then what? You'll have just lived in misery?"

"It's so hard," I say with a tremor in my voice, "I don't want to disappoint him."

"I know Dad is tough on you, but you won't know how he'll react if you never tell him how you really feel. I think he might surprise you. He's not that bad, you know? He's incessant with the football thing, but he does care about you. About all of us.

We're all he has left, and I think he'd rather you be happy over anything," she says, her voice soft and comforting.

"I don't know, Ally. It just feels easier to go along with his plan, play for a few years and then retire," I sigh.

My head and my heart are at war, because in my heart, I know Ally's right. It's what I want to do. In my head though, I want to do everything I can to not disappoint my dad any more than he already has been.

"And waste your time being unhappy? If mom's death teaches you anything, it's that a long life isn't guaranteed. Go after what makes you happy everyday because you never know when it'll be your last."

The fear of telling my dad seems to always annihilate my own needs.

"I just don't know how I'll tell him."

"Tell me what?" my dad's voice pierces through the cold night air. My next breath halts in my lungs as I look up to find him standing in the doorway.

Fuck. How long has he been there? Did he hear our conversation?

Neither of us says anything as our dad stares at us with curiosity. "That girl of yours pregnant or something?"

"No, and her name is Marcela," I grit my teeth, not liking the attitude attached to his tone.

He throws his hands up in defense. "Just asking, son. You never know with these girls."

"She's not like that," Ally defends her as she stands up. "I'm going to go read a story to Mason before bed. I'll see you guys in the morning."

As she stands, she catches my eye and mouths *good luck*.

Yeah, I'm gonna need it.

My dad leans against the barn door, crossing one foot over the other. "What is it, Theo?"

I inhale deeply, keeping my eyes on the floor as I gather up the courage to blow up my entire life.

My head slowly rises, my light-blue eyes meeting his own. "I hate football."

Relief briefly floods my system at finally saying those words to him, followed by panic because of the unknown of what will happen next.

My dad stares at me for what feels like a long time, and then he scoffs. "You're the best quarterback this sport has seen in years. No one who is as good as you can hate what they do."

"Call me the first, then," I reply as I look up at him. "I'm good, because I wanted to make *you* happy. Playing is your dream, not mine. It's the only reason I've worked this hard, despite how much I hated doing it. I only did it for you, because you had already experienced so much loss and I didn't want to be another thing on the list."

He puts a hand up. "Don't."

"Why not, Dad?" I stand as anger begins to simmer below the surface. "Mom passed away nearly twenty years ago, and we never talk about her. It fucking sucks and it's not fair. I'm—"

"I said *don't*," he shouts, his face turning red.

I shake my head, knowing that if I continue he'll just shut down, and I don't have it in me to fight with him. "Fine, but maybe you should talk to someone else about her then."

"Why don't we talk about this football thing? What are you saying, son?" he asks, ignoring my last comment.

I'd been debating what I wanted to do for a long time, but right now, only one thing comes to mind. I'd been afraid in the past because I didn't want to disappoint my father, but I'm tired of keeping up a pretense.

My whole life I've done what he's wanted, but I can't keep playing this game. It doesn't bring me joy and my body is tired. *I'm* tired of always being exhausted and not being able to do the things I like. I want to be able to eat whatever I want and not care about working it off.

I want to just be me without the pressure of meeting someone else's expectations.

"I'm going to finish the season, and then I'm done," I tell him. "I won't be entering the draft. I'm not going to play the game ever again after this season."

My dad's face twists with anger as he throws his hand out in frustration.

"You're just going to throw it all away? You could play ten years in the league, become a world-renowned champion and be set for life. You're an idiot if you give up now and waste what we've worked for."

"That's exactly it. Dad, it's not we. *I* had to get up early to train for hours. *I* had to give up things I love because I didn't have time to do them, or I was too fucking exhausted to do them. You've decided my entire life for me and I'm done being miserable," I shout, unable to contain myself anymore. He's made a lot of sacrifices so I could play, but does that make my misery worth it? "Maybe I'll take over the farm, that way you can find something you actually love, because I know it's not this. We both deserve to be happy."

The idea had been floating around in my head since Marcela and I visited for Thanksgiving, when she pointed out how happy and peaceful I seemed here. And the more I sat with the idea, the more I saw how it made sense for me. How much I wanted that.

"Theo, I've already been in talks with the Denver Lions. They want to draft you. Don't make me look like a fool." I don't miss how he ignores what I said about working here at the farm.

"No, Dad. I'm not doing it. I've already wasted so much of my time doing this for you. It's time I live my life for *me*," my voice drops as I speak quietly. "That's what Mom would want."

When I look over at my dad, I notice something I've never seen before. A tear rolls down his face and he immediately brushes it off.

I take a step toward him. "Dad ... I ... I'm sorry, I didn't mean to—"

"I need a minute," he snaps, turning to face away from me.

I walk to him and place a hand on his bunched-up shoulder, but he shrugs me off. I brush away the sting at him doing that and say, "It's okay to be sad over her. I'd be a mess too if I lost the love of my life. But please stop using me to deal with your grief. I can't do it anymore."

With that, I make my way out of the barn and toward the house, a mix of feelings surging through me. Relief for finally telling him and Allison. Confusion, because I have no idea what the hell is going to happen now. Hurt, because I feel bad for my dad.

I can only hope that in time he'll come to respect the choice I made, and maybe without football and if he can forgive me for choosing myself. And we can finally work towards building a normal relationship.

I've already lost one parent. I really don't want to lose another.

"Ahhh!" Mason squeals excitedly as he rips off the blue penguin-themed wrapping paper on the gift I got him.

"What is it?" I ask, sitting on the floor next to him.

"It's a race track!" he says once the paper is all ripped off. "Thank you, Uncle Teo."

Catch Me

"You're welcome, Sunny boy," I hug him to me, internally thanking my sister for giving us this ball of sunshine. Opening gifts is the perfect buffer after the shit show we had last night.

I passed out as soon as I hit my bed. Despite the tension that now exists between my dad and me, I got the best sleep because of the weight that was no longer on my chest.

I haven't had a chance to fill Ally in on what happened. But by the way she keeps glancing between the two of us from her loveseat, coffee cup in hand and a disappointed look on her face, I'm assuming she's guessed how it went.

The rest of the morning is painfully awkward, with my dad and me exchanging as few words as possible. I spend the rest of the morning watching the magic of Christmas unfold for my nephew, as we enjoy our big breakfast before I help build the race track I got for him.

As Mason plays, I take a moment to pull out my phone and snap a picture of me smiling with the Christmas tree in the background to send to Marcela.

Me

> Merry Christmas, Celly! How was last night?

Celly

> Merry Christmas, Theo! It was good, we got home around one after Misa de Gallo church service and had a huge dinner. And then my mom made us put out our shoes for El Niño Dios.

Me

> That sounds like so much fun and I hope you got to sleep in after the late night. If you had dinner last night though, what is your family doing today?

> **Celly**
> I did and I'm still exhausted, which is unfortunate because the Bass side is coming over. It's going to be a long night.

> **Me**
> I hope you enjoy it the best that you can. Did your mom like the set of olive-themed salt and pepper shakers I got her?

> **Celly**
> She loved it. Thank you, you didn't need to do that.

She sends another text before I can reply.

> **Celly**
> How is your day going?

> **Me**
> Just spectacular!

> **Celly**
> What happened?

I have a love-hate relationship with how well this girl knows me. My thumbs fly over the keyboard as I decide honesty is my new policy from now on.

Catch Me

Me

> I broke down in the barn, my sister found me and I ended up confessing how much I hated football and how much I missed our mom. My dad walked in on us, and demanded to know what I was hiding. So I did, and it went about as well as I expected.

Celly

> Oh, Theo...I'm so sorry. Do you want me to come over or do you want to come here? You know my mom won't mind at all.

Me

> I appreciate the invite but I don't want to intrude. I'm going to still try and enjoy time with my sister and nephew. But then I'm leaving first thing in the morning.

> Also how's it going at your place?

I redirect the conversation because I don't want to spend another second thinking about how I blew up my life and what will come next.

Celly

> Okay, if you need anything you can text or call me anytime. And it's going surprisingly well, but it's still early in the day, I'm not keeping my hopes up.

CARLIE JEAN

Me
> Call me later and we can talk about it?

Celly
> Yes, I'll text you when I'm free.

Chapter 30
Marcela

It's almost midnight by the time I retreat to my room and finally get to talk to Theo. "How was your Christmas?" I hear Theo's tired voice for the first time in only one day, and yet, I find myself comforted as if I … missed him?

I don't think much of it and focus on what he asked me.

"It was oddly good. There was no fighting or rude comments, just a normal Christmas Day. We woke up, had a huge breakfast that my mom made, opened our gifts, and had a few hours to get ready before the rest of the Bass family came over."

Back in Costa Rica, my mom told me that we would have spent the day relaxing on the beach with family, which sounds a lot better than the formal dinner we had.

Bass Christmases are a huge ordeal. My stepfather hires someone to excessively decorate our house, with a beautiful nativity scene in the living room taking center stage.

Our family party lasted till nearly midnight, but I snuck away an hour ago because my social battery was drained.

Not only did I have to socialize all day, but I was dressed up because Chris always insists on it for this party. I usually love wearing heels, doing my makeup, and picking out a cute dress, but for this party, it fails to spark the same joy. The Bass family is great. What bothered me was the demand that I dress like this. It wasn't a choice, and I think that's what grated on me.

"I'm glad you had a good day. Was Santa good to you?" he asks on a chuckle.

"Very good. I got everything on my list," I joke back, laughing along with him. I didn't want to pry about what happened with his dad, so I try to keep the conversation light.

"When can I see you?" he blurts out, as if he couldn't wait to ask.

"We have another Bass Christmas party tomorrow, with some of my mom's family joining us from Puerto Limon as well. So the day after that, if you're free? I'll be heading back to my apartment then. I can only survive so many days here."

"How will I ever survive that long?" He sighs dramatically, making me giggle.

"I know. I miss you," I admit quietly. As soon as the words leave my mouth, I realize what I've just said and how it might sound. I don't miss Theo the way I would miss any of my other friends, and suddenly I want to change the subject.

"Have you heard from Dale? How did it go telling Robin's parents?" I blurt out.

While I don't know them that well, Theo had mentioned he was nervous for his friend to tell her parents, so I'm hoping it all went smoothly.

"Dale texted me not long ago and said that they were very shocked, which he expected. But they're already coming around to the idea and are very excited."

"That's so good to hear."

"Do you want kids?" he asks, making me falter.

"Uhh … what?"

"Do you see yourself having kids? I'm curious, that's all."

I take a moment to mull his question over, and I'm hit with a mental image of me and Theo at the farmhouse, with a baby wrapped in a blanket in his arms as he leans in to kiss me, and—

Oh no. No. No.

Why am I imagining that? I never once imagined it for Hunter and me. More importantly, why do I like how much a future with Theo looks?

"Celly, you there?" I hear his voice become farther away as he pulls the phone from his ear most likely to check if the call dropped.

"Yeah, sorry," I say, my voice higher than it was before. "I have to go."

"Wait—" Theo says, his voice full of panic. "Is everything okay? I was just curious—"

"No, that's fine, you're good. I'm just really tired after the long day," I partially lie.

"That's okay. Get some rest. We'll talk tomorrow," he says, and I can't tell if he believes me or not.

"You too. Good night."

"Good night, Celly."

The second Bass party was underway, and you think it'd be less extravagant than the day before … but somehow it's always more food, more people, more socializing.

And I happen to only like one of those three things, which is why I take my place at the appetizer table that my mother prepared this morning.

"This food isn't going to eat itself," my mom chastises as she slides next to me at the table.

"I'm trying to eat as much as I can. But all we've done the last three days is eat, and I'm stuffed." I laugh as I pat my belly.

"Good, that means I'm doing my job," she smiles, looking more at ease than I've ever seen before.

My mother seems different this holiday. I think it's because she knows it's the last time she'll have to endure all of this with my stepfather since she has plans to leave him once I've graduated in May.

She told me about her plan when I got here on Christmas Eve, right before we went to Misa de Gallo. I couldn't be more proud of her. She's already secured her own lawyer and they're working to get everything ready to go.

Knowing my mom is leaving Chris gives me peace of mind that I desperately needed. I don't think I realized how much I worried about her living with him, until I realized I won't have to anymore.

"*¡Marcela, te ves hermosa!*" My Tía Isabella yells as she makes her way over to me.

"*Gracias, Tía. ¿Cómo estás?*"

"*Estoy bien. ¿Sabías que tu antiguo novio está aquí? Pensé que con ese nuevo hombre tuyo no estaría invitado,*" she says, making the air around me turn frigid as the blood drains from my body.

Hunter is *here?*

"*No lo invité,*" the words somehow escape me as I begin scanning the room for him. Hunter came to this party every year, but he had to know he was no longer welcome, right?

My tía gasps, then reaches for my hand and gives it a squeeze as she says, "*No dejes que arruine tu noche. Estaré aquí si me necesitas.*"

I give her a nod, and she smiles before making her way over to Jade, leaving me by myself.

I decide to head to my room in case Tía Isabella was correct. I'm nearly out of the room when I run right into Hunter.

"We need to stop meeting like this," he says with his signature smile. A smile that would have made me blush a year ago, but now? It makes me roll my eyes.

"Why are you here?" I snap, surprised at my cool tone to my voice, because I never talk to anyone like that. Even Hunter looks surprised.

"Your dad invited me."

"I didn't."

"So?"

I let out a humorless laugh. "So? Are you kidding me? Hunter, you cheated on me with my best friend, and you expect me to be okay with you coming to my family's Christmas party? I don't care who invited you. If it is anyone other than me, consider it void from now on."

All he does is smirk at that. "I kinda like this bossy side of you, Marcie. Hell, if you were like this when we were dating, I wouldn't have looked elsewhere."

"Thank God you did, because I've moved on to better things," I say with confidence. It strikes me then how true of a statement that is. My entire life has shifted for the better since we broke up. Despite how hurt I was then, I've never been happier.

Sometimes when good things are happening to us, they don't always feel good right away. It's like a flower blooming. It doesn't start with beautiful petals, but eventually you get there.

He's quiet for a moment, when he takes a step toward me. "I want you back." He tries to grab my hand, but I back away from him.

I can't help it, a boisterous laugh erupts from my lips, and there's nothing I can do to hold it in. Hunter's face is priceless, a mix of embarrassment and shock as I continue to laugh uncontrollably.

"Stop laughing," he hisses, noticing the eyes on us. "I'm serious. Ruby was the fun fix I needed, but I'm ready to come back to you and settle down. That phase of my life is over. She and I have been done for a week now."

I'm not even shocked that they already broke up, and I don't feel bad for either of them.

It doesn't bring me joy nor sorrow—I simply don't care. The only thing I'm thinking about is how Theo and I don't need to keep up pretenses anymore. We were in this fake relationship to prove to them that I had moved on too, but now that they're over, we can call it quits.

I should be happy, yet no part of me likes the idea of not being his anymore. There's so much going through my mind that I honestly don't know what to think, except that Hunter needs to hear this loud and clear so he gets the point.

"What we had wasn't love. The way you treated me is not how I deserved to be loved. I'm not a phase in someone's life, or a backup plan. I wish you the best in your future, Hunter, but I will never be a part of it."

Hunter stumbles back as if my words physically hit him, while his tongue prods his cheek as his eyes bore into the ground.

I want to say I'm sorry for saying no and hurting his feelings ... but that was the old me. The new Marcela isn't apologizing for setting boundaries and being honest.

"And Miller is that guy?" he finally says.

"He treats me better than you ever did."

Hunter shakes his head and leaves without another word, walking right out the front door.

A tear strolls down my cheek once he's out of sight, but it's not from sadness. Months ago, I never would've had the courage to stick up for myself and tell him how I really felt about how he's treated me. This time when I shed a tear, it's not because of what he did to me, rather it's because of what this situation did for me.

It's the closure that I needed to end that chapter of my life, and I am more than ready to write my next one.

I have a feeling it was about to be a good one.

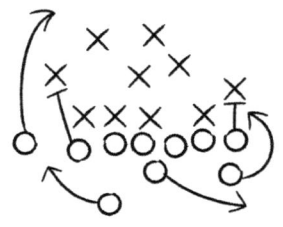

Chapter 31
Theo

Marcela walks out of her building, stealing the breath right from my lungs. It's the first time I've seen her in days and I missed her. She's wearing a white puffer jacket, brown leggings, and white snow boots, with her wavy hair loose under a pink beanie.

I can't seem to form words, even when she's standing right in front of me with a concerned look.

"Theo? You okay?"

My eyes trace the freckles on her cheeks and bridge of her nose, and up to her honey-brown eyes.

"Better now," I smile, handing her the bouquet of roses.

"Theo …"

"You're welcome." I lean in and briefly kiss her forehead before opening the passenger door. "Keep them in the truck. We've got places to be, Celly."

Marcela moves to hop in the truck, but she pauses in front of me. She rests her hand on my chest and places a small kiss to my cheek. "Thank you." When she pulls back, I see admiration in her gaze, which I'm sure I'm mimicking back at her.

My skin tingles where she kissed me and my entire body buzzes with excitement that she could be in this for real.

I lay my hand on top of hers, giving it a gentle squeeze. My mouth parts, the words about to tumble out of me, when I think better of it.

Now isn't the time. I haven't seen her in a few days and the last thing I want to do is push her away by telling her how I feel. If this is going to be the last date we go on, I want to enjoy it.

I let go of her hand as she settles into the passenger seat, and we drive over to the distillery district for the post-Christmas farmer's market.

"So, I saw Hunter yesterday," Marcela suddenly says, nearly making me slam on the brakes.

"What the fuck, *where*? What happened?" I ask, on edge that he may have said something to her that will make me want to hurt him.

"Everything's okay," she reassures me. "Apparently, Chris invited him to the party. He told me he wanted me back because he and Ruby broke up."

A million thoughts run through my mind—from wanting to punch Hunter for wanting Marcela back after hurting her, to the fact that Ruby and Hunter broke up. But only one trumps them all.

What does that mean for us?

If Hunter and Ruby broke up, what happens to Marcela and me? Does this mean we have to stop being together? If she knew about this yesterday, why did she still agree to go out with me today?

"I hope you told him to fuck off," I say, hoping she didn't let him off easy.

"Not in those exact words, but yes."

"I'm proud of you, Celly," I glance over at her, not missing the satisfied smile she's wearing.

"Me too, Theo. Me too."

The entire drive to the district, I keep thinking about how I'm more determined than ever to tell her how I feel after this date. Maybe it will go better than I thought.

Maybe she's done pretending too.

"I think I'm going to keep this hanging up in my room year-round." Marcela gleams with pride as she looks at her ornament.

I took her to Creation Station, a craft store, where we each made an ornament. She painted her round wooden piece with a stack of books wrapped in a big bow, while I painted a night sky with a bunch of stars.

Because they reminded me of her. Bright and beautiful, quiet but powerful.

"Me too," I agree as I pull into the parking lot of her building.

"This was such a fun day. Thank you for taking me there. I think I'm going to be full and tired for the next three days."

She wasn't wrong. We went ice skating, and walked around the entire market three times as we browsed the stands and tried as many festive treats as we could. We drank hot chocolate, ate chocolate-dipped pretzels, and my personal favorite—devoured snowman brownies.

To end the night, we had Indian food from a food truck, making us full beyond capacity at that point. It was worth it though, everything we had was delicious, and not once did I care about what my trainer would say. Because football wasn't my priority anymore.

I will still do my best to win the championship in February, because my team and I deserve it. But then I will be done. Forever.

God, I haven't wanted anything this badly, other than wanting to be with Marcela.

Catch Me

And I think it's time I let her know exactly that. I've kept quiet the entire night, holding back these feelings inside of me. But I'm done doing that. I've done it my whole life and it's exhausting.

"Same," I hum my agreement, as I put the truck in park.

I go to speak, but Marcela beats me to it. "What happened with your dad? I know I usually don't pry, but I need to know that you're okay."

I wasn't planning to keep it a secret from her, I just had more important things I wanted to talk to her about first. But since she's asking, I oblige.

"When I told my dad I hated football, he had a hard time wrapping his head around it. He tried to convince me that I would be wasting all the work I've done, and I should at least go pro to play a couple of years. But I told him that I was done, and that there was nothing he could do to change my mind."

"I am so sorry, Theo," her voice is gentle as she speaks. "But I am proud of you for finally speaking your truth." She places her hand on mine, giving it a squeeze. My body revels in her comforting touch.

"Thank you," I whisper quietly. "I'm not sure what will happen next. And I hope we'll get a chance to mend our relationship. All I know is that I have roughly seven more weeks and I'll never have to play football again. That's what I'm trying to keep focusing on."

"You won't quit on your team," she points out.

And oddly enough, knowing I'd no longer be forced to play beyond this season makes me almost ... excited to finish out the last few games. It's funny what happens when you take away the pressure that's been weighing you down.

"You know me well." I grin as I place my hand with hers.

My stomach rattles with nerves when I say her name.

"Marcela."

The air in the car instantly changes when her eyes flit to mine, wide with a hint of fear of them. "Theo? What's wrong?"

I swallow roughly, but don't look away. "I need to tell you something."

She slowly shakes her head back and forth, as if she already knows what I'm about to tell her, but I don't let it deter me. I've waited and bottled my feelings up for far too long. It's time for me to face my fears, no matter the consequences.

"I love you, Marcela," I say, my voice surprisingly steady. "And not just as a friend. I've been crazy about you since the day you walked into that lecture hall freshman year," I pause as Marcela's face becomes unreadable but since I already started, I need to get it all out.

"I knew fake dating you was going to be a challenge, because I was already so into you. That's the only time I've ever lied to you, and for that, I'm sorry. Because every minute I've spent with you over the last few weeks—where you let me see the real you—I've fallen hopelessly in love with you."

My chest aches and warms at the same exact time, relieved to have told her the truth, yet utterly terrified at what comes next.

Marcela's eyes well with tears. "Theo … I-I can't."

"What are you so afraid of?"

Her bottom lip quivers as her eyes dart from my lips to my eyes. "I'm scared of falling again."

"I'll catch you, Marcela," I say softly.

Marcela remains quiet as she looks away from me. I can feel how torn she is, and I hate that she's so unsure about us. I wish she was so certain about me, the way I am about her, but I can't force her to feel the same.

So as much as my next words will break my heart, I have to do it. For her sake, and mine. "I'm breaking up with you."

Her head whips towards me, shock written all over her face. "W-what? You tell me you love me and then you don't want to be with me?"

"You need time to figure out what you want and how you feel, and I'll never pressure you into it."

My heart shatters at the hurt on her face, but this needs to happen. I can't go on pretending anymore, and she needs space to figure out what her feelings are.

"I guess with the closure I recently got with Hunter, it makes sense that we stop pretending too," she reasons, her face devoid of emotion. She's guarding herself, not letting me gauge her feelings

My chest hollows at her words, even though I knew that's what this was all for. Her falling for me the way I have for her was never guaranteed.

"Yeah," I say tightly, not wanting to break in front of her.

There's an awkward silence growing between us, louder than any words could be. I don't know what happens next, but I need to leave before I take back everything I just said.

"I should get going," I say. "I have an early training session."

"Okay," she responds quietly as she undoes her seatbelt. "Thanks for … everything."

I watch as she opens the door and hops out of my truck.

"Marcela," I call before I can stop myself.

"Yes?" she replies quietly, a hand on the car door frame.

"If you realize that you feel something for me too, I'll be waiting. I've waited this long, and I'd wait forever."

She gives me a nod and shuts my truck door. All I can do is watch as the love of my life walks away, potentially forever. For the second time in a week, tears trickle down my face.

I knew this was a possibility, but I hate that this is how my and Marcela's might end. But that night, as I toss and turn in bed, I usher a silent prayer to the universe that she'll come back to me.

She's all I've ever wanted, and I hope she feels the same way about me.

Chapter 32
Marcela

I officially had the worst night of sleep that I've ever had. Not even the night I found out Hunter had cheated on me with Ruby could top last night.

Theo, the guy I'm—*was*—faking dating, and one of the few true friends that I have, told me he was in love with me.

"Ugh," I groan as I roll over, and plant my face down into my pillow.

I feel like an idiot, thinking we could pretend to be together without any consequences.

I thought I was fine and I'd get over our fake relationship ending. But the gaping hole in my chest that's been there since I walked away from him tells me a different story.

Because not only am I hurting over the knowledge that this broke his heart, but because my own is broken too.

And I didn't even see it coming.

Deep down, I knew that I was developing feelings for Theo, feelings bigger than friendship. I just didn't want to admit it to myself. I thought that the more I ignored it, maybe it'd go away and I wouldn't have to deal with it.

Because I didn't want to fall again, not after getting burned the way I have before.

My mind was at war with my heart.

I'm terrified of falling in love again. I know it sounds like such a cliché, but the idea of opening myself up and being vulnerable to more pain is horrifying.

He said he'd catch me if I fell, but my trust issues screamed at me that he was lying. When you get screwed over by two people you were supposed to trust the most, it changes how you think.

I didn't want to be a scornful woman who never loved again, but I also didn't know how to move past that.

I might have gotten closure with Hunter, but it doesn't mean my fear of trusting someone again was magically restored.

Theo knows me better than I know myself, so I owe it to both of us to process everything and figure out where my head is.

I spend the remainder of the holiday break holed up in my apartment, only leaving for food, since I don't need to report back to work until the start of the new semester. I spend hours at my desk trying to distract myself from my thoughts, but find myself unable to write a single word.

I'm currently wrapped in a blanket watching my comfort show when there's a knock on my door. I sit up, instantly on edge at who could be at my door. There are only three people who know where I live, and I don't care to see two of them again. Let alone at my doorstep.

Which means there's only one person it could be. Theo.

My heart pounds erratically as I untangle the blanket from my body and make my way to the door. I pause when I pass the hallway mirror, noting the messy bun on my head and the outfit I've been wearing for the last two days—an oversized sweater and leggings. It's not my best look, seeing as I haven't showered, but there's nothing I can do about it now.

I peer into the peephole, and I'm surprised that it's not Theo standing in the hallway. As quickly as I can, I unlock the door and am greeted by three faces.

Aurora, Jasmine and Camille.

"How did you know I live here?" is what I blurt out.

"How do you think?" Aurora raised a brow at me.

"Theo told the boys, and they all told us. Obviously. We came to check on you to see if you were okay," Camille says.

"I hope it wasn't supposed to be a secret that you guys broke up, because we all know Theo cannot keep his mouth shut," Jasmine mutters, making me smile faintly.

"No, it wasn't a secret," I shake my head and pull the door open for them to come inside. "Come in, it's not super clean. I wasn't expecting anyone."

They all roll their eyes at me and tell me not to worry, which is all I seem to do these days.

It's not until we're in my living room that I notice they didn't come empty-handed. Aurora sets down containers of sushi on the table, while Jasmine sets out a box of baked goods from the bakery and Camille opens a cooler full of drinks.

"What's all this for?"

"Breakups suck," Aurora shrugs as the girls begin to open everything up. "Not that I'd personally know that, but from what I've heard."

"We weren't actually dating though. It was fake, remember?" I remind them as I pop a sweet potato roll into my mouth.

"Then why are you sporting the whole post-breakup look right now?" Jasmine counters as she eyes me up and down.

"I've been enjoying my holiday break, that's all," I try to defend myself.

Camille gives me a sympathetic look. "Marcela, it's okay to admit that even though this started out as fake, that it upsets you now that it's over."

"I mean, of course I miss having him around. It's just an adjustment, that's all," I say, not sure if I believe the words.

"You're telling me you feel nothing for him? Even if this was all fake, I saw the way you looked at him," Aurora says knowingly.

"How did I look at him?" I ask curiously, wanting to know what she saw.

"You'd always have this smile on your face, and your eyes were full of adoration. As if he put the stars in the sky just for you."

The mention of the sky makes a lump of emotion grow in my throat because we seemed to have all of our moments under the stars.

"It's true," Camille adds. "And he looks at you like you're his entire world."

"That's not something you can fake. The eyes are the window to the soul, if you ask me," Jasmine says.

"I mean, yeah. We like each other as friends, of course we look at each other that way," I say, trying to diffuse their facts.

"Friends don't look at friends like that," Jasmine retorts over the rim of her glass of wine.

"I just don't get what's so wrong about having real feelings for him," Aurora says gently, and I can tell she's genuinely trying to make sense of this. Just like I am.

As we eat and catch up on how our holidays went, I put on *Bring it On Again: All or Nothing* to play in the background.

Jasmine and Aurora spend most of the time talking about their wedding plans, which are coming up in just a few months. Camille tells us all about married life with Ryker, and how she loves being closer to her brother, Quinton.

As the girls chat about the baby, I take a moment to soak in the fact that they showed up for *me*. I've never had friends like this, and it means the world to me.

"Are you okay, Marcela?" Camille asks. "You've been quiet."

"Nothing, just … you guys coming here today, it means a lot. I've never really had friends like this, and I've been so worried the past few days that you all wouldn't want to be friends with me anymore," my voice shakes slightly as my emotions threaten to take over.

Three sets of eyes stare at me with sadness, and Camille is the first one to speak.

"I'm so sorry no one has treated you the way you deserve, but that's all over now. We're your girls for life, no matter what. We don't love you because you were with Theo, Marcela, we love you because of you."

"What she said!" Aurora points at Camille, as Jasmine does the same.

"I love you all too," I sniffle, doing my best and failing to keep the tears at bay. The three of them move in close, enclosing me in their embrace.

"You know you're standing up in both of our weddings, don't you?" Aurora says matter-of-factly, still holding me tight.

"W-what?" I stumble on my words, utterly shocked as I pull back to look at them. "Really?"

"Of course. Neither of us have got around to asking because we figured everyone here already knew," Jasmine explains.

"I'd love that," I tell them, my voice full of emotion.

A sense of happiness washes over me, a foreign feeling after days of feeling like crap. I thought these girls would never want to speak to me again after everything that happened with Theo.

Our conversation lulls as we watch a bit of the movie, until the question floating around in my mind finally makes its way out.

"How is he doing?" I ask, hesitant to hear the answer. What if he's content and has moved on? Does it make me a bad person if I don't want that?

Aurora's features fall slightly, her words careful as she says, "He'll be okay. It's painful right now, but he knew it was the best decision. He couldn't continue faking it, when he felt that way."

It all seemed so easy when we first made our deal. But looking back now, did we ever stand a chance? He wasn't supposed to fall in love with me. No one was supposed to get hurt.

But they say that if you pretend to be happy, eventually it'll become real. I'm starting to think that saying applies to other things too.

"I'm so sorry," I manage to say as I fold my arms across my belly.

"Don't be sorry," Jasmine says, her voice warm. "You can't be responsible for how others feel. Especially at the expense of your own feelings."

"How do you feel?" Camille questions me, her voice gentle.

"I—" I pause as I'm suddenly hit with a flash of memories. Of Theo and I laying under the stars, spilling our deepest secrets. Of Theo sticking up for me. Of Theo smiling at me on horseback. Of me melting into his arms whenever they're around me.

"I don't know," I admit quietly, for the first time.

"Let me ask you this." Aurora rests her forearms on her knees and folds her hands together. "How would you feel if you saw Theo doing all of the things you two have done in your fake relationship with someone else?"

Jealousy consumes my body so quickly that I nearly jump up to shake the odd sensation off. I don't think I've ever felt a feeling so instantly, let alone one of anger. It's not like me at all.

She smirks as she looks at me, "Exactly."

"If your feelings were strictly friendly, you'd be happy for him," Jasmine adds in.

"I agree with them, Marcela. Can you imagine yourself doing those things with another person?" Camille says, making my stomach twist.

Because no, I can't imagine myself ever being with someone else. Over the last few days, whenever I've tried to picture my future after this, I only saw Theo. I just didn't want to admit it to myself and tried to reason that there was another explanation.

My bottom lip begins to quiver as anxiety takes over. "I'm so scared," I whisper.

"What are you scared of?" Jasmine asks, putting her arm around my shoulders.

"Of being in love again. Trusting someone entirely, and giving them the chance to hurt me. I've worked so hard to get myself here after what Hunter did to me. I can't go through that again."

"Love is scary, but Theo would never, ever do that to you," Aurora reassures me.

"Logically I know that, yet at the same time you never know what can happen," my voice shakes as I explain my fears. I'm terrified to put my heart out there again only for it to be broken once more. I'm not sure how many times I can put it back together.

Camille speaks up. "Your fear is valid, Marcela. Shit happens in life, and you might get hurt. You can't hide from the good things just because they have the potential to hurt you. That's no way to live, Marcela. It's okay to be cautious, but you're never going to have love again if you let fear win. I just don't want you to end up regretting things later in life."

She's right. It's the same advice I'd give to either of them, yet taking it myself is terrifying. I'm the one that has to deal with the potential fallout.

"You're right," I sniffle. "And I don't want to live in the shadows of my fears."

"You need to know that you're strong. You've been through some crappy things, and know how to handle yourself. You're more confident now than I've ever seen before, and you also have us. You'll never be alone," Jasmine adds, giving me a hug.

I nod along, resting my head on Jasmine's shoulder as I try to take in all that tonight's talk has revealed to me.

"Of course we will support you in whatever you decide. It's your life. We just want to be here to support you," Aurora says.

"I think I need some time to process everything."

Tonight has been an overload on my brain. Right now all I want to do is relax with my friends.

"Then let's sit back and enjoy some chick flicks," Aurora suggests.

And that's what we do for the rest of the night. We watch some classic girly movies and stuff our faces with food, and talk about anything and everything.

Despite the confusion in my head and the ache in my chest, it's the best night I've had in a while.

After the girls leave, I settle into bed, prepared for another sleepless night. Because I already know the chances of me turning my brain off are slim.

Not when I'm certain I have feelings for Theo.

How exactly did this happen?

There's not one defining moment I can look back on and say *"Aha! Right there, that's when I fell for him."*

I think I fell for Theo a little each day. I fell for the kindness he treated me with. The patience he never stopped giving me.

The small but meaningful gestures. He was my biggest fan, my number one supporter who made me feel like I could do anything.

Theo understood me and could anticipate my needs. He made me feel beautiful, sexy, and desirable. The way my body felt every time he touched me couldn't be faked. That kind of chemistry isn't just two people testing it out for research purposes.

It was real. All of it.

I don't think there's ever been a single thing we've faked. Every touch felt natural. Every laugh was genuine.

Not to mention that I went on two dates without Hunter and Ruby in sight, purely because I enjoyed spending time with him. It had nothing to do with proving anything to anyone.

Plus, how could I not be in love with someone who treated me like I was the center of their world and never stopped trying to prove it every day?

I thought admitting my feelings for Theo to myself would be the hard part, but it doesn't even come close to what comes next.

What now?

I know Theo told me to let him know when I figure it out, but I don't know how to do that. Do I simply show up at his house and tell him that I love him? Do I come up with a grand gesture?

Putting my feelings out there has never been easy for me, especially ones that I didn't want to admit to myself.

That's a weird thing too, isn't it? How did I manage to fall in love with someone a few months after my breakup? Am I just falling for the first person that gave me attention?

I push the endless worries out of my mind and focus on the one thing that matters most right now.

I'm in love with Theo Miller.

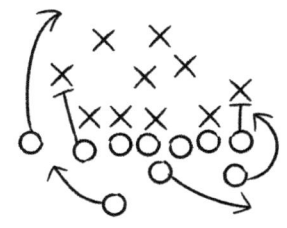

Chapter 33

Theo

If these past few days have taught me anything, it's that the mundane suddenly becomes way more interesting when you're trying to avoid your feelings.

All of the sudden, my personal training sessions with Rob aren't as dreadful as they always were. I even found myself reviewing tape footage for the playoff game in two weeks, and coming up with plays I thought might help our team.

And I hate football, so that's saying a lot.

In hindsight, I did this to myself. I broke my own heart by ending things, but wasn't that always the plan? This pain was inevitable. We were never guaranteed a happy ending, but I lost sight of that with my overbearing optimism that she'd eventually feel the same way I did.

My chest ached so profusely over the past five days that I seriously considered going to the hospital at one point, because there must have been something else wrong with me. I never knew missing someone so much could cause such an intense physical pain.

The only shred of light I could hold onto was that when I'm grey and old, I'll still remember that I got to make memories with the girl who stole my heart.

Although today, the pressure feels extra tight on my chest, and the only thing getting me out of bed this morning is the smell of fresh bread.

I wander downstairs and into the kitchen where I find Dale chopping strawberries on the cutting board. "Morning, sunshine," he sing-songs. "Glad to see you made it out of bed for something other than a workout."

He's aware of what happened and knows exactly why I've been sulking around.

"Are you making bread?" I ignore his comment, focusing on the source of the delicious scent wafting around us.

"Yup. Robin's parents got us a bread maker for Christmas. You can be my first taste tester if you'd like."

"Absolutely," I say as I sit on the bar stool.

Dale looks up at me from the cutting board, doing a quick glance-over before he returns to chopping. "You look like crap," he half chuckles.

"Leave me alone. I'm dealing with heartbreak," I try to make it a joke, but it falls flat.

He sets down his knife and gives me his full attention. "Are you okay?" he asks, feeling guilty.

"I don't know," I say honestly. "I know I did the right thing by ending things, but fuck, I miss her a lot. Do you know how hard it is to go from seeing each other nearly everyday to complete radio silence?"

"I do actually," his voice takes on a reverent tone, as if he's remembering a painful memory. "Robin and I broke up briefly two years ago. We were young and it was over a dumb reason, but the pain of not being with her for weeks was unbearable."

"How'd you cope?" I ask him, desperate for some tips.

"I let myself feel what I needed to feel, but I also didn't let it take over my life. After a few days, I eventually started to get back into my routine. It wasn't easy, but it helped a lot. I had days that sucked, and days that weren't so bad. And eventually, we worked things out. It made me feel more secure knowing I could handle us being apart if it ever happened again. Don't get me wrong, she's the love of my life and I don't want to live without her, but I know I could live without her if anything were to happen. You get what I mean?"

"I do. It'll suck if Marcela doesn't want me back, but I know that regardless of how bad it'll hurt, I will be okay," I tell him, feeling slightly better already.

Hell, the more I thought about it, the more I thought maybe I was being a tad dramatic. She hasn't even told me anything yet. I should stop assuming and wait it out like I told her I would, instead of moping around like a lost puppy.

"Exactly, and I'll always be here if you need me," Dale says, offering me his fist.

I bump it with a smile. "Thanks, man. Same goes for you."

Dale and I spend the rest of the morning eating fresh bread and fruit salad as he tells me all about the baby shower he and Robin are planning, his fears about being a dad, and how he wants to propose to Robin.

"How are you going to ask her?"

A mischievous glint casts over his eyes. "I'm going to take her back to the place where we had our very first date. When we're sitting on the bench where we had our first kiss, I'll get down on one knee."

"That's amazing, Dale. I'm so freaking happy for you two," I smile, bringing a cup of coffee to my lips.

"Yeah, I can't wait to spend the rest of my life with her," he says, right before he shoves a piece of bread topped with Nutella and strawberries into his mouth.

"Can I tell you something?" I ask, wanting to be honest with him. It seems to be my thing lately.

"Of course. What's up?" he says with a mouthful.

"I hate football."

Dale's fork clatters to his plate as his mouth pops open. "What?"

"I hate football," I repeat, keeping my eyes locked on his.

"Theo, you're the star of the team. Hell, the star football player in the country. And this whole time you've hated it?"

"The only reason I've kept playing is because of my dad."

I let the words hang in the air between us, letting Dale put the pieces together when understanding dawns on his face.

"Wow," he says, sitting back in his chair as he looks at me. "How hard has that been?"

His question makes me huff a sarcastic laugh. "Oh, I've been having the best time."

Dale shakes his head at me. "That bad, huh?"

I nod, letting go of my previous humor. "I've hated every second of it. Playing always made me so goddamn anxious. I know I'm good at it, but just because someone's good at something doesn't mean they enjoy it. I'm sure if I had grown up to play recreationally, I might've liked it more. But the way I was raised with it being my entire life, it made me despise it. It took everything away from me. My dad, my childhood, the chance of having a normal life."

"Fuck, man. I'm so sorry. What are you going to do?"

I hold the mug of warm coffee between my hands, trying to let it soothe the pit in my stomach that I get when I think about hurting my dad's feelings.

"I'm going to tell Coach Davis tomorrow that I won't be opting into the draft. However far our team makes it this season will be as far as my career goes."

"I'm sure Coach will understand. I mean, after this you're no longer his player so he shouldn't care much," he comments, and I agree. Coach wouldn't be affected by my decision unless I quit right now, which I'm not.

"So what are you going to do with your life?" he asks, peering at me with curiosity.

"Bit of a loaded question for ten in the morning," I chuckle, and he smirks at that. I shrug my shoulders. "I don't really know. I've been thinking about going back home to the farm and taking over my dad's job. He's getting older, and I'm sure there are other things that would make him happy."

"National football star turned farmer, who would've thought?" Dale cracks a smile and I can't help but laugh along with him.

"Make your jokes now, but next time you eat, remember to thank a farmer."

We both laugh at that.

"Honestly though, Theo. I'm proud of you," Dale says. "What you've done is hard as hell, and to finally choose yourself after a lifetime of not doing that, I commend you."

My body sags in relief at hearing those words from him. "Thank you, seriously. It means a lot to hear that."

Dale and I fall into easy conversation about what our lives will look like in the next few months. Both of us are graduating, and while one of us will become a parent the other has no strict life plans.

The contrast between the two of us should throw me off and make me feel like there's something wrong with me, but the only thing I feel is this overwhelming sense of freedom.

To be who I want to be.

To do what *I* want to do.

To live with my choices for the first time in my life.

Chapter 34
Marcela

A week has passed since Theo broke off our fake relationship and it's been two days since the girls visited me, and in that time, I've gone through a range of emotions.

Confusion and heartache to start, followed by an emotion that everyone searches for.

Love.

Since realizing that I'm in love with Theo, it's all that I've felt. And it's made everything around me brighter somehow. Making my cup of tea in the morning has a little more pizazz than before. Listening to love songs makes my body feel fuzzy with joy from memories of him.

My body feels lighter with each step that I take.

There's a reason they say love is the closest thing we have to magic, because it isn't tangible. It's something we believe in and feel.

My creativity has never been so high, and I ended up finishing my novel. The love and support from my readers throughout this journey has given me the confidence to start working on self-publishing this for real.

The burst of creativity also gave me an idea of how to tell Theo that I'm in love with him. I can only hope Theo still feels the same way, and isn't too upset that I haven't reached out to him in the last week.

I think we both needed the time—at least I did—to figure my feelings out on my own and be sure of what they really were. I also needed the time to finish what I am using to tell Theo how I feel about him.

And now, I'm finally ready to open myself up in a way I haven't before.

Checking the time, I realize I have to leave my apartment now. Robin is supposed to be on her way to Theo's. I reached out to her yesterday and asked if she could do me a favor, since I needed someone to deliver what I'd made to his house.

My stomach rattles with nerves as I get dressed in my peacoat, scarf, hat, and gloves. It's only five in the evening, but it's already dark out and the temperature has dropped significantly.

Minutes later, I make my way out of my building and toward our spot.

The one where we first bared our souls to each other. Under the stars, on top of the hill, away from the world below us.

I walk with an extra pep in my step, excited but simultaneously nervous to see Theo for the first time in a week. I'm lost in my own world, and don't realize how out of it I am until I crash into someone.

I look up to see a familiar shade of purple-red hair, whose green eyes shoot daggers at me.

Ruby.

I decide to ignore her and move past her when she blows a cloud of cigarette smoke right in my face. "Still lame as ever," she snarks.

Something inside of me snaps. I'm fed up with the way she's treated me. I stop in my tracks and turn to face her, squaring my shoulders as I stare her down with a confidence I once lacked. I used to only find power in my words, but I'm learning my voice has power too.

"And you are still as rude and lonely as ever. You've always loved knocking other people down so you could feel better about yourself. You've always said I'm too nice, so I'll be nice one last time. I really hope you find happiness. I hope you never hurt someone the way you've hurt me, for someone who ended up leaving you the same way. I hope you'll find a version of yourself that you actually like, and don't rely on making others feel bad to do so."

I let out a large breath after my speech, watching as her eyes fill with tears she doesn't let fall. Ruby's façade slowly crumbles as a tear escapes, which she wipes away quickly before wrapping her arms around her body protectively.

"I dumped him, you know," she says quietly.

That makes my head tilt in confusion, because Hunter told me he was the one who broke up with her.

"Smart choice," I respond, not feeling bad in the slightest that they didn't work out.

"I found out he got Aspen's football coach's wife pregnant," she says, stunning me into silence.

Theo always wondered why he made the sudden switch to RLU, and now I know why.

"She's five months along, which means he cheated on me. I guess I got what I deserved," her voice drips with sarcasm and sadness all at once.

Old Marcela would have felt bad and jumped to comfort her. But the new me can't find it in me to care.

When I don't move to reply to that, she continues.

"The fucked up part is the coach's daughter told me. Her dad is planning to go public with the information and wants to make sure Hunter's career is ruined, since Hunter ruined his life. Because of that, their daughter's entire life is blown up because of a man who can't keep his dick in his pants," she shakes her head as her voice shakes. "It made me realize how much cheating can really hurt others, so I just want to say I'm sorry. I know it doesn't fix anything, but I needed to say it."

Not that I needed to hear her apologize, but it is a small comfort.

"Thank you. I hope you have a good life," I say in parting as I sidestep her and keep on moving to my destination. My mom always said to kill people with kindness, and that's exactly what I'm doing.

It feels good to have closure with Ruby, and officially end that part of my life.

The only thing left to do now is continue the chapter of Theo and me.

As I make my way to the top of the hill, I peer up at the pink and purple night sky with stars shining across it.

It's a beautiful night, and I can only hope that it gets better with Theo by my side. If he doesn't come, it'll mean he's changed his mind in the last week, and I'll have to piece myself back together once again.

But how do you put yourself back together when the one that helped you through the last time is the one now breaking your heart?

Let's just hope I don't have to find out.

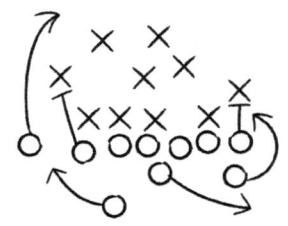

Chapter 35
Theo

A knock on my bedroom door startles me from the laser focus I've had on the racing video game Ronnie boy created.

It's finally out worldwide, and it's wild knowing my good friend did all of this. His creativity is the reason so many people will have fun and make memories. It's amazing what happens when you follow your dreams, and I can't wait to find out what will happen when I do the same.

I pad toward my door, swinging it open to find Robin there with a ... gift in her hands?

"Uh, hi," I say, confused. "What do you have there?"

Robin and I are friends, but we'd never exchanged gifts for the holidays. Or were we supposed to, and I totally missed the mark? Shoot, maybe I could quickly order something.

"It's not from me, calm down. You panicked quicker than Dale did when I told him I was pregnant," she chuckles, handing over a rectangular present covered in pink wrapping paper and topped with a red bow.

My heart stills because I know without a doubt who this gift is from.

"What is this?" I ask, not tearing my eyes off the small sticker that says

To Theo,

It's a little late, but Merry Christmas.

Love, Marcela

"My lips are sealed," she mimes with her finger across her lips as she slowly backs away and heads down the stairs.

I close the door behind me and sit on my bed, my hands shaky as I hold the gift.

Is this a gift she wanted to give me before I broke up with her and it's just getting to me now? Or….

Before I get lost in hypotheses, I rip the paper apart and uncover what looks like a red journal. Unsure what it's supposed to mean, I open the first page, reading the title that says "How I Fell in Love with My Best Friend, by Marcela."

And then everything quiets around me, except for the rapid beating in my chest as I read those words over and over again. I know she considers me her best friend. If this means what I think it means … holy crap.

I flip to the next page, and find a drawing of Marcela and I sitting on our bench. The words below are what take my breath away.

It all started when you were there for me after all that happened.

Next is a picture of us looking at the stars.

I found myself opening up to you when it had never been so easy to do it with anyone else.

After that is a picture of us sitting in a booth at Beers 'n' Cheers, laughing as we sit beside each other.

You make me laugh more than anyone ever has, and your smile brings me an immense amount of joy.

The next page is us in my truck, my arms wrapped around her, the day we went to dinner at her parents' house.

The way you protect and stand up for me doesn't go unnoticed, and makes me feel safer than I ever have.

I flip to see a picture of us on the football field, her wrapped in my arms.

I never realized how a set of arms could feel like home.

And the next image is a picture of me on the horse with Mason.

The way you love everyone around you makes me feel immensely lucky to be one of those people.

My eyes nearly bulge out of my head at the following photo, it's Marcela on her bed, hair splayed on her pillows with her mouth open in pleasure, but the sketch only goes to her collarbones.

No one has ever made me feel the way you do.

The second to last page is a picture of me giving her a bouquet of flowers.

The way you effortlessly made me smile with your small gestures.

My hands shake as I flip to the last one, seeing a sketch of Marcela and I sitting on the bench at our spot, staring at the night sky with the words below,

Catch Me

Those are just some of the ways I fell in love with you.

I choke on a sob, my emotions rearing at the realization that my dream girl actually loves me back. In what world did this actually happen? Marcela is in love with *me*? I get the girl I've always wanted?

I'm about to pull my phone out and call her when I close the book and see that there's a sticky note on the back.

Meet me at our spot. I'll be waiting there - Celly.

My mouth breaks into a widespread grin at her note as excitement fills my veins. I quickly get dressed, and within minutes I'm speed walking down the street towards campus, right to our spot.

It only takes me about ten minutes to get to the bottom of the hill, and within seconds, I'm propelled to the top. My eyes instantly land on her sitting on the bench. And just like that, it suddenly seems easier to breathe and I feel lighter than before, just seeing her for the first time in a week.

"Celly," her name falls off my lips in a breath.

Her head snaps over to me, a wide smile erupting on her face. I jog the last few steps to her, and I pick her up in my arms the moment she's standing, spinning us around as she clings to me.

I'm hit with her scent of mint chocolate, and I revel in the familiarity of it. I let it wash over me, breathing her in and relieved that she's here. That she *loves* me.

We're silent for a few minutes when I set her down as we hold onto each other, her head nestled into my neck while I cradle the back of her head.

"I love you," she whispers, so faintly I nearly miss it.

I pull back and she lifts her head to look at me.

"Say it again," my voice hoarse with need as my hand strokes her cheek.

"I love you," she says louder this time, confident and sure.

I shake my head, in disbelief that this girl loves me back.

"I love you too," I say, my eyes dipping to her lips.

We slowly inch our lips closer, until our breaths become one. Then I take her lips with mine, for our first *real* kiss. She melts in my arms as she kisses me back, this one different than ever before.

It's real, it's raw, and it's full of love.

Each press of our lips against one another are unspoken promises and I love yous.

I've never been so happy, so full of life and joy that it hits me then how goddamn miserable I was before. When I was living my father's life instead of my own. When Marcela wasn't mine.

This is how I should have felt all this time, and now that I know what it feels like, I'm going to do everything I can to keep it.

We slowly part, her eyes flitting up to mine as we drink each other in.

"I missed you," I whisper as I play with the ends of her hair.

"I missed you too."

"Was part of it because I'm ridiculously good looking? I tease, making her giggle.

"Don't get me wrong, you're *so* handsome, but no, that wasn't it," she shakes her head, a shy smile forming on her lips.

"Hmm, was it my ability to make you come more than once?"

Her cheeks flush and she smacks my chest. "N-no … but that's a good point."

She takes a deep breath before locking her gaze with mine again. "It wasn't just that I missed you, which I did. A lot. When I thought back to our fake relationship, I realized that none of it was ever *fake*. I never had to fake being happy with you. And there was no way I could deny how much your kisses made me feel, no matter how much I wanted to play it off as nothing. I was so afraid of falling that I didn't want to admit it to myself. But I'm done denying how I feel."

"I'm here to catch you, Celly. I'll always be here," I say as I plant a chaste kiss to her lips before she pulls away to finish her thoughts.

"That's exactly why I'm here, because I know you'll catch me."

"Always." I smirk, loving the raw vulnerability I'm getting from her. While we've always been open and honest before, I can tell there's a slight difference now. She's fully giving herself over to me now.

"So ..." she trails off, looking adorable as ever. "Do you want to get dinner with me?"

I huff a laugh as my hand caresses her cheek. "I want to have breakfast, lunch, and dinner with you."

Marcela nods as tears pool in her eyes. "Me too. Does this mean we're real dating now?"

"Yeah, we're real dating now. Even though you've always been mine."

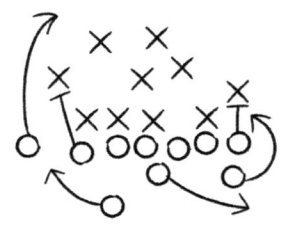

Chapter 36
Theo

Today's my last football game ever, and I never thought I'd ever see this day.

To say I woke up feeling better than I ever have is an understatement. Not only did I wake up with Marcela snuggled at my side, she made French toast for breakfast and then I feasted on her for dessert.

Something I didn't expect was the sadness weighing heavy on my chest as I stepped into the locker room. Even if I hate this sport, I'll always cherish the memories I made with these boys.

"Hey," I shout for everyone in the room to hear. Some of my teammates whip their head my way, while a small group have their eyes glued to their phones. I already know what they're looking at, and as much as I dislike Hunter, there's no room for outside drama here. "Put your phones away. We have a championship to win. Your teammate's a hell of a tight end, and we need him to win today."

It nearly killed me to say that, but it's what they need to hear to go out there and do their jobs today. No one says a word as they hurry to tuck their phones away.

Catch Me

When my eyes land on Hunter, he gives me a subtle nod in what I assume is his way of saying thank you. I reply with a curt nod because I need to be the bigger man. Besides, whatever's going on with him is none of my business. And I need him to be in a good head space to help us today.

"This is our last game together, boys, and we're not leaving without that trophy," I shout, standing on the bench as everyone begins to form a circle around me.

"Coyotessss!" I cup my hands around my mouth, getting even louder. My team starts howling in response, and I yell, "Who's gonna bring all they have?"

The howls boom throughout the room.

"Who's gonna take home that trophy today?"

"Coyotes!" everyone shouts back at me as they slap helmets and backs.

One final game.

Green and white confetti rain from above, clouding my vision as pandemonium erupts around the stadium. The crowd's cheers are so loud I can feel the vibration of it in my chest, but the thing I feel the most is freedom.

It washes over me in one big tidal wave, because I'm finally done.

My teammates are hyped up, jumping on me in a dog pile to celebrate our win against the University of New York. It was a tough match, a constant back and forth until the second half when we got an interception and scored a touchdown.

It gave us the momentum we needed to dominate, and we did just that.

And the best part? I had fun doing it. I finally played a game for someone other than my dad. I played for my teammates, and for myself, to end my career on a high note.

The sea of jerseys disperse, allowing me to stand and make my way to the crowd, right toward where I know Marcela is sitting.

She's smiling proudly, her hands resting on her chest as I approach the rail and tap it.

"Get down here," I call out to her.

Marcela makes the few steps down to the railing, making it easy for me to reach over and grip her hips as I lift her over and into my arms.

Unlike the last time we did this, Marcela kisses me as we spin in a circle, making my chest squeeze with the love I feel for her. I never thought I'd get this, and now here she is, loving me out in the open for everyone to see.

"You can rest now," she says as the confetti is caught in her wavy hair.

I rest my forehead against hers, squeezing my eyes shut as I try to avoid the tears that want to fall. It doesn't work.

"I love you and I'm proud of you," Marcela says, her lips brushing against mine as her thumb wipes under my eyes. "It's all done now."

My arms tighten around her as I kiss her once more. "I love you so much," my voice is hoarse with emotion as I speak.

"Theo!" I hear the familiar voice of Kelly Karson behind me, causing me to set Marcela down and tuck her into my side as I turn to face her.

"Great game you played today. How does it feel to finally bring a championship title home to RLU?"

"It's a feeling like no other. These guys deserve it more than anything, and I'm happy we could get it done this year seeing as it will be my last."

I talked to Coach the other day, so this won't come as a shock to him. In fact, he was very understanding and applauded me for having the guts to go my own way. His support gave me the fuel to do what I needed to do today.

Kelly's face drops, her mouth agape. She snaps out of it quickly, her professionalism taking over. "You're not entering the draft this year?"

"No. Football has been the focal point of my life for as long as I can remember, and it's time that I focus on something else now. This chapter of my life is over," I say with finality.

"Wow," Kelly seems baffled as she turns to her cameraman. "You heard it here first. The best QB in the country is officially done with football," she pans back to me and asks, "What will you do now?"

"Something I'll share if I'm comfortable with it," I say as kindly as I can. Now I turn to her camera, looking it right in the eye. "Thank you to all of the fans who have supported my career, and this team. I loved seeing you guys in the stands and now it's time I do something for me."

And with those final words, I guide Marcela and I off the field as we exit through the tunnel I'll never go through again.

With every step we take away from the field, I feel lighter as if I'm finally shedding that version of myself. I can't wait to mold and create the person I actually want to be, with no limitations or expectations except for the ones I set for myself.

When we near the locker rooms, I spot Ally, David, Mason, and my dad waiting there.

"Theooo!" Mason squeals, running right to me. I bend down and scoop him into my arms.

"Hey, Sunny, did you enjoy the game?"

"Mhm," he nods enthusiastically. "Pops told me that you were playing so good. I'm so happy you won, and then it rained green and white!"

I chuckle at his excitement. "I'm glad you had fun."

"Cela!" he yells, squirming out of my arms so that he can get to her.

Seeing how much Mason has taken to her after the one day they spent together makes my chest pinch. I always knew I loved her, and seeing her become a part of my family only adds to that love.

"Hell of a game, brother," Ally says, drawing my attention to her and David.

"It's about time you won something," he snickers, making me laugh.

"Thanks, you two."

And then that leaves my dad. He eyes me warily, looking nothing like the closed off man I grew up with. I've never seen him so unsure of himself than the way he is in this moment, and I wonder what he's about to say.

He stretches his hand out between us as he says, "Congrats on a great career, son. I'm proud of you."

I take a minute, not saying anything as I make sure I heard him correctly. He gives me a subtle nod, letting me know he means it.

He's accepting my choice.

Emotion bubbles to the surface, unable to be stopped as a single tear escapes me. I pull my dad into a hug, one he reciprocates as he hugs me tightly. "I'm sorry," his words are muffled.

I don't respond, because my automatic response wants to say it's okay, but it never was. I simply accept the apology and let him take accountability.

"I want to talk about——"

"Let's talk about that another time, okay? I want to sit down and be fully present for what you have to tell me, but the team will be coming down here any minute now," I tell him as we release each other.

"Sure, sounds good." He looks away from me, likely embarrassed about showing emotion.

"Thank you for coming today," I turn to my family. "It means a lot."

"We will support you no matter what. Unless it's illegal, of course," Ally quips, taking Mason's hand in hers.

"She's boring. If it's illegal, come to me," David jokes, making us all laugh. We say our goodbyes, while Marcela follows them to wait in the lobby while I quickly shower.

Once done, I empty my locker and make my way to the lobby in search of my girl. A wide smile spreads across my face when I find her waiting for me next to a vending machine.

"Ready?" she asks me, grabbing my hand in hers.

"Ready," I tell her as we start walking out of the stadium.

Every step I take away from the field is therapeutic, more so than I ever imagined. I may have won the championship title today, but she's the greatest thing I'll ever have.

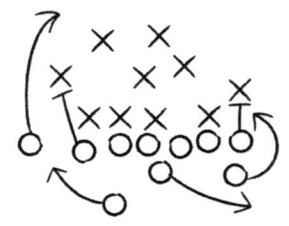

Chapter 37
Theo

One week later

"Why the fuck did you never tell me any of this?" Ryker grumps from the seat next to me. We're currently all lounging in Elio's and Jasmine's new house, who are throwing me a party for winning the championship game.

"I didn't tell anyone," I point out, while leaving out the fact that Marcela knew before he did.

Ryker scoffs. "And you say we're besties."

"Aww, Ry guy, we're still besties. Don't you worry. You're never getting rid of me," I say with a wink.

"Lucky me," he mutters, turning his gaze towards his wife who's standing with Marcela, Jasmine, and Aurora near the kitchen.

"You know, now I feel like a jackass for doing this for you when you hate football," Elio complains as he sets down a charcuterie board on the long, white granite-top island.

"We thought of canceling it after seeing your post-game interview, but we'd already made the travel plans to come here,"

Camille gives me a shy smile, as if them wanting to celebrate would offend me.

"Listen, y'all, you had no idea. In fact," I pause, grabbing a hold of my beer to raise it above me. "Let's toast to the fact that I'm done playing forever."

Everyone settles around the island, and raises their glass. "To no more football!" we all shout, clinking our cups together.

I throw the rest of my drink back, before setting my empty beer bottle down.

Everyone falls back into their conversations as they pick at the food, while I take a moment to soak it all in. My eyes move to each person in the room, reflecting on how far we've all come in these last four years.

Aurora's about to open Fields to Court Athletics this upcoming March, and is heading to the Olympics in Paris this summer. I still remember the day we first met and how in awe of her pure talent I was.

Cameron places a hand around her and pulls her closer to him. Before they met, all she ever cared about was volleyball, and I'm so happy they found each other. They bring out the best in each other and I've always loved being at the forefront to witness it.

Jasmine passes by them, making her way to Elio who's holding a spoon out for her to try his soup. Jasmine's growth since we met is inspiring, having gone from a situation similar to mine where all she did was please her parents, to opening up her dream business.

She gives Elio a thumbs-up, letting him know it's good and he gives her a smile that lingers.

When he catches me staring, he gives me an annoyed glare and I shoot a wink back at him. He likes to pretend he hates me because I might be the reason her dad found out about them, but I know he loves me.

Camille comes over and slides onto Ryker's lap, who's sitting beside me watching a video on his phone that she's been working on, and I'm more than happy everything worked out for them after what happened with her family.

Ryker went from baseball being the center of his world to Camille taking the spotlight. He's been crushing it in the first few months as a rookie, and so is Camille, being the content creator for his team.

They couldn't be more perfect together.

And the fact that I got to officiate their wedding on an island off the coast of France, because she was a literal runaway princess? Yeah, I don't think anything could top that moment in my life.

Besides marrying my girl. That will definitely top it.

I soak her in, watching as she laughs and mingles with our friends. She never liked socializing before, but I love how comfortable she is around them. It makes my heart full seeing her come alive like this.

She makes her way over to me, and I pull her onto my lap.

"Did I tell you that you look beautiful tonight?"

"You have, three times already. But thank you." She blushes, her eyes shining with love as they stare into mine.

I open my mouth to tell her it'll never be enough, when Elio speaks up. "Theo, did you know that your dad was applying for a coaching job?" he asks, looking up at me from his phone.

My stomach twists at Elio bringing up my dad, a lifelong response my body's accustomed to, even though things aren't like they used to be.

"Yeah, he was interested in taking over for the coach at Aspen. Why?"

"The news just broke online that ex-quarterback Randy Miller is returning to the world of football as the head coach at Aspen, starting next year."

"I'm happy he got it," I reply, meaning it.

Our relationship was far from perfect, but we were working on it.

He's going to start living a life he enjoys, as am I. He said that if he got the job, he'd be handing over the farm and house to Allison and would move closer to Aspen.

I've asked Allison if I could come more often and start taking care of the place with her, and she agreed. I think what I like most about this option is that I can still change paths if I want to. I can change my mind and change it again. Knowing that nothing is holding me back is the best feeling in the world.

We spend the rest of the night laughing over card games, old memories, and plans for the future. A future I'm finally excited about.

We've all come from different backgrounds. And all faced unique challenges. We've all made mistakes and learned a lot about life and ourselves. The one constant thing is that we did it together. The eight of us have a bond that can never be broken, no matter how much we stray when life takes us in different directions.

We'll always have the love and support here for each other.

It's something I'll never take for granted.

I kiss the side of Marcela's head and wrap my arms around her waist. "How are you?"

Her smile is effortless and real when she says, "I'm happy, really happy. And you?"

"I've got everything I'll ever need right here."

Epilogue
Marcela

5 years later

My hands wrap around my pink bow mug, savoring the warmth it brings me in this late November chill.

I walk towards the grand window in our kitchen, taking in the sunrise as it climbs over the peak of the mountains. My favorite view, though, has to be my husband coming out of the stables in a pair of jeans, cowboy hat, and boots.

It's something I get to see every morning since we built a house next door to the farm, with our kitchen window facing the horse stables. Working on the farm and being close with his family has been huge for him and his mental health. I've never seen him so at ease, especially when we moved out here.

Our lives have changed drastically in the five years since we graduated.

Theo and I moved in together a few months after graduation, where he went right to work on the farm. I did part-time work for the local library while getting my master's degree, and finally self-published my first novel.

So you could say I've been a bit busy.

Catch Me

My debut novel did well, and I went on to self-publish three more books over the last few years.

I eventually found an agent last year, the way I've always dreamed, and she helped another dream of mine come true. My first traditionally-published book was released last week, and I've been on edge ever since. It's a new world and I really hope people love it.

My phone pings, dragging me from my thoughts as I make my way to the table and swipe it open. I gloss over notifications as I sip my tea, then click on a message that my agent just sent me.

Lisa

> You did it. #1 on the NYT bestseller list.

Tea spray from my mouth as my body goes into shock. I did *what*? Quickly, I clean up the mess from my tea and text Theo.

Me

> Come here please!

Hubbs

> I'll come anywhere you please.

A groan leaves my lips as my hands shake with excitement, making it nearly impossible to text back.

"Cellyyyy," his smooth voice calls out from the back door, making me swing around in his direction.

I set my phone down on the table and run right into my favorite place in the world. His arms. He wraps me up instantly, resting his chin on my hair. "Everything okay?"

A sob racks my body as I nod my head.

"Why are you crying then? I'm kinda confused." He chuckles, sounding nervous.

I take a moment to gather myself, swiping under my eyes at the tears that are refusing to stop. I'll have to thank the extra hormones for that. Yup, I'm pregnant.

We weren't trying, but we weren't preventing it either.

I stare into Theo's light-blue eyes, knowing that he's going to be more happy about this than me, and somehow it makes it even better.

"*Spell Bound* made it to the number one spot on the list."

Saying the words out loud makes it more real somehow, and I'm suddenly sweating at the fact. How the heck did I end up here?

Theo's mouth gapes open, speechless, so I decide to tell him everything.

"And I'm pregnant." I'd planned on telling him with a cute Christmas ornament that had my name, Theo's, and Baby Miller.

His eyes widen, remaining eerily still.

"Theo …"

He seems to snap out of it, his eyes moving to my stomach and then back up to my eyes, with tears of his own.

"Now I know why you were happy crying," he half-laughs, half-cries.

I laugh and cry along with him as he pulls me into his arms once again and kisses me. And I mean really kisses me, the kind of kiss that has me wanting him to take me right here on the kitchen table.

"As much as I'd love to fuck you right now, I need a minute," he says, dragging his hand over his mouth. "There's so much to process. Not only is my wife a goddamn rock star, she's now carrying our child. Our first child."

The way he's looking at me right now, it's like I hung the stars.

"I'm so fucking proud of you."

"Thank you. And congrats on your sperm, it's the reason we're pregnant," I joke, making him shake his head as he laughs.

"Have you told anyone?" he asks, getting excited.

"No, not yet. I'd like to tell my mom and your dad before we tell everyone else, and once we make it to three months. I'm only five weeks along."

My mom left my dad right after I graduated. Since she took the time to prepare and had everything in place, when he tried to fight her on it, she had amazing lawyers who refused to let that happen. They've been divorced for three years now, and we haven't heard from him since. Even Jade, who is growing as an A-list actress, has only rarely spoken to him.

My mom has her own catering business and loves every second of it. She even met someone and I've never seen her this happy. We spend every Sunday night together having family dinner, an event that extends into the evening as we all catch up. And I have to say, it's nice to longer hold your breath every time you sit down with your family to eat. Because when we get together now, it's nothing but love.

"Of course. Anything you want," his voice is soft as he leans in and kisses my forehead. "I do have to get back to the stable, but I'll be back in an hour to make you lunch, okay?"

"You're really strict about that whole breakfast, lunch, and dinner thing, huh?"

"Every day, for the rest of our lives. It was in my vows." He smiles that devastatingly-charming smile at me, that one dimple popping.

My smile mirrors his, knowing that Theo is going to keep that promise and continue to catch me as I fall more in love with him each and every day.

Our story is my favorite that I've written, one I can't wait for us to keep writing together.

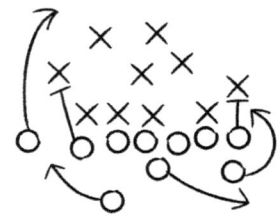

Bonus scene

Theo

THE RLU CREW 10 years later, 2034

"Sam, do not pull on your sister's braids," I chastise my youngest daughter, who's attempting to pull out Sofia's hair that my wife just did.

Sam looks at me from the living room carpet with the same eyes as her mom, her little lip in a pout. "I'm sorry Daddy."

"It's okay, Silly Sam, but all of your aunts, uncles, and cousins are almost here, so Mom will not want to redo your hair. You know Aunt Camille will have her camera out, snapping a bunch of photos," I explain to her, as it was Christmas Eve and we were getting together to celebrate the holidays.

Our lives have been pulled in different ways, but we make it a point to get together as much as we can.

"I can't wait to see everyone!" Sofia squeals in delight, always excited to see her cousins.

The girls had all gotten pregnant around the same time as each other, except for Jasmine who had the twins two years before any of us had kids.

Catch Me

"I bet they feel the same way, Sof," I tell her just as the front door swings open with the entire group piling into the house.

"We're here," Jasmine calls out as she's the first to walk through the door.

It's going to be a loud and busy night, but I wouldn't have it any other way. Our lives were meant to be filled with love and joy, which is exactly what our friends gave to us in the family we've created together.

Marcela emerges from the guest bathroom, greeting everyone as they come in while I ensure all the kids make it into the playroom safely. Once I see that the kids are all settled, I make my way back to the living room where everyone is sitting on our couch.

"Theo!" Aurora gleams, jumping out of her seat to hug me. "It's so good to see you."

"You too, retired superstar."

"Hey, I'm not old!" she protests with a laugh. Aurora decided to retire this year so she could focus on her gym and her family.

"She may not be, but I sure feel like it," Elio mutters, since he's nearly forty.

"Eli Oldi, see the nickname now fits perfectly," I tease him, earning me a lethal glare.

"After all of these years, you'd think I would like you," he jokes, making all of us burst into laughter. He can pretend all he wants, I know he loves me.

"How's life as an MLB legend?" I turn to Ryker, who just set a record for all-time home runs hit.

He tries to appear humble, but I see the smug smirk creeping in. "Meh, the same."

"Whatever man, you're crushing it out there and you know it," Cameron chimes in, shaking his head at his brother-in-law.

"He really is. Whenever I post content about him, it blows up," Camille confirms, looking at her husband with the same glow that she did the day I married them all those years ago.

"Speaking of blowing up," Jasmine pipes up, resting a hand on her belly. "We're pregnant again."

The girls break out into squeals as they crowd her with hugs and questions, while the guys and I clap Elio on the shoulder and congratulate him.

"Baby number four. How do you do it?" Marcela asks, sounding tired at the idea of it.

We'd love to have more kids, but I'll admit being a parent is fucking hard some days. Besides, right now we're happy but busy. Marcela is a best-selling author, working on her newest book, while I handle the farm. Our days are *go, go, go* from start to finish, but I wouldn't have it any other way.

My girls are my whole life, one that I love living every single day.

"I guess we'll find out." She shrugs, not at all worried because she knows that Elio will be by her side.

We spend the rest of the night reminiscing on our days at RLU, our weddings, and the struggles and joys of being parents.

From promises to learning how to trust one another, while keeping each other afloat and being there to catch us when we fall, we've been through it all.

And the best part is? Our story isn't over yet.

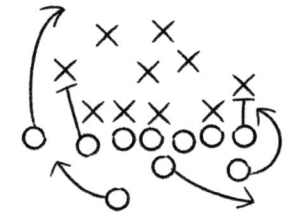

Group chat
Theo

10 years later

Me
I need help.

Eli Oldi
If you need some evidence of why, I have a list going.

Me
Add this to the list then.

Ry guy
Make it quick. I've got about forty minutes before we need to pick Olivia up from gymnastics and I'd like to spend time with my wife.

Ronnie boy

We're at Aiden's soccer game, but I'm here. What do you need?

Me

How the hell do I say no to my daughters? Yesterday, Sam asked me if she could get a pony, and I said yes without a second thought. Marcela had to explain to me why we can't just give them whatever they ask for.

Eli Oldi

For once I understand you. I have two sons and I can say no to them with ease, but when Kiara asks me, it's a different story.

Ronnie boy

I'm with Elio. Daughters have that special effect on us.

Ry Guy

You don't. My little princess knows if she wants something, I'm the one to ask.

Me

So basically I'm screwed???

Catch Me

Ronnie boy

No, you're not. It'll just take some practice. Good luck with that and get back to the rest of us with how it goes. For research purposes.

Eli Oldi

I second this.

Ry Guy

I third this.

Ry Guy

Are we sure we're going to be able to handle this?

Eli Oldi

I'm not mentally prepared for this weekend, don't bring it up just yet. We still have two hours until it starts.

Me

Oh come on, you know you're excited to spend a whole 48 hours with me.

Eli Oldi

That's exactly what I'm not ready for.

CARLIE JEAN

Me

> You know I like it when you're mean to me. Only makes me work harder to earn your love.

Eli Oldi

> It's been 10 years. Giving up sounds reasonable.

Me

> Never, my love.

Ronnie boy

> It's going to be fine, we can handle all of the kids by ourselves. The girls deserve this trip.

Ry guy

> They do, we got this.

48 hours later.

Me

> That was... fun.

Ronnie boy

> All that matters is that we survived.

Eli Oldi

> Barely. I think I have a permanent migraine from the noise.

Catch Me

Ry guy

> We were outnumbered, 8-4. The odds were never good.

Eli Oldi

> And I'm about to have another baby in a few months.

Me

> You can call me if you ever need help.

Eli Oldi

> riiiiight.

Eli Oldi

> I'm sorry Theo, your support and friendship means the world to me.

Ronnie boy

> .... Have you been hacked? I can help with that.

Ry Guy

> What the fuck did he just say?

Me

> Hi, jay bay bay. Miss you hope you had fun in South Carolina.

Ronnie boy

> Ohhh Jasmine is beside him. Not surprised, Aurora's right here too.

Ry guy

> You guys are so soft.

Ry guy

> It's Camille, don't let him fool you. He's been snuggling me since Olivia went to sleep.

Me

> Ooh. Ryker and Camille, sitting in a tree, K I S S I N G

Ry guy

> good night.

Eli Oldi

> bye.

Ronnie boy

> I thought it was funny Theo!

THE END

Want more of Marcela and Theo?

Head to my website carliejean.ca to get a bonus scene.

Acknowledgments

To think I'm sitting here, writing the final acknowledgement for this series is crazy. And I have you, my amazing readers to thank for it. Without your unwavering support and love, these books would not be what they are today. As much as these books come from me, they also come from you, because I couldn't do it without you all. Thank you so much for the love you've shown the RLU series, whether that was falling in love with Aurora and Cameron right off the bat, or joining our world later on in the series. Either way, I'm incredibly grateful. So thank you again, and I can't wait to continue to do this journey with you all.

To my family and friends who share my stories and support me, thank you. I especially love the part where you don't actually read my books. Never change! Seriously. To my friend Sam, who has been dying for this story because she has been a Theo stan since day one, I hope this lives up to the hype. Thank you for always being there for me, and for loving my books as much as you love me.

To my boyfriend, who this book is dedicated to, thank you for being my favourite person to exist. The way I write about love has changed since you've shown me what it's like to be loved so thoroughly. You've always been my biggest supporter, pushing me to do things I never thought I could. You clapped so loud I didn't care anymore about who wasn't. Thank you for being you.

To my editing team - Salma, Emily, Isabella - thank you for all that you did to help get this book to be the best that it could be. Writing books takes a team and I'm so happy you three are a part of mine. Every time we work together I know I'm going to get the best feedback that will improve the story, along with some laughter too. I'm so grateful to have crossed paths with you all and to have you be a part of this story. Thank you so much for all that you did!

To my beta and sensitivity readers, Kylie, Summer, Isabella, Jordyn, and Mariana, thank you for all the love and support for Catch Me. I loved seeing your reactions and love for these characters. It made me believe in this story more than I did before, and that confidence is something I'm so grateful for.

To my cover designer Cat, for always making my mouth drop when she sends over the cover. She never disappoints, and her artistic skills are simply unmatched. Not only is she talented, but she is the kindest and sweetest human. Thank you for all that you do.

To Shaye and Lindsey at GoodGirls PR, thank you for hyping up and loving this book as much as I do. You ladies are not only amazing to work with, but amazing people who deserve the very best.

To Nada at Qamber, you always blow me away with how amazing your services are. Not only is the work you produce of the greatest quality, but it is done in a timely manner and to top it off, you are a joy to work with. I look forward to many more books with you!

About the Author

Carlie is a romance author who loves all things swoon, sunshine, and spice. She lives in Canada. She has two brothers, and a dog named Milo. Some of her favourite things are sunsets, warm weather and iced matcha lattes. She loves to watch and play a variety of sports, which is where her obsession with sports romances originated. When she's not teaching, she loves reading, writing, going for walks, and traveling.

SOCIALS

Check out my website and socials for in-depth book information, what I'm currently writing, and bonus materials!
www.carliejean.ca

@carliejeanwrites on TikTok and Instagram.

Printed in Great Britain
by Amazon